A CHRISTMAS QUINTET

A BLUESTOCKING BELLES COLLECTION

SUSANA ELLIS   SHERRY EWING   ALINA K. FIELD
JUDE KNIGHT   RUE ALLYN

CONTENTS

SHOULD AULD ACQUAINTANCE BE FORGOT
Alina K. Field

MARYANNE AND THE TWELFTH KNIGHT
Jude Knight

HER HOGMANAY SPY
Rue Allyn

Cover Design by Dar Albert

Digital ISBN: 978-1-965509-00-5

Print ISBN:978-1-965509-02-9

❀ Created with Vellum

A CHRISTMAS QUINTET

Five charming stories for your holiday season:

• Friends to Lovers—The farmer's daughter, the viscount's son, and the estate manager reunite as adults. Della is starry-eyed for the viscount's son, but is he really the one for her? (Regency, Christmas)

• Fake Relationship—When the pressure to marry is overwhelming, can a plan put in place at a Christmas house party turn into a love that will last forever? (Regency, Christmas)

• Second-Chance Love—An accident leaves the modiste burned, blinded and in despair until the physician offers hope and stirs memories. (Regency, Christmas)

• Country Mouse and Marriage-Shy Duke—Invited at the last minute to make up the numbers, she expects to be an interested observer. The duke has other ideas. (Georgian, Twelfth Night)

• Two Spies, One Secret—Trapped in a deserted wilderness, will they set aside secrets and past betrayals to rekindle their love and ring in the New Year together? (Medieval, Hogmanay)

DELLA'S CHRISTMAS GIFT

SUSANA ELLIS

A cattle breeder's daughter, Della Paget has always been passionately devoted to her life on the farm. Life as she knows it is about to change, and she's expected to move on to a life as a wife and mother. If she must marry anyone, it would have to be her childhood crush, the viscount's son, who was one of her trio of childhood friends. Meanwhile, the third member of the group suffers in silence as he watches events play out.

PROLOGUE

Paget House
Ibstock, Leicestershire
15 September 1801

"LAUD'S HEIR RETURNS FROM GRAND TOUR. In search of wife, says reputable source."

Della's brother threw down the latest copy of *The Teatime Tattler* and snickered. "Poor sod's too young for a leg-shackle. Doubtless Lady Laud's pressing for grandchildren. Mothers!"

Their father lifted an eyebrow. "If your mother were still alive, you'd be wed by now, Thomas. I suppose I've been negligent on that front. You're what, thirty now? Ought to be settled down."

Thomas's fork clattered when it hit his plate. "And who would I marry? Some farm girl like Della here? If I were a banker's son I could look higher."

Della winced and her father's face turned red. "THOMAS! Apologize to your sister this instant!"

"Sorry," he mumbled. But Della could tell he wasn't sincere, even before he added, "But dammit, *she* should be wed by now too. But what choices does she have, as a farmer's daughter? We should all be better off if we sold out and went into banking."

Thomas Sr. pounded the table hard enough to rattle his plate. "ENOUGH!"

Both of his offspring stiffened and stared at him incredulously. Their father rarely lost his temper, and never at the breakfast table. But there had been more than a few arguments recently, Della mused.

"This farm has provided you an easy life, Thomas. You've been handed everything you need and want, even a chance for a superior education at Cambridge, which you squandered by neglecting your studies in favor of—er—" he swallowed as he glanced at Della, "studies of a different sort."

Della snorted and promptly looked down at her lap when her father gave her a stern look. Well really. She was twenty years old, the same age as Thomas when he returned home from Cambridge in disgrace. Did they really believe she hadn't heard all the stories about his misdeeds there? Rumors had been rife at the time, and although she might not have understood exactly what they meant at the age of ten, she had since apprehended them more clearly.

"I'm inclined to believe that this self-indulgent lifestyle you've embarked on can be attributed to the influence of the useless young lords with whom you caroused first at Harrow and then at Cambridge." He shook his head. "Your mother would be ashamed, Thomas."

His son had the decency to drop his chin.

And well he should, thought Della. He'd had the good fortune to have *had* a mother, at least. *She'd* never had that opportunity, her mother having died at Della's birth.

Their father pushed back his chair and rose from table. "Thomas, your jaunts to London and York and all points in between are now cancelled. Henceforth, you will spend your time at Paget & Sons, employed in furthering the interests of our sheep and cattle."

Folding his arms in front him, he glared at his son. "In case you've forgotten all you've been taught over the years, I'll put the lad in charge to refresh your memory."

With that, he marched out of the room.

Della giggled. The image of Thomas being bear-led around the farm by the much-younger estate manager seemed dubious at best.

He slapped the table. "It's not funny! I don't care a jot about sheep and cattle, and you all know it! Besides, I have a shooting party next week. It's almost the end of the grouse season."

Della's hands curled up. "You *should* care. This farm will be yours someday! It's in your own best interests to ensure its prosperity."

Thomas's lips curled. "It's been losing money for years. By the time it comes down to me, it'll be worth a pittance. Best to sell out now and put the capital where it can do some good."

Tilting his head, he studied her with a gleam in his eye.

"If I'm not mistaken, *you* are out there with the cattle every day. And Kit too. Now *there's* a match for you—the rustic farm girl and the penniless estate manager."

Della tossed the remainder of her sausage at him. "You are horrid, Thomas."

"And you're a twit," he threw back as he exited the room.

Della heaved a sigh. It wasn't that she didn't like Kit. He'd been one of her best friends forever. But as for marriage, she had something else in mind.

Reaching for the *Teatime Tattler,* she smoothed her fingers over the headline. Toby was looking for a wife, was he? Well, she intended that he look no further than the neighboring estate.

CHAPTER ONE

Assembly Hall
Ibstock, Leicestershire
30 September 1801

"Is he here yet?" "I can't see!" "Leave off pushing! You almost knocked me down!"

That last came from Della—Fidelia—Paget, who would never admit that she was as eager to see the entrance of Toby Boxworth as much as any of the other local girls. She was a little miffed that he hadn't come to see her since his return more than a fortnight ago, particularly since they were neighbors and close childhood friends.

Well, not so close *lately,* she had to admit. Not for a very long time, actually, not since he'd gone off to London to Eton, then Oxford, then off on his Grand Tour. In all that time, she and Kit had barely seen him, even during his brief furloughs at home. But now, the future viscount was home at Laud Manor and ready to settle down with a wife, or so the tabloids claimed.

And *that* was why the Assembly Hall was packed with young ladies in their best gowns, all hoping to catch the eye of the most eligible gentleman this side of Leicester.

She grimaced as she considered her own gown, best as it was of her limited wardrobe. It was the same old yellow muslin gown she'd worn to church and assemblies for as long as she could remember. The lace collar had started to yellow, and it was getting harder to tie the laces in front due to her burgeoning bosom. She really should have ordered a new gown. But tending to her appearance was a bore, and she'd assumed her long friendship with Toby would give her an edge over the rest.

Perhaps that was a mistake, she pondered as she finally reached the front of the wallflower flock just as Toby, resplendent in a black jacket with an embroidered ivory waistcoat and fawn-colored breeches, bowed before her cousin Helena and asked her to dance. Helena, her cheeks pink with pleasure, accepted and the couple headed for the dance floor as the master of ceremonies called for a reel.

Della tried not to be envious of her cousin. She and Helena were close in age and had been friends since forever, visiting each other frequently while growing up. Helena lived in Littlethorpe, where her father was a wealthy industrialist, and Della knew her current visit was prompted by the proximity of the young Laud heir. Helena was a beautiful blue-eyed blonde—at a time when blondes were the latest thing—and she had a wardrobe of lovely gowns to dazzle him with. She didn't know Della had set her cap at him as well; just that they had been close childhood friends. She'd met him herself on visits in the early days, before thoughts of marriage had entered any of their heads.

After his dance with Helena, Toby was introduced by the master of ceremonies to a half dozen other young ladies, with whom he danced before returning to Helena, this time a cotillion. He finally caught sight of Della when he returned Helena to her mother after the dance.

"Della Paget! By all that's holy, I didn't expect to see *you* here!"

He didn't? Why not?

He caught her by the hands and pulled her to him in a giant bear hug. "It's been so long! A year, at least!"

"More like three," she corrected him. "I've long since grown up, as you see."

He put her away and studied her intently, lingering longer on her breasts, pulled tight by the laces of the dress. "I see that. Why have I always pictured you as a wild hoyden?"

Della felt like crying. A wild hoyden? Not a close friend?

"You and Kit and I are going to have to have an outing together. For old times' sake," he said easily as he released her.

"Of-of course," she murmured. "Just say when, and I'll pass it on to Kit."

His mouth fell open. "You—and Kit? Don't tell me..."

"Oh no!" she cried out. "Kit works for Papa now. Manages the farm. I see him every day. We're friends—as we always have been."

His face cleared. "I see. His father is dead, then?"

She nodded. "Kit was the natural choice. He's grown up on the farm, after all."

"Of course." That was the moment his face changed, indicating the conversation was over, and he turned to Helena.

"Miss Clare tells me she's staying with you for the nonce. I hope I may be honored to pay you a call on Monday afternoon?"

Helena blushed, or at least deepened her previous blush.

"Yes," said Della bluntly. Could he have made it any plainer that his purpose in calling was her cousin?

She should have bought a new dress. A ball gown. And allowed Helena's abigail to make something of her unruly hair. Courting Toby might require a bit more effort than she'd expected.

CHAPTER TWO

Paget House
Ibstock, Leicestershire
1 October 1801

"Aн, m'dear lassie, your numbers are lookin' fair grand these days," Kit said as he rubbed the triangle between the calf's eyes and forehead. "I don't doubt you'll grow into a fine milker for some lucky dairy farmer in a year or so."

He led her out to the paddock and watched her stroll over to her usual companions. Smiling to himself, he headed over to his makeshift office, where he kept a ledger for recording statistics for the animals. Having studied with both Robert Bakewell and Thomas Coke, Earl of Leicester, he had learned the importance of keeping up-to-date, accurate records in order to optimize the growth and determine the success of the breeding program.

About to move on to the next calf, he was interrupted by the loud slamming of the barn door, which made him wince. Cattle didn't like loud noises; it made them skittish. Must be Thomas Jr., then, since neither Thomas Sr. nor Della would have been so careless. And indeed, it was the younger Thomas who appeared shortly after in the small paddock where the remaining calves waited to be measured and assessed.

"Good morning, Mr. Paget. What can I do for you?"

As a child, Thomas Jr. had been "Tom" to him, but since he'd become estate manager, it was "Mr. Paget" to his employer's son. Which had turned out to be a good move on his part, since the man seemed to resent him—a much younger man than he—elevated to the position left by the death of his father, the previous estate manager. Not that he'd ever aspired to it himself—what he'd learned about cattle breeding over his thirty years of living wouldn't qualify him to be a lowly farmhand. And this, Kit suspected, was the reason his employer was considering giving up cattle breeding to go into banking. Paget of Paget & Sons had only one son, and his interests were elsewhere. Now his daughter was another story. Kit smiled when he thought of Della. The farm was everything to her, but she'd been born a daughter.

"M'father thought you could use some help."

He shielded his eyes from the noonday sun. Kit thought he looked the worse for drink, his legs unsteady and his hand shaking slightly.

"Kammer could use some help mending fences in the north corridor." He knew better than to suggest mucking out stalls in the stables.

"Mending fences, bah!" He righted himself and studied Kit as he pulled another calf into the stall. "What are *you* doing?"

"Assessing the calves, as we do every third month."

Thomas dragged himself over to the calf and slapped his hind end. The calf bleated and skittered away. "I'd prefer to help you. What should I do?"

You could try not frightening the calves.

Kit coaxed the calf back into position, stroking him behind the head until he relaxed. Then he began a thorough examination, measuring his legs, head, and finally the girth. "600 pounds," he announced. "I've my eye on this one to sell for stud. His mam is one of old Sam's offspring. She went to Feldon's Farm last week and is producing about 15 gallons a week, or so he tells me. That's 780 gallons a year. Feldon is over the moon."

"Old Sam! We'll never see another like him. None of his spawn has come close to equaling him. Seems like we're in a downward spiral."

Kit sent the calf back to his friends, entered the figures into the book, and returned to choose the next calf.

"If you mean we haven't sold another steer for 400 guineas, that's a fact. But the stock from our breeding program is consistently bigger and more productive than any other around."

"But what do the books say? Damn long list of expenditures this year, Hall."

Kit's back stiffened. "There's a reason for that. We had to reroute drainage in the south field." He led the next calf into position. "In any case, the deficit is more than erased at the auction in the spring." His lips flattened as he glared at Thomas. "The same is true of last year and the year before."

Thomas crossed his arms. "Ah, but the profits are down since you took over from your father."

Kit was silent. It was true. His father had made some poor decisions during his last illness, and Kit had had to scramble to compensate. It hadn't escaped his employer's notice, but the two of them had agreed to keep quiet about it in order not to besmirch the memory of Kit's father.

"I've told Father cattle breeding is a lost cause. We should sell out before we reach rock bottom. Banking is where it's at. Much more profitable. More civilized. More suitable for a gentleman, in fact."

"Gentleman bankers, eh? That's a new one for me."

Thomas's fist slammed into the fence and startled the calf. "Dammit, Hall, you know what I mean!"

Kit turned to face him, nostrils flaring. "You don't like getting your hands dirty, I know. You'd rather sit in an office and count money and choose who to lend money to. Mix in society and marry an heiress." He shook his head. "Are you not forgetting that to the very top echelons of society, bankers have the 'smell of the shop'?"

"Farming is a respectable occupation. Farming feeds people. The top echelons of society are gentleman farmers—they live off the proceeds of their estates. Even King George has his own little plot to farm at Kew, or so they say."

Kit knew he'd gone too far when Thomas shook his fist at him. "You dare say that to me? You don't know anything but cattle breeding! Just wait until Father sells the farm and you're out of a job. I'll make sure no one in Leicestershire hires you!"

"What's going on here? Thomas, lower your voice. You're frightening the calves."

Della entered the paddock, closing the gate behind her, looking first at her brother, then Kit.

"Father is *not* selling the farm! And Thomas, why are you disturbing Kit at his work?"

"Did you *hear* how he spoke to me? The hired help?"

Della shook her head. "You didn't like what he said, that's all. Thomas, if you're not going to be helpful, just leave! I'm sure your cohorts are already assembling at the local pub."

He snorted. "And what do *you* know about anything? You're just a *girl.*" He raised his eyebrows. "Father sent me out here to work. I was trying to help Kit, but he won't allow me to."

Della rolled her eyes. "If you want to work, then go muck out the stables. You're more of a hindrance here."

"Blast it, Della. You have no right…!"

He gave one last kick to the gate and stomped off.

Della strolled over to the calf and stroked it gently. "I'm sorry, Kit. Father still hopes that Thomas will transform himself into a cattle breeder, but it will never happen." She stared off into the distance. "He won't consider me his successor, because I'm a *girl.*"

Kit's features softened. She was right. If she'd been born male, she'd have had a good chance to inherit the farm, although Thomas was the elder.

"I'm glad you're *not* a boy," he said with a flirtatious smile.

She shook her head, but her mood lightened. "Do give it up, Kit. You and I are friends. I don't know what I'd do without you. You're the only one in the world I know I can trust." She rushed over and hugged him tightly.

He pushed her away before she could notice his heartbeat pounding... and other areas reacting to her close contact. Then he noticed her cheeks were wet.

"What's wrong, Della? Has something happened?"

Della burst into tears. "It's Toby. He danced twice with Helena at the assembly and hardly noticed me at all!"

Spots flashed before his eyes. Toby was an idiot if he preferred Helena to Della. As for Della, well, there were times when he wished they weren't *such* close friends. Times like this, when she wanted to talk about other men as though he wasn't one himself.

Would she *ever* get over her childhood crush?

CHAPTER THREE

Three weeks later
River Sence, Leicestershire

"WHAT A CAPITAL IDEA YOU HAD, Della! The three of us, together again, fishing at our favorite spot! Remember when I caught that four-pound grayling? Put up a good fight, he did. Close to an hour, wasn't it, Kit?"

Kit shrugged. "It was a big one."

"Your father said the big ones like that usually get away, didn't he, Kit?" Della's eyes sparkled with excitement.

"Grayling are intelligent, as fish go," Kit admitted. He almost wished he had found an excuse not to come on this nostalgic excursion. Almost. But he didn't like the idea of Della and Toby alone in the backwoods, and clearly, he'd made the right choice. She had taken more pains than usual with her appearance, and Toby had cast her more than one appreciative look as they'd trudged along the leafy forest floor.

"Oh, there it is!" cried Della as the embankment they knew well appeared in the distance. "The brush is thicker, but the tree branch is still there!"

She started to run until her fishing pole caught on a tree branch.

"Be careful, Della! There are sticks and crevices underneath the leaves that might trip you up," warned Kit.

She frowned at him as she carefully untangled her pole from the tree. "I'm not a child!"

Not a child, perhaps, but she was behaving recklessly and, well, so naïve.

Reaching the site first, she headed for the massive oak tree with a branch extending around ten feet over the river.

"Oh Della! Really?" Kit remonstrated, as she lay her fishing pole down, pulled her skirts up and commenced climbing the tree toward the branch. "You'll regret it if you fall in the river."

She ignored him and was shortly seated astride the branch. "Hand me my pole, will you?"

Kit held it out to her. She pulled a worm out of a bag around her waist and cast the line into the water. "I see some big ones out here. What are you two waiting for?"

"She's a game one, is Della," whispered Toby into Kit's ear. "Hasn't changed a bit, except, well…" and he made a gesture indicating her feminine curves.

"She's changed in more ways than that," Kit retorted. "Not that you'd know, seeing you haven't been around much."

Toby tossed his line into the water and tilted his head toward Kit. "Oh? The wind is blowing that way, is it? The boss's daughter caught your eye?"

"Don't be ridiculous!" Kit lied. "We're friends, nothing more."

"Nonsense," said Toby. "Men and women can't be friends. Not the pretty ones, at least."

"What do you mean by that?" demanded Kit, troubled that Toby found Della pretty in spite of her hoydenish ways.

Toby's mouth formed an ugly twist. "Don't be a dolt, man! You know what I mean. Men get urges around attractive women. It's our nature."

"Oh please!" Kit objected. "We're not animals. And I'd best not hear you referring to Della in those terms."

Toby whistled. "You *have* got it bad. Listen, buddy, she might be a catch for you, but I've got my eye on her rich cousin. In the meantime, there are plenty of lasses around to be had without the wedding vows. You should know, eh? Any recommendations you can pass on?"

He nudged Kit with his elbow in a show of brotherhood. Kit wanted to punch him, when Della squealed that she had a bite. She had both hands on the pole and seemed close to losing her balance. Kit raced over to the tree and was up on top of the limb in a matter of seconds.

"What are you doing, Kit? I don't think the branch will hold both of us!"

"Don't be a fool, Della! You can't fight with a fish from up here! That water is ice cold and you'll catch your death if you fall in!"

She clenched her jaw, but before she could respond, the fish pulled hard at the line and she started to slide. Kit reached over and steadied her. "I'll help you with this one, but you'll come down and fish off the embankment with us after."

Toby was laughing uncontrollably when they returned, Kit's face red with rage and Della triumphantly sporting a ten-inch chub.

"What are you going to do with *that?* Feed it to the pigs? Pigs'll eat anything."

Della's face fell. "I thought we'd have it for dinner."

Blast Toby! Kit was constrained to defend her. "It's a fine fish, Della. Marinated in onion and garlic, chub's a tasty dish for the table."

Della turned soft eyes in his direction, and Kit felt a rush of happiness.

"I WOULD HAVE LIKED to stop in Paris a bit longer, but at least I did get to refine my fencing and riding skills, and spring for a top-notch wardrobe."

By this time, Toby had given up all pretense of fishing and was lying on his side, one hand supporting his head and the other pulling up blades of grass and tossing it as far as he could. Della listened intently to his adventures for the first half hour or so, and then had to force herself not to yawn.

"French fashion isn't that much different from ours," he opined. "It's just the extra touches that make their garments stand out. And the quality of the materials as well. The finest silks, the most exquisite embroidery, buttons that shine like jewels…"

Della glanced over at Kit and caught him stifling a yawn. Was there anything worse than listening to someone prattle on and on about his fabulous holiday? They exchanged knowing looks and made feeble attempts to change the subject.

"The harvest was certainly good this year."

"The new steer is finally cozying up to the cows we put him in with."

"Flirting with them, you mean." Della giggled.

But Toby didn't seem to notice. "But Italy was the best of all. The art, the music, the women—"

Kit reached over and slapped him on the shin and aimed his head at Della.

Toby jerked his head back and gave Kit an incredulous stare. Shrugging, he continued, "Well, all I will say is that the masquerades in Venice were like nothing you've ever seen in your life!"

"Is that all?" Kit quipped, with an eyeroll aimed at Della.

Toby didn't get it. "No, of course not. I bought a few Canaletto paintings and even one by Piranesi." He returned to his previous position. "It's too bad Father didn't provide a bigger allowance, because there were so many beautiful things to be had for relatively nothing. In Florence…"

Fortunately, Kit got a bite, and he and Della became engrossed in the drama of bringing in the fish. It turned out to be a nine-inch perch, which even Toby admitted was a prize of a catch. After the excitement petered out, however, he continued on with his travel tales.

"Now in Rome, we were invited to dinner at the home of Prince

Yusupov, you know, the Russian nobleman? There I saw the most beautiful sculpture ever created. Psyche Revived by Cupid's Kiss, the masterpiece of Canova. It was so realistic I almost believed it was real. Psyche, you see, was told not to open the vessel she was taking to Venus from Proserpina in the underworld…"

Della blew out a puff of air and tried to imagine what it would be like to be Toby's wife. To be a viscountess. The balls. Being presented to Her Majesty the Queen. But… she didn't really want a life like that. It came to her suddenly that Toby came with the sort of social obligations to which she'd never aspired. But if she wanted Toby, somehow she would manage the rest of it, wouldn't she?

"And so, the vessel, instead of making her more beautiful, put her to sleep. Cupid drew away the sleep and woke her with a delicate prick of his arrow. It's a romantic story, isn't it, Della?"

"Indeed."

"I haven't been able to get it out of my head," he mused. "And then, wonder of wonders, when I first set eyes on your cousin Helena, I knew immediately that she was Psyche to my Cupid."

Della nearly dropped her pole. Kit secured it for her and rose to his feet.

"I think that's enough fishing for today. Come, Della, I have work to do, and you can take both our fish to Cook to prepare for dinner."

Toby, completely oblivious to the distress he'd leveled on Della, continued expounding on his favorite subject, with a side forecasting of his glorious future with the lovely Helena at his side.

Della wanted to cry. But she waited until she got home, and then she locked herself in her room and cried her eyes out.

CHAPTER FOUR

Paget House
Ibstock, Leicestershire
Early November

"So, what do you have planned for today, Fidelia? Another fishing expedition? I do hope you and Master Toby don't monopolize my estate manager's time. I depend on Kit to keep everything in good order, you know."

"So it fetches a good price when we sell it," mumbled Thomas Jr., with a mischievous glance at Della, who gave him a glassy stare.

"I thought I'd check on Sally. Kit saw some mucus pooling yesterday when she was lying down."

"Excellent. A new calf is always a happy event. I'll look forward to meeting the newborn when I return from town."

Della stopped playing with her shirred eggs. "You're leaving, Father? For what purpose?"

"A meeting with other prospective investors in the new bank in Leicester. Thomas, if you promise to behave yourself, you may accompany me. I believe Della and Kit can manage the farm without us."

Her brother hooted. "Capital, Father! I'll go and gladly."

Della's face paled. "Is it... final, then? That you are selling the farm?"

Her father gave her a thoughtful look. "Not as yet, my dear. But you'd best prepare yourself. Your brother wants it, and I'm looking to the future." He leaned over and patted her hand. "Don't fret. You'll be wed and settled before long. You can trust Thomas and me to handle the business."

Because you're a female and couldn't possibly manage a cattle farm. Della had heard it over and over. It wasn't true and it wasn't fair. But that's how the world was run, at least for now. Someday perhaps... Her fists tightened under the table.

At that point, Kit was announced. His eyes sparkled and he forgot to take his hat off.

"Sally's had twins! A bull and a heifer!"

His gaze met Della's. "You'd best come and help. They appear to be healthy but need a bit of help feeding." He grinned. "Good old Sally. Twins indeed!"

Della's despondency vanished. "I *thought* she was carrying heavy. Do you think she can feed both of them?" She gulped the rest of her tea, hurled her napkin toward the table, and vaulted out of her seat.

"Don't get too excited," drawled her brother. "They're likely to be too weak to be useful for breeding. And the heifer is probably sterile. Best sent off for veal when the time comes."

Della glared at him. "I know where I'd like to send *you,* dear brother, and it's not to a bankers' meeting in Leicester!"

"Della!" roared her father.

But she and Kit were already gone.

"It's quite possible your brother is right, Della. Twin calves aren't usually favorable for cattle breeding." Kit and Della strolled to the barn.

Della dabbed at her eyes. "Oh, I know! But it's—it's the *way* he said it! As though money is the only thing that counts! And... the way he keeps taunting me about the farm being sold. And there's nothing I can do about it!"

She broke into tears and Kit drew her into his arms, lightly stroking her back while she sobbed. He wished he could make things better for her. She deserved so much more. But there were some things he was powerless to do for her. Things she would have to manage on her own.

As the sobs slowed, he drew away from her, offering her his handkerchief.

"Better now?"

She gave him a teary-eyed smile. "Yes. Thanks, Kit. I don't know what I would do without you. I think you're the only one who truly understands me."

Kit's heart felt full. *Don't you know I would do anything to make you happy?*

Taking her arm, he resumed their path to the barn.

"Your brother isn't all bad, Della. He's not a farmer. Never has been. He's been playing farmer for your father's sake all his life. And now he wants to do something he feels more suitable for him."

"He doesn't have to crow over it, though!" she snapped.

"No, he does not. But have you ever thought how he's felt all these years? Feeling out of place. Watching his very much younger sister take to cattle breeding in the way he should have done. He's never adapted to farm life. Or country life, either."

Della went still. "I never thought of it that way." She scrunched up her face. "But Papa *would* send him to Harrow and Cambridge. I don't suppose he met many farmers there!"

She studied him intently. "How have you learned all this? I never thought you and Thomas were bosom buddies."

He chuckled. "Hardly that. But we have worked together over the years, and it was obvious that he wasn't happy with his life. And he resented the fact that you were."

Della blew out a puff of air. "He wanted what I had and I wanted what he had. Why is life so complicated, Kit? I should have been him and he should have been me. If I were a man—the firstborn male, at least—I should not be in the position of losing everything I care about."

I'm glad you're not a man, thought Kit.

By that time, they had reached the barn, and Della broke into a run toward Sally and her newborn twins.

CHAPTER FIVE

Laud Manor
Ibstock, Leicestershire
Late November

"KELLER, Miss Paget's cup is empty."

It was a royal command. Della did not particularly wish for more tea, but she was not about to risk censure from her hostess for refusing it.

"Thank you, Lady Laud."

"Durand baked these lemon cakes this morning, from a receipt given to him by his cousin, who is employed at Kew Palace."

As a cook or a gardener? Della mused. Still, if the King enjoyed them, who was she to argue?

"They are delicious," she lied, as she accepted a second one. Either the Lauds' cook had misread the receipt or the King preferred his cakes dry and crumbly.

A moment later, Lady Laud set down her cup and touched the sides of her mouth with her napkin.

"I hear your father is selling the farm," she said with a thoughtful look at Della. "I wonder what you will do with your time when you move to town."

Della swallowed her annoyance. If this woman were to become her mother-in-law, she would have to learn to control her tongue.

"Nothing is set in stone, my lady."

Lady Laud sighed deeply. "I understand your reluctance to accept the situation, my dear. But it is time for you to put away that life and think of marrying and setting up your own household."

Della went completely still. Lady Laud speaking to her of marriage? Marriage to her son, perhaps?

"To that end, I have decided to host a ball on Christmas Eve. There will be many eligible young people in attendance, from Leicester and further afield, in attendance." She smiled, her eyes twinkling. "Never let it be said that I am a matchmaker. No indeed, I should never wish to take on the responsibility of deciding the happiness of any person."

"Of course not, my lady." Della's eyes narrowed.

"However, it has occurred to me since the recent return of my darling son that putting young people in the way of eligible partis is a rather obliging method of encouraging them toward matrimony." Lady Laud looked at her as though expecting a response.

"Of course, Lady Laud," she said with a weak smile.

"You are invited, of course, along with your brother. The two of you will move higher in society once you move to town. Your brother should have wed long ago, but you know how gentlemen are." She shook her head. "I shan't allow Toby to play man-about-town as long as that, you may be certain. His father and I expect him to settle down and do his duty to the family."

Her brother? A man-about-town? Della stifled a giggle. But where was her ladyship going with all this? The conversation wasn't going the way she'd originally hoped.

Lady Laud leaned over and smiled. "I don't approve of gossip, of course, but I must tell you that he was so charmed by your cousin Helena at the harvest assembly that he has been to call on her several times since, and that is the reason he is not here now."

Della felt numb all over. "He's-He's gone to Littlethorpe?"

Fortunately, Lady Laud didn't seem to notice the devastating blow she'd just delivered to her guest.

"Yes indeed. Of course, I don't know if anything will come of it. There will be many lovely young ladies at the ball that he will have to choose from, but I do see it as a sign that he is serious about settling down, don't you?"

Della managed to nod, her throat too thick to allow speech.

"It will be so exciting to have a party again at Laud Manor! The decorations in the ballroom will be much remarked upon, I assure you. Greenery and colorful ribbons and all sorts of beautiful hangings about. I say, my dear, might you be willing to help the servants with the preparations? I'm sure you will know all the best places for finding the holly and mistletoe and such. I shall be far too busy writing the invitations and ordering the food and music, but if Toby is home, he might help you, I suppose."

Acceptance was expected and Della gave it. Should she be grateful that the possible presence of Toby was thrown into the mix? Doubtful.

"And oh, my dear Della," her ladyship tossed after her as she rose to leave. "Do have a new gown made up for the occasion. You won't wish to be outshone by the other young ladies."

"Yes, my lady."

Would Toby notice her if she had a new gown? Seemed unlikely, but she didn't want to be seen as Helena's frumpy cousin either.

BY THE TIME she'd reached the end of Laud Manor's long, winding driveway, Della's despair had turned to anger. If she were a man, she wouldn't have to find a husband. She could do whatever she wanted to do, given the proper resources. She knew without a doubt that if she were born male—even the second male in the family—her father would have found a way for her to carry on with the farm. She was good at it—no, she was utterly marvelous at it—and he would know that putting her in charge would be a damned good financial decision (and he wouldn't quibble at her using the word damned either!).

But having been born female had limited her future to marriage and subservience to a husband. How many husbands would tolerate her involvement in animal husbandry, even if they had the resources to finance such an operation? A wealthy man would want a proper wife, who socialized with his friends, managed the household and the children, and essentially made his life comfortable.

Toby would want those things in a wife too, she mused. But if by some miracle she could have Toby, would she *mind* becoming his possession and losing herself? After all, it seemed she was doomed to losing herself no matter who she married.

BY THE TIME she returned home, her anger had dissolved into despair once again, so she headed to the paddock to check on the now two-month-old calves. She loved watching them frolic around the various groupings of older cows, chasing after each other like gleeful children. Children should be happy, she mused, because one day they would be grown up and have to face the hard truths.

"Frolic and play while you can," she murmured aloud. "The day will come when you're sent for slaughter."

"A case of the dismals, is it? Care to talk about it?"

Kit joined her at the fence where he tilted his head in her direction, his eyes making contact with hers.

She grimaced. "No. Yes. I don't know. I'm just... frustrated, I suppose."

He smiled sadly and turned to look at the frolicking calves. "I think I know what you mean. I've been pulling out steers for the abattoir. Seems harsh, but the English do love their beef, don't they?"

"We do indeed. And the farm needs the income. That's the way it is."

Her tone was flat, and he twisted his head back to her.

"Why do I suspect this isn't about cattle?"

Della jerked her head around to face him. "Oh Kit, it's just not fair! If I were a man, I could do any number of things. But a woman... Well, there's only one choice, isn't there? I'm so mad I could just spit!"

KIT POUNDED a fist on the desk in the estate office. *It's not fair!* she'd said, and she was right. Della was not the sort of woman to be content with a life of marriage, fashion, and afternoon teas. Perhaps it came from being motherless and loosely supervised by her father, but he rather believed those circumstances simply allowed her to grow into the woman she was intended to be. Intelligent. Capable. Honest. Determined. Self-confident. Independent. Such qualities in a man would have been considered appropriate and worked in his favor. But in a woman... not so much.

Her womanly qualities were there, however. She kept them hidden because she considered them weaknesses, but she was kind, compassionate, and nurturing—he knew from seeing her with the animals that she would be a good mother. And she did like getting new dresses even though she'd never admit it.

Now this fixation she had with Toby... He didn't believe it was love. It was more of a childhood infatuation that had become an obsession. He was wealthy and heir to a viscountcy. Those things alone would make him a target for marriage-minded young ladies, but he was also handsome, sophisticated, and a man of the world.

He shook his head. Clearly, Della would be miserable as a viscountess, for many reasons. She didn't really know Toby. The Toby of their childhood had been absent for many years, and during those years his character had radically changed. As with so many aristocratic youth, he had been let loose on the world to pursue his own pleasures as he wished. Now his father meant to rein him in, get him married and settled into his responsibilities, but it wasn't working so well. Toby frequented the local pub, flirting with the wenches, drinking to excess, and brawling with the patrons. Any young lady who wed Toby would soon become aware of her folly. But then, she'd be a wealthy viscountess, so perhaps that was enough.

Kit ran a hand across his face and tried to concentrate on the estate books. He and Della were so well suited. If only he had something to offer her. All he had was his employment as land manager, and as soon as Della's father sold the farm, he wouldn't even have that.

CHAPTER SIX

Madame Celeste Modiste
Leicester, Leicestershire
12 December 1801

"Well, I do think the white satin trimmed in gold would become you well, Della, with your dark hair. White is the fashionable color these days. Mama says white is the only appropriate color for young girls to wear in the evening."

Helena held up the shimmering fabric against Della's chest while an employee obligingly carried the remainder of the bolt.

"I told you I shan't wear white," Della insisted, pushing the fabric away. "White isn't even a color. I prefer the lavender sarcenet."

Stepping off the small stool, she selected the lavender bolt and held it under her face in front of the mirror.

Helena took a step back and studied her for a moment. "I must say, it does flatter your coloring. Perhaps with a delicate white handkerchief tied about the neck."

Della frowned at the white handkerchief idea, but eventually agreed that white was the best trim color for the dress. Necklines for evening were lower than she was accustomed to, and she wasn't eager to show off too much décolletage. She found her full breasts some-what embarrassing, not to mention inconvenient when she was out tending the stock. She was secretly envious of Helena's more elegant figure that better suited the current styles. *Her* bosoms didn't jiggle when she moved quickly or danced, nor was she ogled by members of the male sex wherever she went.

After hearing her grumble about this, Helena laughed. "My dear, you don't know how many young ladies envy your-er-fullness." She glanced down at her own meager chest. "Mama kept telling me mine would fill out in time, but I haven't seen evidence of it so far, and I'm a full year older than you are."

Della's eyes widened. "But... *why?* They are so... unwieldy! I've tried binding them to my chest, but it's not at all comfortable, and Thomas and the farmhands laugh at me behind my back."

A shocked gasp came from behind her. "Oh *mademoiselle*, you must never do such a thing again! You have lovely high bosoms that should be cherished and prized, even exploited!"

Madame Celeste grinned at Della's white face. "Poor dear, it is such a *dommage* you have had no *maman* to guide you. For she would have advised you that a chest such as yours is highly attractive to gentlemen. Your husband will convince you of that, when you are married."

Well! Della couldn't understand that at all. In any case, she didn't want a husband, unless it could be Toby Bosworth. But he seemed to prefer Helena's more modest figure.

While she mulled over this contradiction, Madame Celeste and Helena discussed a way of using boning under the breasts in her short stays to provide more support. Following this, the young ladies sorted through ribbons and trims for the neckline and sleeves, purchased a small length of white satin for the headdress, and headed for the haberdashery next door for a few sprigs of silk lavender flowers to dress it up.

"As for slippers," Helena suggested when they entered the ladies' shoe shop across the street, "Purchase at least two pairs if you plan to dance. I've had mine shred to pieces at a ball and would have had to return home in my stockings had my maid not brought along a spare."

"Perhaps they should be made sturdier," Della mumbled as the proprietor approached with a bow. Helena gave her a warning glance before she smiled and spoke to him.

"My cousin wishes to be measured for two pairs of white silk dancing slippers, if you please. They'll be needed soon, for a Christmas Eve ball."

"Ah, for the ball at Laud Manor. Come this way, miss. We will get you fitted up in good time for the event."

"Please, do make them as stout as you can. Miss Paget is extraordinarily fond of dancing, you see." Helena smiled wickedly at Della, who rolled her eyes.

The shoemaker clenched his jaw. "Our footwear is *always* sturdy, miss. We serve the best families in the shire, and they never have cause to complain."

"Perfect. When should we return for a fitting?"

LATER THAT DAY

"Oh look! There is Mr. Gooding with the greengrocer's cart!"

Della waved and called out to him. "Good day, Mr. Gooding! I hope your wife is feeling better!"

She couldn't hear his reply, as she and Helena were following the winding path along the river and he was a distance away on the road out of town, but it served her purpose in distracting attention from Helena's endless chatter about Toby Boxworth's call on her that morning while Della was out assessing livestock with Kit.

Horse and animal doctors being what they were—namely idiotic drunkards—the Pagets kept extensive records on the growth and health of each of their animals. Kit's father had taught them both many natural remedies and cures to treat and prevent common ailments. Keeping a close eye on each and every one was essential, and one of Della's favorite tasks was to accompany Kit on his rounds and carefully take down a written record.

But if she'd known Toby were coming to call, she'd have remained at home, dressed in her best day frock to sit in the parlor and pour tea and chat with him and Helena. Which sounded somewhat less appealing than what she had been doing instead, but at least she could have diverted some of his attention from Helena to herself and avoided Helena's silly prattling about his intentions toward her.

"Did I mention that he expressly requested *two* dances at the ball and forbade any of his friends from asking for more than one!"

"Yes, you did," replied Della dryly. "More than once."

"I wonder if he will declare himself at the ball. Mama will be in alt when she arrives tomorrow. I simply cannot wait to tell her all!"

No doubt Mrs. Clare would be eagerly planning the wedding, Della thought enviously. An engagement to a future viscount could mean a triumphant Season in London leading up to a fashionable June wedding at St. George's, none of which was likely for a young lady whose father was in trade, no matter how large her dowry might be.

That thought led Della to wonder how much of Toby's interest in Helena could be attributed to her wealth. An only child of doting parents who stood to inherit everything of theirs, in addition to her generous dowry. As soon as it came to her, she banished it from her mind. The Clares were fabulously wealthy and Helena, well, she was a close friend and cousin, a wonderful person and deserved to be desired for herself.

"Remember when we were children and lay outdoors and specu-lated on our future husbands? I was smitten with the fetching butch-er's son who used to smile at me in church." She chuckled. "Imagine *me* as the wife of a butcher!"

She tilted her head at Della. "What kind of husband did *you* dream of back in those days, Della? I can't recall. Someone more practical, I suppose."

A future husband? Della couldn't think of anyone. Most girls had mothers to fill their heads with thoughts of beaux and marriage and the necessity of it, but Della had not. It had all seemed rather irrelevant to her life, until her governess had suggested that she might set her cap at Toby Boxworth, since he and Kit were such devoted playmates of hers.

Della went still. Was that where the idea of marrying Toby originated? She hadn't paid much attention to it at the time—or at least she hadn't thought so—but why, as time passed, had it seemed as though she and Toby were meant for each other? She liked Kit as well, and somehow, he'd never crossed her mind as a potential marriage partner. Which was all quite astonishing, really, because she had much more in common with him. Toby's wife would be a grand lady, and she'd never aspired to that. No indeed. If she were ever to marry anyone, Kit would be the perfect choice.

Still musing over this surprising conclusion, she didn't hear the quiet sobbing until Helena pulled her over behind a clump of bushes.

"What—?"

"Hush, they'll hear us."

Della huddled down beside her cousin and followed her line of sight to the back of the church and the churchyard, where not twenty feet away on a memorial bench sat Mrs. Timmers, the vicar's wife, and her daughter Cassie, a girl of tender years, perhaps fifteen or sixteen.

"I'm so sorry, Mama. I never meant to—it happened so quickly. If I'd known, I'd never have let him—"

"Hush, child. You need not explain further." Mrs. Timmer swung her head about to check for listening ears.

Oh dear. We really should not be here. But if we move away, our presence will surely be discovered, the result being embarrassment on all sides.

Della and Helena exchanged anxious glances. Helena covered her ears and motioned for Della to do the same, but it was no use. Cassie's sobs and her mother's frantic attempts to console her were clearly audible.

"What shall be done, Mama? I am ruined!"

Her mother put an arm around her shoulders and patted her arm. "Oh, my darling child, I know not what to do."

Her daughter erupted in renewed sobbing.

"But we shall think of something, Cassie dear. Perhaps your father can persuade him to marry you. To avoid a scandal, you know."

Cassie pushed her mother away. "He'll never do that, Mama. The scandal is mine alone! He says a future viscount must look higher than a vicar's daughter for a wife, and that the fault is mine since I didn't stop him!"

Toby? Toby was the one who had molested poor Cassie? Surely not!

Helena went pale and mouthed the word NO, but Della clapped a hand over her mouth before she could utter a sound.

"Oh, what a rogue he is, that Toby Boxworth!" Mrs. Timmers shook her fist. "Your father will have something to say to Lord Laud when he finds out, of that I am certain!"

Cassie leapt to her feet and took a few steps toward the greenery that concealed Della and her cousin before turning on her heels and facing her mother.

"No, Mama! I won't have him forced to wed me! I hate him!"

"You hate him now, but you apparently didn't always hate him," replied her mother sensibly.

Another wave of sobs. "But-but I thought he liked me! He was so k-kind and attentive. The things he said... I thought he loved me!"

"I know you did, my dear, but in the heat of-er-the moment, young men say things they don't mean. Surely I warned you about such things when you were younger!"

"But... this was different! I was certain Toby loved me! I wanted so much to make him happy..."

Her mother rushed over to take her daughter into her arms. They were close enough to the girls' hiding place as to make Della hold her breath.

"Come, my child. I believe your father must be finished with his tutoring lessons. Once he has learned all, I am convinced he will know what can be done."

Della breathed a sigh of relief as Mrs. Timmers led her daughter toward the vicarage amidst further sobs from one and soothing words from the other.

After they had disappeared into the house, Della and Helena turned and ran through the woods until they were in sight of Paget Farm. When they finally stopped, Della turned to Helena, whose face was wet with tears.

"I never dreamed Toby could be such a blackguard, Helena! Oh, he was somewhat full of himself after his gadabouts in London, but I was sure the old Toby was still there somewhere, and he'd settle down once we-er-*he* married." Della hoped Helena had not caught her slip of the tongue.

Helena stomped her foot. "And to think, I might have unknowingly tied myself to that scoundrel! For life! Oh Della, I swear I will never wed anyone ever!" She shrugged her shoulders. "Well, at least not until Papa has investigated him inside and out and we are certain he wants me for myself and for no other reason!"

Della pulled Helena into her arms and laughed shakily. "Oh Cousin, I am so glad your heart is not broken. For you are absolutely right that you deserve only the best of husbands!"

Joining hands, they made their way toward the farm quietly discussing poor Cassie and thinking up appropriately dreadful punishments for her ravisher.

Upon encountering Kit bending over to check a sheep near the paddock, Della found herself staring at him. How had she never noticed his wide shoulders and muscular thighs?

"Kit..." she began abstractedly, stopping in her tracks.

Kit stood up immediately, eyebrows drawn together. "What is it, Della? Are you well?"

For the first time, she looked deeply into his blue eyes and saw—concern, perhaps—or was it something more?

Kit. Kit's the one. Not Toby, never Toby. It's always been Kit. But—why? How?

She couldn't have spoken had her life depended on it.

Helena's gaze bounced between one and the other, her eyes narrowed.

Finally, she pulled at her arm. "She'll be fine, Mr. Hall. Just had a touch of the sun. You know how careless she is about removing her bonnet."

Clearly, he did not, as he continued to stare after them as they moved past him toward the house.

Della was stunned. In addition to his other stellar qualities—which she'd shamefully taken for granted—Kit was an exceedingly handsome young man.

The perfect man for her. Was it possible he returned her feelings? Or had she left it too long?

CHAPTER SEVEN

Laud Manor
Ibstock, Leicestershire
23 December 1801

"I won't do it! You cannot force me! I am not a child to be ordered around, Father. I shall do as I please, marry whomever I please!"

The study door slammed, and Kit heard Toby stomp out of the room and dash down the stairs where he nearly crashed into Kit, who was just leaving the house after a consultation with the Boxworths' estate manager.

Kit put out his arms to ward off the impact. "Steady on, man! What's happened? Take a breath and calm down before you do something rash."

Toby pushed him away. "I've got to get out of this place." He accepted his overcoat and hat from the hovering butler and stomped toward the front door. "This place is so stifling. I'd trade places with you in a minute, Kit. You can do what you want, marry where you want—or not marry at all, which seems to be the best choice of all."

Kit blinked. Toby thought he wanted to be him? Not a chance! He followed his friend outside.

"Where are you going? What are you planning to do?"

He expected to hear something along the lines of the pub or the gentleman's club in Leicester, but stopped in his tracks when he took in Toby's words.

"Over to Paget's to propose to Della."

Propose to Della?

"What did you say?"

Toby halted and turned toward him. "I'm headed over to Paget's to propose marriage to Della Paget."

He had heard correctly. Kit's heart sank.

"Della? But why?"

"Because I can, that's why. I shan't marry that slut Cassie, in any case. Who's to say the babe is mine? I shall wed Della and install her at Laud Manor while I kick up my heels in Town and live my life as I please."

A sudden coldness formed in his core. "Cassandra Timmers, the vicar's daughter? You molested that child? Good God, Toby, tell me you did not!"

Toby's nostrils flared. "Molested? Not on your life! She begged for it! I'm sure the whole thing was a plot to trap me into making her a viscountess." He snickered. "Well, the joke's on them. I shall wed Della instead and that'll teach them, and Father too!"

He spun on his heel and continued his trajectory toward the stables.

Kit took a deep breath and tried to control his emotions. This wasn't the Toby he'd known as a child. Toby the boy had been a tease and a prankster, but never cruel. He'd recognized the not-so-subtle changes in Toby over the years, his self-centeredness, his recklessness, his irresponsibility—but he hadn't expected *this*.

He wanted to talk sense into his friend—perhaps *former* friend was the more accurate term—but discerned that it would be wasted effort. Whatever had passed between Toby and his father had created a raging inferno that had to play itself out, no matter who or what was destroyed in the process.

An uncontrollable shudder swept through his body. *Della.* Toby was going to see Della and ask her to marry him! No, in this frame of mind, he would *demand* that she marry him. If she refused, there was no telling how he would react. Violence was not out of the question. She could be seriously injured before the other occupants of the house could rescue her.

There was no time to waste. Kit mounted his own horse and raced after Toby, his heartbeat racing. Della was no fool, but he knew she was infatuated with Toby. She might even *accept* his proposal!

Which would be disastrous for all concerned. Somehow, Toby had to be stopped.

BY THE TIME KIT ARRIVED, the Pagets' groom was leading Toby's horse toward the stable and Toby had presumably already been permitted entry into the house. Throwing himself off the horse, Kit was about to follow suit when the groom called out to him.

"If it's Miss Della yer after, she's in the barn with the twin calves."

"And Mr. Boxworth?"

"Bolted into the house loik 'e had a banshee after 'im."

Kit let out a huge breath. "Thanks, O'Neill." What to do now? Go after Toby or warn Della? Della, he thought. And then she appeared from inside the barn

"Kit! Do come and see Reuben and Rebecca. They're simply adorable!"

"Della!" He sprinted toward her. "I must speak with you. Now!" He gave an anxious look toward the house before grabbing her arm and pulling her into the barn.

Della blinked. "What? What's wrong, Kit? Is Father well? Thomas?"

"No! Yes! It's not that, Della. It's Toby!"

"Toby? What's happened to Toby?" She clutched her hands. For some reason that infuriated him.

"Toby! It's always Toby with you, isn't it? And you must know he doesn't deserve to be in the same room as you!"

Della flinched. "Kit! Calm down and tell me what is going on? Something to do with Toby? He's not hurt, is he?"

She took both his hands and led him to sit on a bale of hay, where she laid an arm around his shoulders. She was so close he could feel her heart beating in her breast, and his breathing began to normalize.

"I hardly know how to begin, Della, but Toby has had a row with his father and has ridden over in a fury to propose to you!"

Della went completely still. "What?" Her body slumped against him and he propped her up with his arm.

He described his recent interaction with Toby, and she began to recover from the shock.

"So he thinks he can propose marriage to me to spite his father?" Her back straightened and she spoke in a carefully controlled tone.

"Well… That's the gist of it. But Della, I hope you don't take it the wrong way. It's nothing against you."

She glared at him. "What other way is there to take it? Clearly I am nothing to him but a weapon to punish others!" She rose and began pacing the floor with fists clenched. "You know, Kit, I *should* actually wed him and proceed to make his life utterly miserable."

Kit's eyes widened.

"But I won't, of course, because in doing so I should make myself miserable as well… and Cassie's poor babe would grow up a bastard. Although with *such* a father, one wonders if having none at all might possibly be better."

Kit drew a deep breath. "And Della, you might warn your cousin as well. I know he came to call on her the other day…"

Della snickered. "Never fear, that shan't ever happen. Helena knows about Cassie"—she explained the conversation they had overheard the previous day—"and she'll never tie herself to a man like that."

Then her shoulders slumped. "But he was my *friend*," she said sadly. "*Our* friend, Kit. How did this happen?"

They commiserated for a few minutes before they were interrupted by one of the housemaids.

"Miss Della, you have a caller. Yer father says to get upstairs and dressed for company right away!"

DELLA STOOD UP, nostrils flaring. How dare Toby think he could use her to punish his father!

Then she sat down again. Toby was going to propose to her! The very thing she'd dreamed of from childhood! But it wasn't right. Toby wasn't the man of her dreams any longer—and probably should never have been in the first place. A young girl with stars in her eyes could be excused for having her heart set a-flutter by a handsome young lordling. But to keep the illusion going for so many years in spite of the burgeoning evidence of his poor character... that she couldn't forgive herself for.

"Della! You're shaking! You must not go alone to face him. He's in a fury and there's no telling how he will react when—if—you refuse him!"

He began rubbing her back and when she looked into his eyes, she saw worry and tenderness and something else that made her heart skip a beat.

"Kit—" she began. "I've been a fool. It's not Toby I want. It's you. It's always been you."

Kit let out a huge breath. "Thank God," he said. "I've loved you forever."

He pulled her into his arms and kissed the top of her head. "I'll go with you," he said definitively.

"No," she said pulling away reluctantly. "This is something I need to do myself."

Kit shook his head. "He's like a raging bull. He might hurt you." He gave her a tender look. "I can't let him do that, Della. Not... now, when I know you are mine."

"Now Kit," she said, her jaw tightening. "By now you surely must know that I cannot be dominated. I must tell him myself. In terms that he could never mistake as feminine melodrama."

Her face softened when she saw the fierce protectiveness in his eyes. He loved her! It gave her such joy and happiness to know her life was secure with him as her partner. From now on, it was the two of them together, not just her alone.

"You can be right outside the door," she proposed. When his face didn't change, she added. "With the door cracked open so you can hear everything that happens."

"What the hell is going on here?"

The raving maniac who burst through the open barn door was Toby, red-faced and disheveled, nostrils flaring, an engorged vein twitching in his neck.

"Your father assured me you'd be waiting in the morning room to hear my proposal, Della! And here you are wallowing in the hay with the hired help looking like a stable boy!"

"How dare you speak to Della that way!" Kit stood up and made a move to confront him, but Della's hand on his arm caused him to pause and notice the warning glance on her face.

"Kit? Hired help? He's your friend, remember? We both are. Why do you come in here thundering at us in this manner?"

Toby's lips curled. "And you! You're a disgrace to all womankind, Della. I must be off my head to offer for *you,* of all women in the world. Remaking you into a proper wife will be a formidable task, let me tell you!"

This time there was no stopping Kit. He was on the other man with the speed of lightning, with a punch to the chest that sent him backward into a pile of straw-covered horse manure. Stunned for a moment at the indignity of his position, Toby was unable to fully rise and prepare himself for Kit's next attack, which resulted in the two of them flailing in the manure, throwing punches and exchanging epithets.

"Stop it!" Della moved forward and was about to attempt to pull them apart, when someone pulled her back.

"What the hell is going on here?" Her father thundered. "Stop this immediately or I'll call the constable and have you both locked up!"

All motion ceased.

"He punched me first!"

"He insulted Della!"

"I just wanted to propose to her!"

"I wouldn't marry you if you were the last man on earth!"

Her father whirled around and glared at her. "I'll talk to *you* later. Go back to the house and tidy yourself while I deal with these two miscreants."

"But Papa..."

"Do as I say, Fidelia!"

Della's eyes widened. She knew when he used her full name in that tone of voice that no further argument would be tolerated.

"Yes, Father." She sighed and shook her head at Kit before she turned and left the scene.

What would he do to them? Surely he wouldn't sack Kit! He'd been expecting her to hear Toby's proposal. Would he be disappointed that she would not agree to marry the most eligible bachelor in the county? And how would he react to her attachment to Kit instead?

Della climbed the stairs slowly and flung herself on her bed in a flood of tears.

CHAPTER EIGHT

ONCE DELLA HAD DEPARTED, her father ordered the two combatants to 'remove themselves from the damned shite' and explain themselves.

"He insulted Della in a most grievous manner." Kit gave his adversary a menacing look.

"I was about to propose marriage to her!"

"When there's another girl who *deserves* the dubious honor of your hand in marriage," spat out Kit.

Toby's eyes widened. "How do you know—" and then shrugged in defeat. "I suppose Della knows as well."

"She does."

Thomas Paget stroked his throat and grimaced. "And you were about to offer marriage to my daughter when this other girl—" he glanced at Kit.

"The vicar's daughter."

"The *vicar's* daughter?" His eyes threw daggers at Toby, who flinched in shame.

"When the *vicar's* daughter is expecting your child?"

Toby crossed his arms in front of them as though trying to make himself smaller.

Thomas approached him menacingly. "You really are a blackguard,

Boxworth. To offer my daughter such an insult after all your years of friendship!"

Toby edged backward toward the barn door. "Perhaps I'd better take my leave..."

"Yes, do go, and quickly, before I have you removed from the premises. And don't come back until you have rectified matters with the girl and changed your ways. My Della deserves far better than a bastard like you!"

"And so does the vicar's daughter," he mumbled under his breath, after Toby had scampered away.

"Now as for you, Hall," he said as he turned to Kit, "do explain how it is that you became ensnared into this imbroglio."

Kit's face, neck, and ears became impossibly hot. "I beg your pardon, sir. I should not have assaulted a guest of yours."

"Balderdash!" His employer scowled at him. "I would have done the same in your shoes. Defending my daughter's honor and all that. No, I want to know how you fit into all this. The whole story."

Kit bit his lip. *I love your daughter. I want to see her happy. I want to see her happy with me.* Somehow he couldn't get those words out. Because Della deserved the best, and he had nothing to offer her.

"It's a long story, sir."

Thomas studied him intently, then offered him a hand, which was just as quickly withdrawn.

"You smell of shite," he said with an upturned nose. "Get yourself cleaned up. I'll send Ellerbee to prepare a bath for you. After that, I'll see you in my study at—" he consulted his watch" —half past four. Is that acceptable to you?"

"Yes sir. Of course, sir." As his employee, Kit could hardly refuse. In fact, it seemed odd that Paget would put his request in the form of a question. Kit had been expecting to be sacked..., and he might still be sacked.

He sighed and followed his employer to the house.

KIT WAS MISSING at dinner and both her father and brother looked at her apprehensively when she appeared in the dining room.

"Where's Kit?"

Her father pulled at his cravat. "He… had some work he had to do. Said he'll get something in the kitchen later."

"Reckon he's hightailed it to the pub, considering he's out of a job," quipped her brother.

"What?" Della felt an overwhelming sensation of dread. "Kit's been sacked? But Papa… he didn't do anything wrong!"

Her father glared at his son. "Thomas, didn't I tell you to let me handle this? You have all the subtlety of a pig in a parlour."

Thomas rolled his eyes and leaned back in his chair.

"Handle what?" Della turned suspicious eyes back and forth between the two of them. "You sacked Kit, did you not? Is there more?"

Her father put up his hand. "Patience, daughter. Ellerbee is waiting to serve the soup."

"I'm not hungry." Della crossed her arms in front of her.

When the soup was served, Thomas Sr. ordered the room to be cleared of all servants. "I'll call you when we're ready for the next course."

All eyes were on Della. Nobody even looked at the soup.

Her father cleared his throat. "My dear, Kit has not been sacked. It's just that—the farm has been sold—you knew that was coming, did you not?"

Della sagged back in her chair. "So all is gone… and Kit is out of a job."

"Quite possibly, unless the new owner decides to keep him on." At her angry protest, he added, "Della, Kit will get through this. He's the best estate manager in these parts, and everyone knows it. I shall do my best to make sure he is… amicably settled."

Della pushed back her chair and started to rise. "I'm going to find Kit."

"SIT DOWN, DELLA!"

Both of his offspring stared at him. Thomas Sr. rarely raised his voice, and Della had never heard him thunder at her in such a way.

She sat down.

Her father narrowed his eyes. "We will speak more of this in my study after dinner. For once in your life, Della, do as you are told, and EAT YOUR SOUP!"

Della picked up her spoon, while still eyeing her father with suspicion. More? What more could there be? The farm would be sold and her life would never be the same. And Kit? They might never see each other again!

The meal continued in silence. Della ate sparingly, head down, avoiding the eyes of her father and brother. When the servants came to clear the table, they all rose, and Della headed toward the door.

"In my study, Della. Now!"

CHAPTER NINE

DELLA'S STOMACH roiled from the tension at dinner, and the last thing she felt like doing was listening to a lecture from her father. She'd heard it all before: moving to the city was in her best interests; she could go to parties and meet eligible partis and marry and then she would learn to be satisfied with her natural role as a wife and mother. It didn't matter to anyone that she had dreams and desires of her own, desires that now she knew included an estate manager soon to be out of work. No, the important thing was that her brother be granted *his* desire to escape the farm and become a banker and socialize on a higher level where he didn't have to get his hands dirty.

Neither of them understood her or even thought twice about her. She was only a female, after all. By the time she forced herself through the door of her father's study, she had worked herself into a fair rage.

He was seated behind the desk in the center of the room.

"Sit down, my dear."

My dear?

"I'd prefer to remain standing," she replied, her eyes studying the floor.

"As you wish."

Her father rose.

"I had a long talk with Kit this afternoon."

She jerked her head back. "You did? So, you know…"

"Everything, I believe."

He moved toward her and put a hand on her shoulder.

"Everything?" She crossed her arms and squinted at him.

"You and Kit."

He bit his lip. "It never occurred to me, Della. I'm a failure as a father. It was clear you carried a torch for young Boxworth over the years, but it never occurred to me that your affection had shifted to Kit."

It hadn't occurred to me either.

"I only just discovered it myself, Father." She shook her head. "My tendre for Toby was an illusion, a childhood fairy tale that persisted for years in spite of all evidence of his vanity and superficial nature. I was a blind fool." Tears pricked her eyes.

Her legs weakened and she would have crumpled to the floor had her father not caught her and half-dragged her to a nearby armchair.

"Nonsense, child. Young Boxworth fooled us all, even those of us old enough to know better. I do hope his father manages to rein him in before he becomes a black mark on the Laud heritage."

Della looked up at him through the tears. "I should have known better ages ago, Papa. I should never have made a proper viscountess. No—don't argue—it's true! I would have had to miss calving and lambing time in order to dance at balls and make morning calls. It never occurred to me that Toby would not wish his wife to be involved with livestock."

Her father fell into the chair next to her, laughing heartily. "No indeed!" He handed her a handkerchief. "But Della, if I had been paying attention, I might have had some idea that Kit and you were perfect for each other. Instead, I took for granted that once we were in Leicester you would turn your attention to marriage and children."

He clasped both of her hands with his. "My dear, the blind fool here is me. If your mother had been here—no, I shan't use her absence to justify my ignorance. I knew I had a remarkable daughter with extraordinary talents and abilities, and instead of encouraging her, I made her feel deficient, as though her wishes counted for nothing."

"Because I'm female."

He sat back in the chair and furrowed his brow. "Well... yes, I suppose so. Well, Della, I don't know any girls who took to farming like you did. I never had sisters myself, of course, and it seemed to me that eventually you would outgrow it and take interest in gowns and balls and beaux and such."

He sat forward, looking pensive.

"I never meant to neglect you, my dear. I expected the governess would take you in hand and turn you into a proper young lady, as a mother would do."

Della sniffed. "She was a stodgy old maid who was always shrieking at me and striking me with her ruler."

Her father blanched. "I'm sorry for that. As soon as I discovered that, I got rid of her, and agreed to send you to the village school with Kit."

Della's mood darkened. "Papa, about Kit..."

His face took on a grave expression. "My dear, I spoke with him at length and told him of your dowry—no, I didn't entirely forget about you in all this business with your brother and the farm—and also a bit of land near Loughborough that belonged to your maternal grandmother that I planned to settle on you."

She shifted in her seat. "Papa..." Her feelings for Kit were too new. Kit had not spoken of marriage. And yet, the thought of marriage to him made her toes curl.

He gave her a sharp look. "You *do* want to marry him, do you not?"

Della straightened up. "Yes. Yes, of course I do! It's just that... he hasn't asked me yet."

Her father sighed heavily. "Nor is he likely to any time soon, my dear. He is adamant that he won't do so until he can afford to support a wife and family with his own two hands."

Seeing her face fall, he added quickly. "A man has his pride, you know. I'm certain he will find a post in no time at all."

"Pride!"

Della rose and paced in front of the desk. "What use is pride? Kit knows very well I'm not a useless female who will be a burden on him. I'll work by his side as I have always done. We'll be together. That's all that matters, really. Isn't it?"

Her breath quickened as she imagined a cozy life with Kit on a farm where they could retire to their own cottage and relax in each other's arms in front of a toasty fire.

She paused and regarded her father. "Help me, Papa. Surely there must be some way to convince him that his pride need not be an obstacle to our happiness."

He scratched his chin. "I wish your mother were here. She had a particular talent for managing situations like this."

Della grimaced. She'd never had a mother, knew very little about the one who'd given birth to her. Except...

"I've got an idea!"

Her father jerked his head back.

"Remember that box of things Mama made for me before I was born?"

"Yes, but..."

Della rushed out of the room, exclaiming behind her.

"I think there's a way she can help me get through to Kit!"

CHAPTER TEN

Christmas Eve
The Vestibule
Laud Manor

"How do I look, Helena? Is my gown wrinkled? Is my hair falling down? Oh, where is a looking glass when you need one?"

Her cousin smiled. "You look beautiful, Della. Trust me, I've seen you when you didn't care a jot for your looks and I know the difference. Your Kit will be enchanted."

She had confided all to Helena the previous evening, and the pair of them had remained awake half the night talking about Kit and her plan to convince him to ask her to marry him at the Lauds' Christmas Ball. Helene was enchanted when she heard it. Their excited chatter continued all morning and into the afternoon, as the two of them prepared for the ball.

Della *was* feeling quite pleased with her looks that evening. The lavender sarcenet flattered her coloring, and the short stays gave her a pleasing feminine figure that didn't jiggle when she moved (she hoped). The white lace kerchief tucked around her shoulders preserved her modesty while revealing a subtle glimpse of décolletage.

Helena's maid had tied the white satin turban around her head, leaving out longer curls in front to rest on her shoulders, as was the latest style. The dark curls behind the turban were tied up and arranged to give the illusion of carelessness.

There was a difference, Della learned, between true carelessness and *arranged* carelessness. Now that she had a beau, Helena said, she would have to learn to care about these things.

Privately, Della didn't think Kit would expect such things, but then, she hadn't really had a beau for all that long and wasn't entirely sure he could officially be considered her beau, so she didn't argue.

By the time they arrived in the family carriage, the long drive was congested with carriages and wagons and pony carts, with neighbors and villagers lining up to be admitted to the elegant Georgian manor, the entrance lit up with gold-rimmed glass lanterns on sturdy black poles. The Lauds' Annual Christmas Ball was a celebration of the harvest as well as the traditional holiday season. Everyone was invited, from the baker to the butcher, and they all came dressed in their best to participate in the festivities.

The vicar was there with his wife and daughter, which gave Della a bit of a jolt. Nevertheless, she greeted them both with genuine pleasure. Cassie seemed a bit pale, but was nevertheless in her best looks, in an ivory gown that complimented her blonde locks. She was a sweet girl. Della hoped her appearance that evening anticipated a happy conclusion to her troubles.

Lady Laud greeted her with pleasure. "My dear, I know I have you to thank for organizing the beautiful decor. I'm told that you and your cousin were responsible for the lovely curtain representing the manger scene."

Della flushed. "Helena—my cousin—painted the curtain. I-uh-decorated the chairs."

Her hostess chuckled. "So clever too, sheep, cows, goats, horses, pigs, even a dog or two—all waiting for our guests to sit in them. And the lamps as Wisemen, how amusing!"

Della wasn't sure if her ladyship actually approved of her unconventional design, but at least she was polite. Della had put in a great deal of time assisting the servants in arranging the holly, greenery, colorful paper chains, and strategically-placed kissing balls around the ballroom, lobby, and card room.

"Thank you, your ladyship."

She herself wasn't looking forward to facing Toby, next in the receiving line. Apparently, he felt the same, bowing and saying her name without making eye contact. *Coward!*

She did notice his father giving him a stern look and a nudge when Cassie reached him; this had the effect of putting a smile on his face, and a "You are looking lovely tonight, Miss Timmers."

Well, well. Perhaps there was a *tiny* bit of Christian charity in the man. Even if most of it was forcibly placed there by his father, or so she suspected.

Helena was soon led to the dance floor by a blushing young gentleman, and Della was left searching the room for Kit. He'd promised her father he would attend. Where was he?

She'd just caught a glimpse of him near a potted plant, sipping a cup of wassail she guessed. Her heart fluttered as she caught sight of him in a perfectly-fitted bottle-green coat, yellow waistcoat, and beige breeches. He was magnificent!

Just as she caught his eye, the greengrocer's son touched her arm and asked her to dance. Declining being not an option in an event such as this, she agreed, tossing a grimace in Kit's direction as she was whisked off to the dance floor.

With all the twists and turns and hops and her efforts to protect her feet from her partner's heavy steps, she lost track of Kit altogether, and when she was free, he seemed to have disappeared. Not dancing, not chatting, and not in the card room either.

He wouldn't have left, would he? Not before they'd had a chance to speak to each other!

The terrace. He must be on the terrace. She hesitated a moment in case he might suddenly appear from another room, but then hurried to the terrace door. Other than the embracing couple in the far corner, he was the only one out there. No doubt because of the extremely frosty evening.

"Della! You should not be out here. You'll catch your death of cold!"

Suddenly his coat was around her shoulders and he was holding her in his arms. Which was just where Della wanted to be. She leaned in and breathed in his scent, earthy and clean with a hint of bergamot. Mostly just... Kit. She closed her eyes and reveled in the moment. Surely she wasn't dreaming when she felt his arms tightening around her.

"Oh... Kit!"

"Della..." His voice was raspy, and when she opened her eyes, he was looking down at her with all the love and tenderness she could hope to see.

His mouth came down on hers and while they kissed her heart soared and she knew all was right with the world.

"Kit," she managed to get out when the kiss had ended. "I have something for you." She pulled away slightly in order to reach for the reticule on her wrist and pull it open. "It was a bit difficult to fit it inside, but I'm sure it'll come out."

Kit gave her an anxious look. "We should go inside. If we were to be found here..."

"It wouldn't matter in the slightest," Della quipped, still rummaging in her bag. "Ah, I have it now!" she exclaimed, clutching a red cushion-like item in her hand, while allowing the reticule to fall and blow away in the breeze.

She held it up to show him a stuffed heart, beautifully embroidered in shades of red and pink.

"What is it?"

She smiled brilliantly, feeling a prickle of tears forming. "It's a heart. My mother—whilst expecting me—made it for me. Which she was never able to give me, since—" She sniffed.

"Yes, I know, darling." He hugged her tightly to him. "I'm sorry you never knew her." Taking out a handkerchief, he used it to wipe her eyes.

"When I was old enough, my father gave me some of her things he'd saved, some baby clothes and linens and such, and this was one of them. He said her intent was for me to keep it until I had met the man I loved and wanted to marry. And then," she said solemnly, "I was to give it to him as a pledge of my love and commitment."

She closed his hand around it and beamed at him. "It's yours, Kit. It's always been yours, but I didn't see it until I grew up enough to realize it."

KIT'S HANDS trembled as he accepted Della's heart. What to say, what to do? Only one thing came to mind, and that was to kiss her again, hard and fast and urgently as his arms reached around her back and felt the pounding of her heart against his chest. He'd loved her for so long, since they were children. While helplessly watching her pine after the viscount's son, at the same time instinctively knowing that Toby would never make her happy.

And that he himself, an employee of her family, had so little to offer her.

But she'd given him her heart! He saw the truth in her eyes, felt it in her lips, her heart, her entire body. She risked her pride, potentially her reputation—her everything—to prove it. His mind raced as he struggled to find a response to equal her heartfelt gesture.

He moved away, lowered one knee to the ground, and clasped her hands in his.

"My heart is yours, has always been yours, my love. Will you agree to marry me and be my love for the rest of our lives?"

Della squealed and pulled him up. "Yes! Of course, I will, you wonderful, incredible, *perfect* man! I was just about to propose to you, if you hadn't done it first!"

They fell into each other's arms and celebrated in the normal way of happy couples, until a familiar voice interrupted from the doorway.

"Dear, dear, I thought the pair of you would never get this thing settled," said her father. "Now do come inside before you catch a chill."

Della and Kit smiled at each other, as they moved toward the door. "I'm not cold. Are you cold?"

"Not at all," she chuckled.

Thomas Sr. followed behind, closing the door firmly.

"You might find this worthy of notice," he whispered. "I believe the Viscount is about to announce the betrothal of his son to Miss Cassandra Timmers."

Kit and Della stared at each other with widened eyes.

"So soon?"

"I'm happy for her... I think."

"His lordship has finally taken his son to hand."

"Do you suppose they'll be happy together?"

Kit shrugged. "Who knows? I'm sure it won't be easy."

Thomas Sr. motioned for them to tidy themselves. "I've hinted to Lord Laud that the Pagets might have an announcement to make this evening also."

A flush of adrenaline rushed through Kit's body. "Of course. Yes, let's. Della?"

"Now? Yes... indeed." Her cheeks were flushed.

Shielded by Thomas Sr. and a convenient potted plant, Kit removed his coat from her shoulders and replaced it on his own, while each of them smoothed out wrinkles and wayward curls.

When his future father-in-law nodded his approval, Kit held out his hand to her and they marched forward together to face their future.

EPILOGUE

Willow Branch Farm
Loughborough, Leicestershire
21 January 1802
Following the wedding breakfast

THE FESTIVE CARRIAGE drew to a halt in front of the entrance to a modest brick cottage, whose roof had seen better days and whose garden was seriously in need of a major spruce-up.

A dapper-looking gentleman emerged and lifted his beautiful bride out of the carriage. She turned to him and giggled. "It's *ours*, Kit. Our very own home. I can't believe it!"

He gave heavy sigh. "It's not what you are accustomed to, my love. But it is indeed *ours*, and I will devote my life to making you happy."

"I'm happy *now*, and will always be as long as we are together!"

She pulled his head down for a long kiss. When they broke apart, she lifted the skirts of her wedding gown with one hand and reached for his with the other. "Let's go inside! I can't wait to be inside alone with you!"

He resisted. "Wait." Then reached down to lift her up in his arms.

She resisted. "Oh Kit, you can't think of… no, I'm far too heavy. Put me down."

Nevertheless, the stronger of them prevailed, and Kit carried his bride to the door. Which was promptly opened by their new cook.

"Don't mind me, Mr. 'n Mrs. Hall. I'm just here to tell ye there's food 'n wine in the pantry, 'n I'll be stoppin' by every mornin'—early—ta clear up and whip up more victuals. I'll be as quiet as a mouse, ye'll see. Or, ye *won't* see." She winked and bustled past them to the waiting coach.

"At least we aren't going to starve," said Della. "I *do* know how to boil water, though."

"So we'll have tea, then," Kit said as he stepped over the threshold and whirled her around before setting her down.

"Welcome home, Madam Hall. Have I told you lately that I love you?"

"Not for at least five minutes," she quipped. "You know I love to hear you say it, darling." Later, after another passionate kiss, "The fire looks lovely. Let's test out the enticing bear skin rug in front of it, shall we?"

"I couldn't imagine anything I'd rather do."

And they did.

ABOUT SUSANA ELLIS

Susana Ellis is a retired teacher, part-time caregiver, sewist, cook, and fashion print collector. Lifelong reading and a fascination with history led her to writing historical romances. She is one of the original Bluestocking Belles and a member of Regency Fiction Writers and the Maumee Valley Romance Authors Inc.

SUSANA'S SOCIAL MEDIA

Facebook: facebook.com/susana.ellis.5
X(Twitter): @susanaauthor
Instagram: instagram.com/susanaellis3
Newsletter: http://eepurl.com/u5u3X
Blog: susanaellisauthor.blog
BlueSky: @susanaellis.bsky.social
Bookbub: https://www.bookbub.com/authors/susana-ellis
Goodreads: https://www.goodreads.com/user/show/26248675-susana-ellis
Website: www.susanaellis.com
Regency Fashion Facebook Group:
https://www.facebook.com/groups/2216340281934103

AWAY FROM THE HOLIDAY CROWD

SHERRY EWING

When the pressure to marry is overwhelming, can one Christmas house party provide a love that will last forever?

David Chadwick, Marquis of Lockhart feels burdened by his title's responsibilities. Heir to a duchy, he knows he must marry but seeks a genuine connection beyond wealth and status. A chance encounter by the lake with his neighbor's eldest daughter opens his eyes to the possibilities that might blossom between them.

Lady Elinor Lacey has yet to find a man she would consider for her husband. But time is running out when her father demands she pick an eligible lord by Christmas. When the Marquis of Lockhart shows up at the edge of their property, she sees him in an entirely new light, giving her hope.

Their conversation becomes easier the longer they converse. David and Elinor begin concocting a plan to give them more time to find their perfect match. What could possibly go wrong? But as love begins to enter the picture, can the two of them go beyond their original plan and let love into their hearts?

CHAPTER 1

Langridge, England
November 1817

LADY ELINOR LACEY sat at her vanity watching as her maid completed the finishing touches to her hair. Her reflection exposed that her sleep last night was restless, with dark circles heavy under her light brown eyes. With those added to her pale complexion and dark brown hair, she looked quite the sight. No amount of pampering would improve what she saw. Not that it mattered. There was certainly no one coming to call on her, at the ripe old age of thirty, especially since she and the family had taken up residence in their country estate for the Christmas holiday. She had resigned herself to being a spinster, and she was all right with that.

"Thank you, Jane. That will be all," Elinor said with a wave of her hand. She turned on the stool to stare at her sister Alice. Unlike herself, Alice appeared bright eyed and ready to take on whatever the day would bring.

"You didn't sleep," Alice said, stating the obvious as she swung her legs that dangled from the edge of Elinor's bed. "Too much on your mind?"

Elinor heaved a heavy sigh. "What could be weighing on my mind?"

Alice shrugged. "Seeing Celia and her husband here for the holidays could be one reason."

"Why would that bother me? I'm happy Celia found happiness with Adrian."

"Mother still hasn't gotten over the fact that you should have wed first since you were the oldest daughter," Alice declared, dropping from the bed and going to the window. She pulled back the drapery to peer outside.

A snort escaped Elinor's lips. "Why should Celia wait to wed because of some old-fashioned custom mother grew up on. Besides, it's not like I have any potential suitors waiting to ask for my hand in marriage."

Alice frowned. "And why is that, I wonder? You're still young and beautiful. Being a duke's daughter has given us both an advantage over others who are looking for husbands."

Elinor pointed a slim finger toward her sister. "And *that* is exactly the point! Those men only see me for my dowry and what being associated with our parents might bring them. They never see *me*. What's your excuse?" she said with a frown.

Alice shook her finger at her and tsk tsked. "My... you *are* in a foul mood this morning. I hope having breakfast and a cup of tea will change your disposition."

Elinor shook herself from her melancholy mood and went to give Alice a hug. "I'm so sorry. I know I should be looking forward to the upcoming holiday but I'm feeling *off* this year."

Alice took her sister's arm as they left the bedroom and began making their way downstairs to have breakfast with the family. "You used to love Christmas, Elinor."

"I still do, but you know what's going to happen." Elinor pulled her sister into an alcove before they came upon the grand staircase. "Mother and Father will invite the entire countryside for a holiday gathering. Every bedroom in this house will be occupied with guests since our parents like everyone to stay here even if they live but a few miles away."

"But that's half the fun," Alice protested. "The house brimming with family and friends to celebrate together."

Another snort left Elinor. "Maybe when we were younger, but you also know they'll invite every eligible lord whom they think might make a suitable husband for us."

"Maybe this year will be different," Alice suggested with a weak smile.

"It won't," Elinor fumed. They once again began making their way downstairs. "Father is getting impatient even though Mother tries to soothe him with words of allowing her daughters to find love on their own."

"Mother always did understand how we wanted a love match much like her own," Alice said with sparkling eyes. "What woman wouldn't want such a relationship?"

"I've about given up on love. Like I said upstairs, those who show any interest in me only see Father's money, title, and what they'll be marrying into."

Alice squeezed her arm. "There has to be someone who can over-look all of that. The world is a big place."

A huff escaped her lips. "Well… let me know when you find him and point the gentleman in my direction."

"Ha! I might steal him for myself," Alice teased. "Now, smile or mother will take you to task for starting the day off with a bad omen."

When they entered the dining room, their parents were already seated at the table with their youngest brother Christopher, or Kit, as he had been nicknamed. At only four years of age, the boy's birth had been an unexpected surprise. He was heir to the Duke of Ashbury title and all that would go with such a responsibility. After having three girls, their father's disposition seemed to lighten when Kit was born. Well… in most things.

Father was reading the paper, but he set the newsprint down after they sat. Servants came to place their plates before them and poured them tea. Elinor took a sip from her cup, sighing in pleasure before she started eating her eggs.

"Good morning, girls," their mother said wiping Kit's face with a napkin.

"Good morning, Mother," Elinor and Alice said in unison.

Elinor smiled at her younger brother. Her mother had no objection bringing Kit to the table with adults as long as it was just family. The boy was well loved and Elinor's parents wanted to spend as much time with the lad as possible.

Father pushed the paper further aside and reached for his cup. "Your mother has been busy planning this year's festivities for the Christmas event and ball." This hardly came as any surprise to Elinor.

"Do you need any help, Mother," Alice asked before Elinor could chime in.

"Everything is in order. At this point the event tends to pull itself together all on its own with the help of the staff." Their mother tossed a glance at their father that could only be termed suspicious. Elinor took another sip of her tea. This year was going to be worse than she thought!

Their father cleared his throat. "Yes, well... as your mother stated, she has all the planning well in hand. What we expect of you, Elinor, is an entirely a different matter."

"You know I'll do more than my fair share to help any way I can." Elinor tried to take another bite but almost choked on the food. She raised her eyes to her father who stared directly at her with a grim look set upon his face.

"What I expect of you is to choose a potential husband by Christmas," her father ordered. "You have had more than ample time to find someone who might suit you."

"But that's only a little over a month away! How do you expect me to just pick someone in such a short amount of time?" Elinor cried out. "You're being unfair!"

"Unfair?" her father bellowed. "My God, young lady, you are thirty years old and should have already been married with children at your feet. I do not care who you choose, only that you pick someone among the eligible men that we have invited."

"Jonathon, please be more understanding." Her mother's calm tone usually worked on placating her husband but apparently this would not be the case today.

Her father pointed his finger at their mother from across the table. "Caroline, you and I have had this discussion. She's well past her time to wed and I will no longer stand silently by while she tries to find love. Clearly, she is too picky to find a suitable mate on her own. No daughter of mine will remain on the shelf. If she doesn't choose someone by Christmas, I will pick someone for her myself."

"You can't make me marry someone I don't love," she yelled while tears rushed to her eyes.

"Watch me," her father warned.

Elinor pushed her chair back from the table and rushed through the door leading to the kitchen. A sob escaped her while she pushed her way through the busy servants. She reached the rear door and grabbed at a cloak hanging on a peg. Before she could open the door, Cook came to her and thrust a napkin into her hand.

"It's your favorite, Lady Elinor, still warm from the oven," Cook said smiling.

Elinor opened the linen to see a gingerbread biscuit before she wrapped the treat again and put it away in a pocket she wore under her dress. She nodded her thanks and escaped out the door. She quickly made her way to the stable and ordered her horse to be saddled. Not waiting for a groom to accompany her, she fled the manor house, knowing her life would be forever changed upon her return.

CHAPTER 2

DAVID CHADWICK, Marquis of Lockhart, donned his leather gloves while he waited for the stable hand to finish saddling his horse. He needed to escape his responsibilities of the estate and the duties that had been drilled into him since birth. At least for a short while. He could never really forget what was required of him. He understood he needed to marry, but at four and thirty, he was still young. He saw no need to rush the matter. He had stayed away from London for a reason, since he could barely tolerate the simpering women who batted their eyes at him knowing he would one day hold the title of duke. Eh gads! The horror of being married to such a woman near drove him mad.

David, instead, left his younger brother George to indulge his every whim with the ladies this season. It was good for the lad to experience the many balls and endure the insufferable mothers pushing their daughters at him, hoping to gain his favor. George had more freedom to find a love match, while David had obligations. He knew what he wanted in a woman, but he had never found her.

His father's gentle nagging was becoming more insistent and had caused him to rush from the manor house. A ride in the countryside was just what he needed to clear his head.

"David," his brother's voice called from across the yard.

George was the only person who ever called him by his given name. David had insisted upon it when they were both young, wanting at least one person that he cared for to think of him as a person more than a title.

"Care to join me?" David asked when George walked over to him.

George inspected his clothing, immaculate as always, and grimaced. "Do I look like I'm dressed for a ride in the country?"

David smirked. "You never do. I could wait if you want to change."

A short laugh left his brother. "And deprive you of another hour when you'd rather be gallivanting across the land? I think not. Besides, it's too bloody cold to be out for any length of time."

"Then why are you out here talking to me when you could be sitting by a nice fire with a brandy?" David asked in amusement, knowing George's aversion to anything too taxing.

George thrust a small satchel at him, and David took hold of it. "From Cook... He said you shouldn't go without your luncheon and thought you might like a snack."

From the weight of the bag, there was enough food inside for at least four people. "Go change and join me. We can have a picnic by the lake."

George shook his head. "You go ahead, and I'll return inside to divert Father from asking the Duke and Duchess of Ashbury to invite half the eligible ladies near Bath to their event in a couple of weeks for your benefit."

"So, you heard our latest argument," David sighed going to his horse and attaching his luncheon to his saddle.

George shrugged. "It's an old disagreement that will never end until you finally chose a bride. I certainly understand your dilemma but you're not getting any younger. Father does want grandchildren someday."

"Then you go ahead and marry someone, preferably one you can love," David said, grimacing at the emotion that had evaded him his entire life. He was getting ready to resign himself to marrying for the convenience of it all instead of falling in love with some woman he had yet to meet.

"You think Father would be satisfied with his younger son marrying before his heir?" George asked with wide eyes. "You must have drunk too much brandy. Maybe you shouldn't be riding in your unstable condition."

David laughed. "I am far from drunk, little brother. I'm just not looking forward to spending a whole month at the Lacey affair when I could come home and sleep in my own bed."

George grinned. "You know how we must appease the older folk around here. They have their traditions and like to stick to them. Maybe one day we'll create our own, once we finally settle down with the women of our dreams."

David raised one dark brow. What a thought. A wife and children and Christmas traditions that they made together... He could only wonder who might fulfill the dreams he had conjured inside his head of a woman who would see him for himself and not the title.

David took hold of the pommel of his saddle. "Are you certain you won't join me?" he asked one last time, before he lifted himself up.

George waved him off. "Enjoy yourself. I'll see you at dinner."

Nudging the horse's side with his knee, David trotted through the stable yard until he came to an open field. He flicked the reins, sending his steed into a gallop as the scenery flew by. He became lost in thought about his father's demands for him to find a bride, the many responsibilities of running the multiple estates and business dealings his father had begun to turn over to him, and even the holiday party he was trying desperately to find a way to not attend.

He was surprised when the lake finally came into view, and he realized he had ridden longer than he thought if he had reached the water at the edge of his family's property that joined the Laceys. He slowed his mount when he neared the place he planned to have his lunch. He pulled on the reins, realizing his spot was already taken. He narrowed his eyes trying to determine who the woman was when recognition dawned on him. He hadn't seen this particular lady since the last holiday party the Laceys had a year ago.

He dismounted and the lady quickly came to a stand while wiping at her eyes. Oh no. She had been crying. Looping the leather straps around a tree trunk, he swiftly stepped forward, pulling out a handkerchief from his jacket and offering it to her. She hastily dropped down into a curtsey.

"Lord Lockhart..." she croaked out, giving evidence of her distress. She lifted the linen to the corner of her eye and dabbed at it. "Thank you."

"No need for formalities, Lady Elinor," he said, wanting, for once, to escape from his status and just be himself. "My apologies for intruding on your solitude."

She gazed around her and gave him a weak smile. "It seems I'm the one intruding on your excursion, my lord, since I'm on *your* property."

"You and your family have always been welcomed to make use of the lake. Now is no different."

She gave a small nod. "I should be heading back. I never intended to ride this far."

He pondered her for a moment. Some of her dark brown hair had come undone from her coiffure and several loose wisps billowed in the breeze around her head. He watched as she attempted to tame the tresses, tucking them behind her ears before she gave up. Soft brown eyes stared up at him and he swore he could see hints of gold in their depths. Smooth porcelain skin, a straight nose, and the perfect bow shaped mouth that just begged to be kissed made his heart skip a beat. Kissed? Where had such a thought come from?

He cleared his throat and his thoughts, remembering the lunch he had. "I have a sizable banquet from our cook attached to my saddle. Would you care to join me for lunch?"

Her breath hitched at his words. "I really should be getting home."

"I understand, but you must know you are safe with me and if you could spare the time, I'd enjoy the company. Unless you've already eaten," David suggested.

"Oh, I appreciate the invitation, but I'm... I'm not hungry," she said in a soft tone. Her stomach rumbled in protest to her words causing her eyes to widen in embarrassment. "Good heavens!"

David hid his smile, went to his horse, and untied the satchel. "As I said, I have enough here for an army. You must help me with some of the meal so Cook doesn't take me to task for not eating my fill."

"If you insist," she said, taking his arm that he offered.

"I do and afterwards I will see you home myself," David declared as they went to the log she had been sitting on when he first arrived.

"That won't be necessary, my lord."

"You will have to indulge my whim, Lady Elinor. I can hardly leave a damsel in distress alone and unescorted now, can I?" he teased her with a smile.

Her smile this time reached her eyes and as he began to set out the repast before them, he wondered how he had never truly noticed how lovely his neighbor had become.

CHAPTER 3

Elinor sat enjoying the company of Lord Lockhart while he made her laugh with stories of him growing up on his country estate. It wasn't as though she hadn't known of him. After all, their lands joined. It was just that she had never been this aware of him before now. While he had come each year with his father and brother to their Christmas house party, she had never really spent any time with him except for the occasional polite conversation. He had always kept to himself.

With a house full of people, her duties were to speak to everyone and ensure her parent's guests were having a grand time. Her mother's insistence made Elinor front and center to being *seen*... as if she could ever hide herself away. She supposed the part she played in every aspect of her parents' event might prove to any suitor, if they looked close enough, that Elinor was more than capable of running a large household.

The man sitting next to her began to intrigue her and she wasn't sure why she had never noticed how handsome he was. Black hair curled at the edges of his coat while he kept sweeping his hand through a lock that continued to become displaced across his forehead. Blue eyes that could rival any clear sky sparkled mischievously as he continued to keep her entertained. When he had dismounted from his horse and come toward her, there could be no mistaking the fine figure he cut with those broad shoulders and lean hips. This was no idle man of leisure, as some of the men of the *ton* appeared. She had heard the whisperings during the Season that he liked to work the land himself. A rarity amongst titled gentlemen to be sure.

"Can I interest you in a gingerbread biscuit," he said with a smile flashing across his features that warmed her heart. "Cook makes the best in the county."

She gave him her own smile as she reached into her redingote and pulled out the wrapped linen showing him her own treat. "I might beg to differ, sir. I'm certain our cook makes the best."

The marquis broke his biscuit in half and offered her part of his dessert. "Perhaps we can share and then compare between the two."

Elinor also broke her biscuit into two pieces and offered Lord Lockhart his half. She took a bite of his biscuit and was surprised at how good it was. "That *is* a good biscuit, although I would never admit it to my parents' cook. She knows this is my favorite treat."

He chuckled. "Mine too," he answered, taking a bite of the biscuit she had offered him. He gave a sigh of pleasure from deep in his chest and the sound sent a shiver of delight racing through her. "We may have to keep this a secret between us. Our cooks may never make them for us again if we divulged how tasty someone else's recipe was."

Elinor nodded before she finally found her voice. "Yes... just between us."

He studied her for several minutes before he spoke what was on his mind. "I hate to ask or intrude on the private moment you were having when I first arrived, but what caused you to be so upset?"

She heaved a sigh. "It's an old issue with my parents."

"Ah yes. Something all of us must endure. The ruminations of our parents," he replied, waiting for her to continue.

She should have kept her private thoughts to herself but for some reason, she felt comfortable telling him what had caused her tears. "My father is tired of waiting for me to pick my own husband and has given me until Christmas to find someone suitable or he will choose one for me."

A snort of disdain left him. "He cannot force you into marriage. Those days are long since over."

"My father is… adamant that I wed before I become more on the shelf than I've already become," she said softly. Her face flushed in embarrassment. "I shouldn't be telling you all this. My apologies for being so frank, your lordship."

"Call me David," he urged.

A gasp escaped her. "But we barely know one another."

"Nonsense! Why, we've been neighbors our entire lives and that should count for something," he suggested, with a smile that crept up at the corner of his lips.

"My parents would never approve," Elinor answered honestly.

"Then let us call one another by our given names whenever we may have a private moment together. There can be no harm in that, can there?" he asked as one dark brow arched upward. "Another secret between us, much like our gingerbread."

Snowflakes began to fall gently while Elinor pondered his suggestion. Something within her shifted. Call it something reckless or maybe something even daring but, whatever the cause, she welcomed the change from always doing what was expected of her. "David…"

"You do me a great honor… Elinor," he murmured reaching for her hand and bringing it to his lips. She thought he would kiss the air between his mouth and her skin but when his lips touched the back of her hand, she held back another gasp of pure delight.

Those blue eyes of his pulled her into a mesmerizing spell almost making her forget anything else existed except this moment between them.

She tore her gaze away to look up at the darkening sky as the snow began to fall heavily. "There's a storm approaching and I fear it will get worse before I make it home. I suppose I should start heading back."

David looked upwards before he returned his attention back to her. "As to your plight… I understand completely what you're going through as I seem to be in the same dilemma with a parent who wants to see me wed."

"They're relentless, aren't they?" she asked, surprised that he was in the same situation.

"I have a crazy idea," he said, with a devilish grin reflecting in those blue eyes.

"More than calling each other by our given names?" she teased.

David gave a short laugh. "Just so! Maybe we can buy ourselves a bit more time until we find someone suitable that we feel we can marry," he said, appearing as if he had become lost in thought.

"What did you have in mind?"

"Your parent's house party will begin shortly. I'm certain both of our parents will be tossing possible spouses in our direction from the start. Maybe what we can do, instead of being thrust into unwanted company, is spend time with one another during the free time you're allowed. That might put them off pushing us toward people we detest. They will think we may be considering a match between us."

Elinor's eyes went wide. She was never one to play games and she was unsure if her heart might begin to betray her if she came to have feelings for this man only to have him wed another. "That could be dangerous and cause more problems."

"Or this plan could offer us the opportunity to sneak away from the holiday crowd. I detest the women who only see me for the title I will one day inherit. I prefer the country to town, and they only wish to be *seen* during the onset of each Season. Besides… I've never been able to enjoy myself with a young lady as much as I've enjoyed conversing with you today. I wouldn't mind spending more time with you, Elinor, if you're willing," he declared. He sounded sincere.

Considering the short amount of time they had conversed today and how comfortable she felt in his presence, Elinor gave into the whim and nodded her acceptance. "I would like to spend more time with you as well, David."

"Splendid!" He stood and offered his hand to help her rise. She was suddenly hypnotized by his blue eyes, and she wondered what spell he was casting over her. And then he once again raised her fingertips to his lips. "Let me see you home before the snow gets any worse."

David helped her onto her horse before he mounted his own steed. Galloping across the countryside next to this handsome gentleman gave Elinor hope. Hope for more time to find a husband but more so hope that maybe, just maybe, she had finally met her match!

CHAPTER 4

TWO WEEKS LATER, David found himself in a bedroom at the Lacey country estate, his valet Felix dusting off an imaginary speck from his coat. Dinner would be announced shortly, and David was looking forward to seeing Elinor this evening. For the first time in a long while, he was excited for the next few weeks. Tonight was the first night of a house party that would last for several days past the Christmas holiday. Every year, David, George, and their father had attended this event and he wondered why he had never noticed Elinor in the past. She was hard to forget.

In fact, Elinor had been all David had been thinking about since he had taken her home that fateful snowy day when they had met by the lake. Call it an accident if he must, but something inside him had changed that day. Elinor Lacey was a rare gem.

After she had wiped away her tears, David had done his best to ensure she was laughing at the tales he told her of his childhood. Anything to make her smile and she seemed genuinely interested in his stories. Not like some of the other women from his past who had plastered simpering looks upon their faces as they tried to show interest in whatever he had been saying. There was nothing fake about Elinor from what he could see, and she hardly appeared as though she was looking to snag what many would term one of the most eligible titled bachelors in England.

"Will I do, Felix?" David drawled as he looked at his reflection in the full-length mirror.

"Most assuredly, my lord," Felix droned in a monotone David was used to. His valet had been with David as long as he could remember and certainly wouldn't allow him to leave his room without looking his best.

His valet went about cleaning up the discarded clothing while David left the bedroom. He headed down the grand staircase that was decorated in boughs of greenery with bright red bows. The foyer held a twelve-foot decorated Christmas tree that David knew was in celebration of the Germain ancestry in the Lacey family. At the entrance to the front parlor, a bouquet of mistletoe with red and green ribbons hung from the archway. David would give everything to get Elinor beneath it.

The low murmur of voices prompted David to continue toward the center of the house. A banquet of food was being brought in from the kitchen to put on a sideboard where the guests could serve themselves. The room was already crowded with guests and David continued to search for the one lady who had captured his attention with just one smile from her lips.

He finally spied her in the farthest corner of the room where she was instructing one of the servants on something that must have been overlooked. The girl scurried away to do the lady's bidding and when Elinor glanced up and their eyes met, a becoming smile swept up at the corner of her lips. She began to make her way toward him, and he pushed through the crowd to reach her side.

"Lord Lockhart," she began dipping down into a curtsey. "I'm so happy you could make our little gathering for the Christmas holiday."

David bowed before her and then chuckled. "Little?"

She gave a bright laugh. "You've been here each year, but I suppose it might be smaller than anything my parents previously held."

He gave a light laugh. "I will take your word for it. May I say you look lovely this evening, Lady Elinor." His eyes roamed over her amber colored gown, which complimented her eyes. The candlelight from the room set the diamonds at her ears and neck to sparkle brightly. The bauble centered in the middle of her cleavage caused David to remember himself and keep his eyes from dipping lower.

"May I return the compliment, my lord. You look resplendent with that colorful holiday waistcoat," she said, reminding him of the vest George had given him last year that was a dark green with colorful red roses printed on the fabric.

"A gift from my brother," he murmured, wondering if the vest was too much. George always did have elaborate taste in his finery.

"It's lovely," she replied, taking hold of his elbow and ushering him toward the far part of the room where they could speak somewhat privately. "I was hoping to have a word with you but this might be my only chance before the rest of the evening takes over."

"I am at your service, my lady," David said enjoying the sensation of having her close to him. He was becoming smitten. When did he start to have feelings for this lady. Falling in love certainly hadn't been a part of his original plan.

"My mother has a biscuit-baking contest planned for tomorrow. I thought perhaps we might team up to begin putting our plan into place?" she suggested shyly. "That is, if you're still interested. I will certainly understand if you've changed your mind."

"Since it was my suggestion in the first place, I would be a cad to renege now. Besides, I have honestly been looking forward to any amount of time you can offer me," David said with what he hoped was a sincere tone.

"You have?" she said in what appeared like startled surprise.

"Yes, I have. I may have had ulterior motives when I concocted our outrageous plan but perhaps something more will come of it," David said, aghast that he uttered his thoughts aloud. "My apologies, my lady. I may have spoken out too soon."

She squeezed his arm, causing him to be surprised again. "You may have read my mind, David," she whispered softly, as she stole a quick glance at him, "but let us see how we get along in the next week, shall we?"

"I would like nothing better," he replied, as he gently laid his hand over the top of hers. He was about to say more when her little brother Christopher ran through the room chasing a small puppy.

"If you'll excuse me, I best attend to Kit," she exclaimed releasing his arm. "I'll see you later?"

"You can count on it, my lady," he replied before Elinor hastily left his side.

He continued to watch her retreat until she was gone from his view. He immediately felt her absence and once again he could only wonder what was coming over him. Was it all this holiday cheer that suddenly caused him to be so moonstruck?

"You've made a conquest I see," George said with a laugh, as he slapped David's back bringing him back to reality.

"I don't know what you're talking about," he grumbled, realizing he'd been caught staring after the lady.

"No need to explain to me. She's lovely and I can only wonder why you haven't noticed her before now," George replied, before he gave another chuckle. "Let's go see what's at the banquet table for dinner. The Laceys always provide the best food at their house party."

David allowed his younger brother to lead the way and he was soon sitting at a table trying to eat the meal before him. But it wasn't until he saw Elinor again with her own plate as she sat with her younger sister and her husband that David finally found his appetite. God help him, but he was doomed. And as he watched Elinor look his way he could only think that if he was going to fall for the lady, then this could be the start of something truly grand.

CHAPTER 5

LAUGHTER RANG out in the room. People talked over one another as they created their treats for the biscuit contest. Although everyone had been invited to participate in the morning event, clearly there were those who were not up to the task of rising at such an early part of the day. As Elinor rolled out the dough, David stood next to her holding a biscuit cutter in the shape of a gingerbread man. Considering their conversation at the lake, there really was only one choice on the type of biscuit they would make together.

"Promise me you won't tell my Cook that I was baking anything other than his own recipe or else I'll never get another decent meal at home," David teased, causing Elinor's heart to flip end over end.

She leaned closer and realized how tall he was compared to her. "Your secret is safe with me, my lord," she replied before stepping back. "I think this is ready and the dough thick enough. What do you think?"

"As long as they're soft and chewy once they come out of the oven, they'll be perfect," he answered before leaning down to whisper in her ear, "just like you."

She gave a bright laugh. "I am far from perfect, Lord Lockhart, and you best know from the start I can be very… opinionated when I need to be."

He chuckled. "As long as you're not one of those demanding women with no thought in their head beside what to wear for the evening, I believe we'll get on just famously."

David began cutting out the biscuits while Elinor placed them on a baking sheet. When they were done, she was a little bit sorry that this part of the contest was over. She was truly enjoying spending time with this man who, up until now, had always been reserved and quiet every year at their house party. To help the servants, David went to give the tray to the kitchen staff, while Elinor began cleaning up their work.

Upon his return, he studied her for a moment in silence until he reached out. When he ran his thumb over her right cheek, her heart once more betrayed the growing feelings she had for him.

"You had a dusting of flour on your cheek," he said quietly as he took his hand away. The low baritone of his whispered words nearly made her knees weak. She had never been one to swoon but David might make her do so if he continued looking upon her as he was.

"Thank you," she murmured, suddenly shy herself at the immediate loss of the warmth of his thumb gently rubbing her cheek. She was about to say more when her mother clapped her hands to draw everyone's attention.

"I hope everyone had fun making your Christmas treats. The staff will take care of the rest of the cleanup. We'll be decorating the ballroom next for anyone who would like to participate. In respect to the Duke's German heritage, we've had a tree brought in to decorate and there will be sledding later this afternoon," the duchess proclaimed as her guests began to leave the room.

"Another Lacey tradition?" David asked, looking down at her.

"Yes, although I don't ever remember you participating before," Elinor said as she raised her head to stare into blue eyes that continued to watch her intently. She couldn't help the blush that rushed to her face.

"I admit I tended to keep to myself every year except the occasional requirement of the evening events," David confessed honestly. "Until now, I never cared for the crowds at a house party."

"What has changed your mind?" she asked since she enjoyed spending time with this man.

"You."

The startled gasp that escaped her lips caused her to raise her fingertips to her mouth. She tore her gaze away from his intense blue eyes. "I can hardly be the reason why you're suddenly taking part in my mother's activities, my lord. As her daughter, I have always been here performing my duties by participating in all her plans for her guests."

She widened her eyes when he took her chin to turn her head, tipping it upward so she had no choice but to directly stare at him. "Maybe for the first time I'm seeing the lady who has always been right before my eyes."

"You could scarcely miss me, my lord."

"And yet I did, but I see you *now*, Elinor." He rubbed at her cheek with his thumb again causing her body to become flushed with excitement.

She gulped, taking a chance that perhaps this unmistaken connection they had found with one another was more than a plan hatched by the lakeside. "I see *you*, too, David."

"Elinor," her mother called from the doorway, breaking the spell that had momentarily been wrapped around herself and David.

They quickly broke apart. "If you would excuse me, my lord," she whispered, dropping down into a curtsey.

"I will see you in the other room?" he asked quietly.

"Yes... of course," she replied softly.

She watched as he left the room, nodding to her mother who rushed across the room to take her elbow. "Do my eyes deceive me or do I see something happening between you and the Marquis of Lockhart?"

Elinor shrugged not wishing to give voice to her inner feelings just yet. "Maybe."

Her mother gave a heavy sigh. "While I don't have anything against the man, he hasn't ever shown the least bit of attention to any young lady at my house parties in the past, yourself included."

"What is your point, mother? Don't you approve of him? I thought you would think he was the perfect suitor for my hand," she grumbled, wondering if anyone would be good enough for her in her mother's eyes. She inwardly cursed, knowing that wasn't a fair assessment of her mother. She only wanted what was best for her daughters.

Her mother leaned forward to kiss her cheek confirming Elinor's thoughts but seconds ago. "It's not that I don't think he would make you a fine husband, dear girl. It's only that David Chadwick has always been a bit of a loner, hiding away at his country estate and missing the London Season every year. You would miss out on so much if you were to marry him."

"There is more to life than rounds of balls and being *seen* each year in London, Mother," Elinor said, defending the marquis.

"I just never saw you enjoying the country life, dear heart," her mother declared as they began to leave the room arm in arm. "But as long as you are happy, then so am I."

Her mother's words only confirmed how much she really didn't know Elinor. A country life sounded perfect to her and, as she entered the ballroom and her gaze automatically went to David, she knew in her heart that this Christmas would be different. For the first time in a long while, she had something to look forward to during the holidays.

CHAPTER 6

FOR THE PAST TWO WEEKS, David enjoyed himself more than he ever had in his past. Having always been one to stand on the sidelines at events like this, Elinor seemed to bring out another side of him that he hadn't even known existed. He hated crowds and this was the reason he preferred living at his country estate instead of town and attending the parties that occurred every Season. Well... and avoiding the grasping women and their mothers who threw themselves at him as the future duke.

His father and brother more than approved of him spending time with Elinor. In fact, when he'd become fully aware how much time David was spending with the lady, he'd taken to singing her praises at every opportunity. Duty had taken her away on several issues that only she could apparently resolve, and each time David had immediately felt her loss. If he had a Christmas wish it would be that Elinor was never parted from his side again. He had become that taken with the lady.

From decorating the Christmas tree to finding the perfect yule log. From singing Christmas carols to sledding down a snowy hillside and ice skating on their frozen pond. Elinor was a bright reminder that beneath the solemn surface he showed the world lurked a man hungry to celebrate everything about the holiday season.

And the reason? Elinor. Plain and simple. It was the lady who drew him from his lonely room and into the festivities. And should this be his life, he would gladly accept it. She made David yearn to be with her from the moment he woke each morning, until he closed his eyes each night and being apart from her became sheer torture. Yes... it was safe to say, David was falling in love with Elinor Lacey.

Now he waited for her to come outside and join him on a sleigh ride. When the front door to the manor opened and she walked toward him, he swore she took his breath away. A dark red cloak with a white fur trim on the hood covered her gown. Her smile was radiant when she met him next to the sleigh.

"Are you ready?" he asked when he held out his hand to assist her into their conveyance for their excursion in the countryside. Her gloved fingertips slid easily into his palm.

"I've been waiting all day for our outing, my lord," she said in a breathy whisper.

Once she was settled inside, he placed a blanket over their laps, took up the reins, and gave them a slap to put the horses into motion. A light snow began to fall as he left the front entrance to her manor home.

"You've been busy of late," he murmured when the silence stretched between them.

"I'm sorry I missed you at breakfast. Mother was having a hard time with Kit this morning and I seemed to be the only one who could calm the boy down," she stated, with a look of disappointment that she hadn't been able to join him.

"I understand. I can hardly occupy all your time even though I wish it was otherwise."

"I must admit, it's lovely to get away from everyone for a while. This is the perfect outing," she declared with bright eyes.

David looked ahead of them. "Well... as much as I would like it otherwise, we are hardly alone, my lady, since other people are also enjoying sleigh rides both ahead and behind us."

"Nevertheless, I will enjoy this time where it's just the two of us for as long as it lasts. Inside the house it feels like a hundred pairs of eyes are constantly watching me."

"It never ends, does it?" he said agreeing with her. "I suppose people inspect us because we've spent so much time in each other's company this year."

"You would think they had better things to do," she grumbled before smiling in his direction. "But let's not worry about what others think. Instead, let's just enjoy our outing."

"I couldn't agree more, Elinor," he said quietly. He stole a glance at her from the corner of his eye before he returned his attention to the path before him as he maneuvered the horses through the snow. "I have enjoyed spending the holiday in your company this year."

"As have I, David."

"Would it be presumptuous of me to say that I hope that our conversations go beyond the plan we concocted by the lake?" he asked, hoping he hadn't spoken too soon about what he was feeling.

"I would think things between us are more than just conversations, David... at least I hope so."

He gave her a smile. "I didn't want to speak too soon but yes... I certainly have developed feelings for you, Elinor, beyond any plan I came up with that day. I didn't want you to think this was all only a game to deceive our parents anymore."

She glanced at him while a blush rushed across her cheeks and she began fidgeting with the fabric of her cloak. "I'm glad to hear you confirm my worst fears. I was afraid that I might become heartbroken by the time the holiday house party came to an end."

"I would never intentionally hurt you, Elinor."

"Neither would I. I can't really explain it, but something inside me shifted that day at the lake. I had never felt anything like it before in my entire life and perhaps that's why I was skeptical if what I began to feel for you so rapidly was real."

"So, you do have feelings for me," he teased her with a wink.

She gave a light laugh. "I was certain I had made that obvious, my lord, but I guess I will have to try harder if you aren't aware that I care for you by now."

He pulled on the reins bringing the horses to a halt while the other sleighs behind them moved onward. When they were at last alone, he turned in the seat and took her hands.

"You don't need to try any harder, Elinor. I can see for myself that you care, and I hope you know I feel the same. I don't know why we never noticed each other before but I am glad we have now." He leaned down to capture her lips in a gentle kiss.

Her hands went to his shoulders and one wound around his neck as he deepened their kiss. It became an exploration of two souls who had somehow found one another as their breaths connected them as one. He pulled her closer and heard a soft moan escape her before he finally broke the contact of their lips. He stared into her soft brown eyes while their breathing returned to normal.

When David heard another set of bells jingling from the harnesses of another team of horses drawing near, he knew they were once again about to have company. He took up the reins and was about to set the steeds back into motion when she pointed upwards.

"Did you deliberately plan to stop beneath a bunch of mistletoe?" she asked before giggling.

He followed her gaze upwards and a smile lit his own face. "A happy accident, I assure you."

She laughed again and clapped her hands together. "I will take your word for it, my lord, given that I know you would never lie to me."

"Perhaps by the time Christmas finally arrives, we might come to an understanding between us?" he asked, hoping she would be open to the possibility of becoming his wife.

"I think that would indeed make me very happy, David," she beamed happily.

He leaned forward to give her lips another quick kiss before he slapped at the leather reins, moving the horses and sleigh forward.

The remainder of their ride was filled with laughter as they continued retelling stories of their past and their hopes for a future together. For once in his life, David was thankful for the miracle of a Christmas holiday and a woman who unexpectedly came into his life.

CHAPTER 7

ELINOR STOOD before the mirror in her room marveling at her reflection. The red velvet gown with green trim was everything she could have wanted in a dress for a Christmas evening ball. Rubies sparkled from her ears, throat and wrist, a gift from her parents this morning as if they had known what she would be wearing tonight... which her mother probably did since she had been with Elinor when they picked out the fabric at the modiste's.

A brief knock on the door came and before she could answer, the door swung open and in walked both of her sisters.

"You look lovely, Elinor," Celia declared coming to kiss her cheeks.

"Beautiful for your handsome marquis just waiting downstairs," Alice chimed in.

Elinor rolled her eyes. "He's not *my* marquis," she huffed in an attempt to not be overly confident. Her sisters broke out into laughter.

"Of course, he is!" Celia answered going to the mirror and patting her blonde hair into place, not that Elinor could see that even a strand needed it.

"Everyone can see for themselves the two of you are in love," Alice stated before coming over to squeeze Elinor's hand. "I'm so happy for you."

"Let's not get ahead of ourselves. It's not like he has proposed," Elinor scolded them.

"Yet..." Celia said with a bright smile. "Adrian has spent some time getting to know him over a game of billiards last night. He has nothing but good things to say about your marquis."

"And I overheard Aunt Grace and Uncle Nicholas saying what a fine gentleman Lord Lockhart has become. I know they approve, too," Alice added with another bright smile. "I have the feeling he'll propose any day now."

"Why, he might even do it tonight at the ball!" Celia said in excitement.

"Stop speculating on what might or might not happen or else I'll become a nervous wreck and won't be able to enjoy the ball," Elinor warned them. "Now, let's head downstairs before mother and father send the servants to see what's taking us so long."

As they entered the crowded ballroom, both her sisters left Elinor to her own agenda. Her eyes traveled throughout the room searching for a glimpse of David. When she finally located him, she was pleasantly surprised to see him conversing with her father who looked entirely pleased with their conversation. A very promising outlook, given the conversation she just had with her sisters upstairs.

When the two men broke apart, Elinor made every attempt not to frown or let the green-eyed monster of jealousy sweep across her features. David was a handsome man, so she shouldn't have been surprised that he was immediately surrounded by beautiful women who were looking for a husband. But one lady in particular worried Elinor, for the blonde seemed entirely closer to David than would be deemed as respectable.

"Do not allow my sister Anne to ruffle your feathers, Lady Elinor. She is no match for your beauty," a male voice purred into her ear.

Elinor distanced herself from the man who also became entirely too close. He had blond hair and his blue eyes twinkled mischievously as though he knew a secret. She dropped into a curtsey. "Lord

Barlingham," she began as he bowed before her. "I hope you are enjoying the ball thus far."

"Now that you have arrived, I cannot help but enjoy myself. As to my sister, you have no need to worry. She can be a frivolous thing flitting about trying to snare one lord over another."

Elinor frowned at his words. "I have never known Lady Anne to be anything other than kind whenever our paths have crossed. You do her an injustice, my lord, with your words."

"I see my sister has a champion coming to her aid," he murmured. "Such an admirable trait, I must admit. But I meant no disrespect as far as Anne is concerned. She needs to marry, and the Marquis of Lockhart is only one of many she has set her cap for."

"Then I wish her the best with finding a husband in the coming Season," Elinor replied tearing her eyes from David.

"I understand you are in the same... predicament," Lord Barlingham replied as his grin widened.

"My personal life is none of your business, my lord," Elinor huffed feeling put out that this man dared to mention aloud that she was yet unwed.

"My apologies for being blunt, Lady Elinor. Perhaps I can make things right between us. Would you permit me a dance this evening?" he asked with a roguish smile.

"Of course, my lord." As a guest in her parent's home, she couldn't refuse the man. She reached for the dance card dangling from her wrist and handed it over to him.

"I consider myself a lucky man that I am to be the first to have my pick of your dances," he drawled filling his name on the card. "I shall look forward to claiming you later in the evening, my lady."

Elinor dared not look to see which of the several dances Lord Barlingham chose. Alice came rushing to her side.

"Do you make another conquest, Elinor?" she teased. "I always thought Orlando Barlingham was a handsome devil."

Elinor gave a huff. "And he *knows* it, Alice. I could hardly deny him a dance. Mother would only take me to task for it once the ball is over."

"Who's to say she'd ever find out?" Alice asked with a worried look set upon her features.

Elinor gave a light chuckle. "Mother always knows everything going on under her roof. You know that." Alice took hold of Elinor's dance card and gave a squeal of delight.

"He chose a waltz!"

Elinor sighed. "Of course, he did. If only I had reached David first, but he seems a little preoccupied at the moment." She observed him from across the room, but it was the sly grin Anne Barlingham placed on her lips when she stepped even closer to the marquis that almost caused Elinor to growl her frustration.

"Oh my!" Alice whispered feverishly. "You're jealous."

"I am *not* jealous."

"You *are* and it's written all over your face, sister," Alice said taking her by the elbow and steering her into the banquet room. "Fill a plate to compose yourself or you'll never make it through the rest of the ball."

Alice began making choices for her and before long there was enough food on her plate to feed several people. "I am *not* going to eat all this, Alice."

"You don't have to. Just take a seat and appear like you're enjoying yourself."

"Then you best help me since you're the one who put all this food on one plate. You know how I hate things touching," Elinor complained taking a seat at one of the tables.

Alice giggled. "Never did understand that whole issue you had, but you are who you are, and I love you."

The two women began nibbling on the feast that Alice had provided for them and when Elinor couldn't eat another bite, she pushed the plate away.

"Feeling better now?" Alice asked with a knowing smile.

"Yes… and thank you."

Alice shrugged. "What else are sisters for if we don't look out for each other's best interests? Besides, I couldn't let you continue standing there looking all moon-eyed over your marquis while Lady Anne was trying to gain his attention."

"She gained it, along with the other women fawning over him," Elinor grumbled.

"And if you hadn't let jealousy rule your head, sister, you would have noticed the poor man was miserable."

Elinor raised her head to peer at her sister who suddenly had a smug look upon her face. "Truly?"

Alice laughed again. "If you're now finished here, let's go find your marquis. He can probably do with a bit of rescuing."

With a new frame of mind, Elinor was able to assess the situation differently when she entered the ballroom. This time, Elinor observed what Alice had quickly deduced at a moment's glance. David was indeed looking like he was needing an excuse to escape the women who were clinging to him.

Elinor decided to take matters into her own hands and walked straight over to their group. "Good evening, ladies... Lord Lockhart," Elinor said dipping into a brief curtsey. "My lord, I believe you promised me the first dance and the musicians are about to begin. Shall we?"

"I could not forget such a commitment, Lady Elinor," David replied holding out his arm. "Excuse us, ladies."

They left the women complaining amongst themselves as David moved them toward the dance floor. "How can I ever thank you enough, Elinor?" he said quietly. "I wasn't sure how much more I could take."

"You can follow me from all the prying eyes to steal a few minutes away from this Christmas holiday crush," she declared as she gently pulled on his arm and took him to a salon that was empty of guests.

David took her into his arms. "You have my undivided attention, my lady."

"I must admit I allowed jealousy to overrule my clear thinking when Lady Anne all but attached herself to you," Elinor admitted as she placed her hands lightly on his chest. She felt the muscles beneath the fabric causing her heart to beat fiercely.

He cupped her cheek with one hand and she leaned into the warmth of his palm. "I am happy that you care enough that another woman could bring out such an emotion in you. But you should know there is no need to be jealous, especially now that we have found each other." He bent down and placed a chaste kiss upon her forehead

"My sister told me that if I had looked hard enough, I would have seen that you were miserable."

He gave a light laugh. "I had hoped that you would rescue me from their attention. Instead, you deserted me for the banquet table," he teased her. "Can I dare hope that I have put any fears to rest as to my intentions?"

"Your intentions?" she asked with wide eyes.

"I spoke to your father."

"I saw you with him when I entered the ballroom," Elinor replied waiting for him to continue.

"I spoke with him at length last evening," he said with a roguish smile.

"You did?"

"Yes. I did."

"And…"

"And I asked for his blessing so I could ask you to marry me. That is, if you'll have me." He pulled away from holding her and went to the window to stare outside before he turned back to face her and continued. "I know that some ladies might find spending the majority of their time in the country when the London Season is in full swing not appealing. But based on our conversations, I know you're not one of them."

"Being seen during a Season, is hardly what is important to me, David," she said quietly. "I don't give a fig where we live as long as we would be together."

He rushed back to her side and took her hands. "And that is the reason why I know we would suit. You give me hope for a future together, Elinor. And I would be honored if you would have me as your husband."

Her eyes began to shimmer with unshed tears of happiness. "And I would be just as honored for you to have me as your wife, David."

"Then you'll marry me?" he asked and she could hear the uncertainty in his voice.

"Yes, of course, I'll marry you!"

He quickly took her in his arms and sealed their words with a kiss. There was nothing chaste about this one. No. This time, David gave in to all he had apparently been holding back and she rejoiced in knowing that she had at last found someone who would love her for just being herself.

Someone clearing their throat at the entryway to the salon caused them to quickly break apart. His brother and father stood there with suspicious smiles on their faces.

"Are congratulations in order?" the duke inquired.

"Lady Elinor has agreed to become my wife," David said proudly after Elinor dipped into a curtsey.

George clapped his hands in glee. "Then you should let the rest of the guests know, especially Lady Elinor's family. The Laceys' Christmas ball just became an engagement party!"

The two men left them alone but Elinor knew they needed to return to the ballroom as well.

"I've never been so happy," she declared giving David another quick hug.

"I am so glad we found each other, my love," he replied taking both her cheeks in his hands and leaning forward to give her another kiss.

"I like the sound of that," she answered gazing up into his blue eyes. "I love you, too, David."

"Then let us make our announcement to your parents and their guests and never again will we have to worry about running away from the holiday crowds."

David offered Elinor his arm and she gladly accepted it as they returned arm and arm to the ballroom. The rest of the evening became a blur of well wishes and enjoying her time with her future husband. Her future for the first time in a long while looked grand.

EPILOGUE

One Year Later...

David tried to grab hold of his wife's arm as she left their bed and only came up with holding air. He leaned up on one elbow as she gracefully made her way across the room. A wicked smile crept across his lips as she inspected the clothes scattered carelessly on the floor. She finally found the silky robe he had removed from her body last night in his eagerness to have her in their bed. Once the garment floated over her to cover what he wanted, she tossed him one of those looks over her shoulder that was usually his undoing.

"Come back to bed, Elinor," he said in a husky whisper.

"David... we're late and expected downstairs," she scolded although her eyes told him she'd rather be between the sheets with him instead of downstairs with a houseful of her parents' guests for another Christmas house party.

"They won't miss us," he suggested, patting the empty space on the bed where she just left him.

"Are you never satisfied, my lord? After last evening, I'm surprised you even have the energy for another round of making love to your wife," she teased with a laugh.

"Never!" he declared and decided enough was enough. He tore the sheet from his naked body and left the bed shortening the space between them until he wrapped his arms around her and began kissing her neck. "I could never get enough of you, Elinor. You're like the sweetest drug."

"You're not playing fair, my love," she answered in a breathy whisper as she pushed her back into his chest. His hands moved down and around to her stomach. She might not be showing that much but he couldn't mistake the hardness of his baby within her.

"You should know by now, I never do," he said nuzzling her neck again. "Is the baby giving you problems this morning?"

"Not even a little," she answered moving her hands over his as they linked their fingers together.

"No morning sickness?" he inquired again holding her tight.

"I'm as fit as can be," she said with a light laugh.

"Good!" He pulled the robe from her body and watched it float back down to the floor as he swept his wife off her feet, up into his arms, and started carrying her back to their bed. "One day I look forward to building little gingerbread houses with our children."

"It shall be a new family tradition."

"New traditions sound wonderful," he replied in a husky tone until a breathy sigh and his name left her when he began kissing her neck again. "And I like the sound of my name leaving your lips even more."

"David! For goodness sake. We have obligations downstairs," she said, playfully swatting at his chest as he gently laid her back down before joining her.

"Let them wait. I have an obligation to my wife to ensure she knows how much I adore her," he answered her. He began kissing any further protests she might have had as she wrapped her arms around his neck.

An hour later, David and Elinor joined their families downstairs for the traditional gathering that had originally brought him and his wife together. It was hard to believe that just a year ago, he was seriously wondering if he would ever marry. And then Elinor swept into his life by accident at a chance meeting by the lake. His life hadn't been the same since and he was grateful to her and for the life they had started to make together.

He pulled Elinor closer to his side and kissed the top of her head. Christmas time would always be a joyous occasion now that he had Elinor in his life and a child coming in the New Year. There would never again be a reason to hide away from the holiday crowd since life had become all the brighter now he had found the love of his life. Life with Elinor was indeed grand!

I HOPE you enjoyed this delightful little Christmas story with David and Elinor. You may remember Lady Elinor Lacey when she made her first appearance in *A Kiss For Charity*. David Chadwick has been mentioned in my previous stories from his brother George's perspective. When it came to writing this novelette, these two secondary characters stood out for having their love story told next. I hope you enjoyed their journey to finding love. You can learn more about all my work that includes my medieval, time travel, and Regency era stories on my website at https://www.sherryewing.com/.

ABOUT SHERRY EWING

Sherry Ewing picked up her first historical romance when she was a teenager and has been hooked ever since. An award-winning and bestselling author, she writes historical and time travel romances to awaken the soul one heart at a time. When not writing, she can be found in the San Francisco area at her day job as an Information Technology Specialist. You can learn more about Sherry and her books on her website where a new adventure awaits you on every page at www.SherryEwing.com.

SHERRY'S SOCIAL MEDIA

Website & Books: www.SherryEwing.com
Bluestocking Belles: http://bluestockingbelles.net/
Dragonblade Publishing: https://www.dragonbladepublishing.com/team/sherry-ewing/
Bookbub: https://www.bookbub.com/authors/sherry-ewing
Facebook: https://www.Facebook.com/SherryEwingAuthor
Goodreads: https://www.goodreads.com/goodreadscomsherry_ewing
Instagram: https://instagram.com/sherry.ewing
Pinterest: http://www.Pinterest.com/SherryLEwing
TikTok: https://www.tiktok.com/@sherryewingauthor
Tumblr: https://sherryewing.tumblr.com/
X: https://www.x.com/Sherry_Ewing
YouTube: http://www.youtube.com/SherryEwingauthor

Sign Me Up!
Newsletter: http://bit.ly/2vGrqQM
Street Team: https://www.facebook.com/groups/799623313455472/
Facebook Official Fan page: https://www.facebook.com/groups/356905935241836/

SHOULD AULD ACQUAINTANCE BE FORGOT

ALINA K. FIELD

Dreading meeting an old enemy at a Yuletide house party, Madame Marie La Fanelle, an acclaimed London modiste, has a clumsy encounter with a lamp that leaves her burned, blinded, and in terror of the future.

But then a kind German physician appears, offering a hopeful diagnosis, and stirring memories of the man she once loved. Can the magic of the holidays heal Marie's blindness and soften the hardened hearts of two prideful lovers?

CHAPTER ONE

December 23, 1822
The Black Horse Inn, Kent

Too groggy to open her eyes, Marie La Fanelle stirred and raised a hand to sooth an ache in her cheek.

Pain shot through her, startling her wide awake.

"No, miss, please don't touch."

The high-pitched voice, like that of a child, was oddly familiar.

She opened her eyes. One of her eyelids had met resistance. With the lightest touch of her fingertips, she gingerly traced the coarse cloth extending diagonally from her forehead, across her right eye, and down to her jaw.

"*Lumière.*" She choked out the word, and then remembered this was England. "Light. I must have light." The murkiness of her vision, the unfamiliar bed, the scent of smoke, all had panic rising in her.

"There now," the child said. "The innkeeper's sent for a doctor. You're at The Black Horse Inn. I'm Libby, one of the maids here."

Libby. The Black Horse.

Marie shivered and gripped the blanket covering her, remembering. The sudden snowstorm had come from nowhere and hampered her journey. They'd stopped for the night, she and the coachman of Lord Shaldon's carriage, and the two grooms who'd insisted they'd been ordered to accompany her. She'd been traveling to Hazelcombe Lodge, the home of Shaldon's heir, Lord Bakeley and his lady, joining the family party for the Yuletide christening of the latest member of the large, happy, extended family.

Her business partner, Miss Enid Barton, had traveled there weeks earlier at the request of her old employer and friend, Lady Shaldon, the former Lady Jane Montfort. Marie had stayed in London to oversee the few last-minute orders from ladies keeping Christmas in town and to add the final touches to the christening gown.

The christening gown.

Marie struggled to sit up.

"Shhh, miss." The child gently nudged her back.

"I am no miss," Marie said. "I am Madame La Fanelle. What has happened here? Why am I in darkness?"

"Oh m-miss—I mean madame." The tiny voice warbled, followed by a loud sniff. "You don't remember. The lamp, it... it fell. Last night there was a fire... A small one, but... You were doing close work on... on the loveliest gown I'd ever seen and... Oh, madame, I'm afraid the gown was r-ruined."

A fire. The gown she'd been working on was indeed one of her best, a crimson *peau de soie* meant to be worn at the Christmas fête planned by Lady Sirena Bakeley.

"My trunk. My clothing. What else has burned?"

"Your dressing gown, the tiniest corner afore I doused it. Naught else, *madame*."

Her nightclothes did not matter, nor even the red frock. She had other gowns to wear at the Hazelcombe Yuletide parties.

As long as the christening gown was safe.

"A lamp, please," Marie said.

"Oh m-madam, what with the snow and all, it's bright sunshine outside and there's no cause for lighting a lamp right now."

Her heart thumped wildly, and she opened her uncovered eye wide, straining to make out the room around her, trailing her fingers over the cloth—a bandage it was—that covered her from jaw to forehead.

She'd been burned. Her face and—she touched her temple where there should be hair.

Burned, bald, and even worse... She was blind.

Sainte Marie, mère de Dieu. What was she to do? What would she be without this work that she'd given everything for, that had become her life? Her business depended on seeing. She could not sketch a design, could not study the drape of a gown on a lady, could not... even if God granted a miracle and her sight was restored, she couldn't see clients when she was horribly scarred.

Her breath caught again. *Or him.* She could not, *would not*, see him, and must not be seen by him, not this way: weak, helpless, ugly.

A message from Lady Jane Shaldon had been left for Madame La Fanelle at the inn, where his lordship kept horses for changes when traveling. Lady Jane knew Madame well, knew she would want the news the note conveyed, knew the choice would be hers whether to continue on to Hazelcombe Lodge or return to London.

She might have done just that: sent the christening gown on to Hazelcombe with one of the grooms while she returned to London.

But her pride had niggled at her, along with a sense of obligation. Lord Bakeley's financial support had eased La Fanelle and Barton through the shaky start of their partnership. Plus, she and Barton dressed all the ladies of the extended Shaldon family, making them shine in London society. In return, their beauty and elegance enriched the little business that had grown to challenge the London modistes and even the fashion houses of Paris.

And this baby to be christened... She'd prayed long and hard for both mother and child. For Lady Jane, at such an advanced age, to be blessed with a baby girl? La, but how it had stirred her childless heart with a longing to hold a babe. One of her own—but oh, that was a useless longing.

When Lady Jane requested that she and Barton stand as godmothers, the honor had incited rare tears. She would hold this baby, cherish this little girl, dress her in beautiful clothing.

That *he* had been named godfather was unfortunate but since he was off somewhere destroying someone's trust for the sake of the Crown's business, it was planned that someone would stand proxy for him.

Lady Jane's note informed her the plans had changed; the godfather had arrived in Dover and would appear not by proxy, but in person.

She had endeavored to take the news calmly. With the great honor of serving as godmother, the Shaldon family would be, in a sense, her family too. The mere presence of Angus Kincaid must not keep Madame La Fanelle away.

Since that long-ago betrayal, they'd had one heated conversation, a conversation with more accusations and renewed recriminations.

Lady Jane had been in trouble, had needed her and Barton to help. The beastly man had accused her of misbehavior again.

He hadn't been entirely wrong. She'd been helping Lady Jane's failed attempt to betray Lord Shaldon after the lady stole his prized painting.

Lord Shaldon had forgiven his lady, unlike…

Merde. It was too late. Kincaid had betrayed her, had used her, and she must not forget it.

And this injury, this blindness… it could not be borne. She must return to her comfortable lodgings above their elegant Mayfair shop. Lady Sirena would stand proxy for her at the christening, or one of the other ladies.

She heard the door creak, and a draft of air swept over her.

"It's frigid in here," a man said. "Fetch more coals, girl. What of the doctor, innkeeper? Has he seen her?"

"Nay, milord. Sent for him, but he's off to a daughter's in Surrey so 'twill be a while."

A hand took her own and squeezed it. "La Fanelle, I came as quickly as I might," a woman said.

The voice was Barton's.

"What do you mean, trying to burn down the inn," her business partner teased.

"*Comme c'est drôle*, Barton. I am not in the mood for *amusement*. Which lordship accompanied you?"

"Lord Bakeley here, *madame*," the man said, and she turned her head to his voice next to her bed. He smelled of fresh air, cologne, and as usual, horses. "The news of a fire frightened the ladies half to death. Barton and I came as soon as we could. I am glad to see you are, er, much better than the message would have us expect. Innkeeper, what treatment has been done?"

"My wife cleaned it with good clean snow water, applied a salve to the burn, and then bandaged it."

The innkeeper's voice came from the foot of the bed.

"I do not appreciate being hovered over," Marie said. "Go and prepare me an accounting of the damages, *monsieur* innkeeper."

The room went quiet, except for the opening and closing of the door.

"Do you feel well enough to travel, *madame?*" Bakeley asked. "We've brought a comfortable traveling chaise. We can reach Hazelcombe by nightfall."

She shook her head and winced at the pulling of the skin on her jaw.

"I'm returning to London."

"But the christening," Barton said.

"Lady Sirena may stand proxy for me."

"But Lady Jane will be so disappointed." Barton squeezed her hand again. "The innkeeper's wife told me the burn is not a deep one. If we keep it from festering, you shall be fine by the christening on Twelfth Night. If you're worried about your appearance, I can fashion a veil—"

"Barton, *non*."

"We can provide you the best of care," Bakeley said. "You need not mingle until you feel ready."

"I am returning to London, Barton, my lord. Because..." She inhaled deeply. "Because I cannot see."

Silence reigned for long moments, and then the door creaked again, and the latch clicked shut. She heard Barton's sharp indrawn breath.

CHAPTER TWO

Paris, 1793

MARIE CLUTCHED her basket tighter and threaded her way through the crowds surrounding the bakery. The stale roll slipped to her by her friend Jeanne nestled underneath layers of cloth, the muslin gown discarded by the mistress of one of the members of the Committee of Public Safety. She would savor each crumb of bread while she remade this scandalous robe into something more élégante. A seamstress for the respectable Citoyenne Raspal must continue to turn herself out fashionably.

Footsteps fell in next to her, the long legs and muscled frame belonging to her downstairs neighbor. A French-born Scotsman, he worked at the Tuileries as an engraver and printer for some bureau of government—a dangerous job in France in these times.

James Murray claimed to have been from a large clan of Jacobites who'd found refuge in France. Or perhaps he was lying. La, everyone in Paris lied these days. For herself, she simply kept her mouth closed and her opinions to herself.

Monsieur Murray was probably a spy, but Marie hadn't worked out for whom. The Hebertists? The Dantonists? Or perhaps the

English whom he claimed to despise. He was elusive about who he favored.

Except that he'd made it clear that he favored *her*. In all of her sixteen years, she'd never had a man pursue her with such determination, nor with such courtesy. He hadn't once tried to kiss her, and she very much wanted him to do so. She was young, but like most French girls, she was old enough.

"Will you have dinner with me, mademoiselle?"

"Dinner?" she countered, stalling for time and sorely tempted. She'd had no meat in more than a week. And yet... She shared her sweltering attic lodging with Jeanne, who had taken up with a gentleman and was often gone. She was sure her Scotsman had noticed. A kiss was one thing, but she wasn't willing to offer the rest of herself.

"Yes, mademoiselle. Come with me for a restorative broth at Boulanger's. Or there is another café near the Palais Royale that I know of. You need not fear I am asking for more than your conversation and company."

They turned a corner and encountered a crowd of women and men surging in their direction. Mr. Murray pulled her into a doorway and nudged her behind him.

Her nose poked the wool of his coat. It was not as fine a fabric as one of the deputies of the Convention might wear, yet better than a laborer's Sunday coats.

Or what would have been Sunday coats. She had to remind herself that the government had eliminated Sunday, along with the God meant to be worshipped that day.

She pressed closer, inhaling his scent—the fabric itself, of course, along with a fragrant tobacco, and the gamey scent of horse. Monsieur Murray had a horse?

"Come out with us," a man shouted nearby, distracting her from her thoughts. "Why are you hiding in the doorway?"

Monsieur Murray pivoted, facing her, and turning her sideways, yet shielding her face from the lout. *"Vive la révolucion."* He pointed to the cockade on his hat, tipped his head toward her, and grinned.

"Ah ha ha," the other man laughed and moved on.

Heart pounding, Marie lifted her chin, willing him to bend down and kiss her. His big body pressed, taut and hard, ready to spring, and she sensed the danger in him. He would keep her safe. At a price, perhaps.

When he turned his head toward her, she went up on her toes and pressed her lips to his.

December 1822, Kent

With its half-timbered exterior, The Black Horse Inn surely dated to Elizabethan times. He'd stopped here before, though so many years had passed he couldn't expect to be remembered.

The front step had been cleared of snow, and a wreathe of cheerful Yuletide greens adorned the scarred oak door. Inside, the scents of musty wood and roasting meat greeted him. He peeked into the tap room, where a crowd of locals gathered with their pints near the crackling fire.

A maid entered from a side door, carrying a pail of coal. She plopped it down and would speak, but another voice interrupted.

"Up you go, Libby, I'll see to this guest. A room for the night?" he asked.

"If one is available. I heard from a traveler I met on the road that the inn caught fire here last night. I hope all is well."

The innkeeper's eyes narrowed. He would not want the story spreading far and wide and ruining his custom. "Naught but a tipped lamp and a few sparks. Quickly put out by a well-trained maid. The one carrying the coals, in fact. You have nothing to worry about, sir."

He set his black traveling case on the counter.

"Here now," the man said. "Is that a medical case?"

In fact, it looked just like the sort of bag surgeons or physicians carried, stuffed with equipment for bleeding. He himself had always carried medical supplies in it, along with his shaving kit and an extra shirt.

As the silence lingered, the landlord wrung his hands. "'Struth, sir there was a guest hurt, and we've sent for the local doctor. Don't know if he'll arrive before Twelfth Night. If you are a doctor, might you have a look at the lady? She's in sore need and, er, what with her noble friends, your fees will not be a problem, I'm sure. Sent word to them right away and his lordship rushed over from Hazelcombe this morning immediately the news arrived, the roads being better."

Though it was still cold, the fine sunny day had cleared the roads of the worst of the previous day's snowfall.

"She was burned?"

"Aye." The ruddy face moved close enough he could smell the fellow's breakfast. "My wife treated her. Seen enough burns in the kitchen, she has and keeps a white ointment on hand. Cleaned the burn and used that ointment. Gave her a wee drop of laudanum to calm her and help her sleep. Burn's on her face, you see, and... Well, the wife's afeared summat is wrong with the lady's eyes too."

Alarm bolted through him. He struggled to compose himself before finally asking, "her eyes were burned?"

"No." He shook his head. "But she can't see."

Ah. That might be hopeful. He'd encountered such injuries before in men dealing with explosives.

"I will be happy to examine her." He accepted the inn's register and signed his name.

The innkeeper squinted at the page. "Dr. Louis Huber from Augsburg?"

"It is a city in Bavaria."

"Ah, good, good. I'll show you up to your room and then take you to see the lady."

"I will see her directly."

With a look of relief, the innkeeper picked up the black case, led him up the stairs, and ushered him into the room.

He handed his greatcoat to the innkeeper and made a quick study of the small bedchamber. The maid, Libby, knelt before the hearth, tending the fire. A tall, thin woman, middling in age and plain faced stood by the bedside. She looked his way and gasped.

"What is it, Barton?" The voice came from the small figure in the bed.

The well-attired man standing on the other side of the bed sent him a look of shock and opened his mouth.

"This here is Dr. Huber." The innkeeper replied, thankfully before the other man could speak. "Happened to be traveling down from London and said he would gladly have a look at Madame's injuries. If you'd like milord."

"Dr. Huber," the nobleman said, lips twitching. "You're a, er, physician?"

"I have much experience tending such injuries. Place my bag on that table, my good man, and take my coat to my room, please."

The woman who had gasped, Barton, moved closer to the bed, a quizzical look on her face. Neither visitor voiced opposition to his examination of the patient.

He stepped closer. There was no need for a candle or lamp. The window curtains framed a blaze of light from the snowy landscape outside.

The small figure on the bed lay very still. Hair spilled over her pillow, the color a brown so dark it was almost black, thick and begging a man's touch, a man's fingers to rake through the soft waves. A cream-colored bandage swathed her diagonally, forehead to jaw, covering one eye. She squeezed the uncovered eye closed, and her full lips formed a frown. Hands fisted, her arms froze at her sides, pressing the counterpane tightly over a still shapely figure. Tension rippled through her, palpable in this chilly room.

Blindness was frightening; he prayed it would not be permanent.

As he drew closer, the medicinal smell of the innkeeper's wife's salve rose up, unable to entirely drown the scent of lilacs and oranges.

Memories stirred. He shook them off and nudged Barton out of the way. A gurgling sound came out of the tall woman's throat as he reached for the patient's hand.

"Whaт *is* it, Barton?" Marie felt a hand at her wrist and clasped it.

It wasn't Barton's hand. It was a man's hand, large, long fingered, and warm. Not clammy and soft, as some men's hands were.

Her breath caught and she dropped her free hand away. A man with such hands had once touched her in intimate ways.

Oh, how gleeful that man would be to see her like this.

This, she reminded herself, was not him, else Barton or Bakeley would have recognized him.

"I will take your pulse now, *madame,*" he said, with the slightest of accents. "Or is it *mademoiselle?*"

Dr. Huber, the innkeeper had called him. His accent was neither English nor French. If only she could make out his face.

Her eyes ached, her whole face ached, and frustration ate at her. "You should like me to introduce myself before I know who you are?" she scoffed.

"Huber, *madame.* Louis Huber."

"Louis Huber," she said dropping the h and the ending consonants and pronouncing the name in the French way. "You are French."

"*Bayerisch,*" he said. "Bavarian. *Bavarois,* if you will."

She'd never met a German who could speak proper French, and his pronunciation was atrocious.

A *soupçon* of relief trickled through her. As defenseless as she was, she would not want to encounter a strange Frenchman. She had never been tortured by a Bavarois.

"Now please, quiet yourself a moment while I the beating of your heart measure."

Pah. He was not fluent enough to put the words in the right order when he translated them into English. She huffed again and grumbled through the long pause as her wrist was held in what was surely a large hand.

"Rapid," he said. "May I proceed, madam? You are French, or Belgian?"

Fingers still curled around her wrist, sending an unwelcome warmth through her. She sensed a challenging masculinity about him that she could not do proper battle with in her vulnerable state. "You are impudent, monsieur. Do what you must."

"Marie," Barton said. "Perhaps he can help you."

"We should like to know if Madame La Fanelle can travel to my estate not more than a few hours from here while the road is still fair."

Bakeley spoke with such pompous authority, she had to gather herself to keep her voice from shaking and speak firmly.

"I am returning to London," she said. "I will rest here one more night and then the earl's coachman may carry me back."

"I've sent him on to Hazelcombe," Bakeley said. "Barton and I have a larger coach. You may travel comfortably with her to look after you, while I ride outside. When you are more recovered, you may return to London. My servants and family shall ensure your care during your convalescence. I must insist on this, *madame*. My stepmother would have my guts for garters if I sent you to London any sooner."

Bakeley's stepmother was Lady Jane, who Barton had served as lady's maid until she left the post to set up in business with Marie. She reminded herself again, it had been Bakeley's investment staking the endeavor, and Lady Jane and the other ladies of the family displaying their craftsmanship in society. She and Barton had been able to pay back his lordship in full with a fair rate of interest. Still...

"I never thought you to be a bully, Lord Bakeley," she said, and the words sounded more waspish than she meant.

"That is not my intention," he said.

"Do not concern yourself, my lord," Huber said. "This peevishness in the patient is an excellent sign. But now, Madame La Fanelle, may I remove the bandage and examine your burn?"

Peevishness, was it? "*Oui*," she huffed.

Fingers slid painlessly through her hair, the touch easing a tension she'd not been conscious of. The bandage must have been tied at the top of her head. Ever so carefully he worked the cloth without pulling a single hair on her head.

Cool air hit her cheek and pain rose with it. She raised a hand, wanting to feel the raw spot of singed skin, but he took her fingers in his. "We will not touch. You must keep the burn clean. Some hair has been singed and that will grow back. I observe red skin and some blisters. Those will heal, and I do not believe you will have more than a minor scar which you may cover with a cream until it fades."

He traced a finger along her uninjured jaw. She winced.

"You have pain there?"

"I have pain everywhere but..." She sighed and shook her head. It hadn't been pain she was feeling.

"You are very beautiful, *madame*. This slight injury will not change that."

"Fustian," she said. That was a good English word she'd learned from Barton. "*Les balivernes*. Nonsense." Or—what was the word her Hanoverian customer used? "*Quatsch*."

"I do not lie, *madame*."

"I am helpless in bed, grossly burned and bald. You are..."

A memory sprang to mind. A conversation like this from many years ago. Happier times before the betrayal, when she'd learned a new word. He would not know the word's meaning. "You are havering."

His fingers stilled. They'd been gently massaging her shoulder. "Havering."

"Talking nonsense. A word I once learned from someone who spoke English as badly as you."

A gurgling sound came from somewhere in the room.

Tears sprang to her eyes. Now they were laughing at her.

"*Madame*," Huber said, his voice a whisper. "Shall I have the maid fetch a looking glass so you can see that I am not havering, as you call it?"

She turned her head toward his voice and gasped as her burned cheek pressed against the pillow. The tears welled and, blink though she might, she could not hold them in.

"I'm sorry, my dear." His hands soothed her shoulders, and a weight pressed down on the bed at her side.

"*Mon Dieu*," she spluttered. He had seated himself on her bed. "You are impertinent."

"Yes, *madame*. Will you tell me, please, if you are able to see me?"

"*Non.*"

"Open your eyes, please, *madame*."

She pressed her lips closed on a curse.

"What can you see?"

She squeezed her eyes shut and shook her head.

"SHE SAID SHE IS BLIND." Barton had moved closer. "Perhaps we should let her rest before talking more."

Marie's partner was the practical sort. Right now, he could see that her face displayed a healthy skepticism along with genuine worry.

"It will help to know what happened," he said, gently.

Barton sighed and nodded.

"I can tell you what happened, sir." The maid who'd carried up the coals was still here.

"Ach, yes. Libby, is it? The innkeeper said you put out the fire. Come out in the corridor and we will talk."

He moved to stand, but Madame swung wildly and clutched his arm. "You will make this discussion in my presence."

He patted her hand and stood anyway. "As you wish, *madame*."

The maid took little prompting to describe how Marie had been working on embellishing a gown—the most fetching gown the girl had ever seen—adding delicate beading so fine that *madame* had turned up the lamp and moved it closer. The girl had been filling a bath, her back turned, when the lamp fell, spilling hot oil and catching the gown and the table on fire. She'd doused what she could with water and beat out the rest with a blanket.

"You saved Madame's life," he said. "Well done. Were you overtired from the journey, *madame?*"

"Sommat upset her," the girl said. "A letter was left here. She was fine until she read it and then she went all shaky, pulled out the dress and sewing things and had me light the lamp."

"Yes, thank you," Marie said, "and begone with you girl."

Her eyesight might be faulty, but her spirit was undimmed.

"You may go, Libby," he said. "Have the kitchen send up a light meal for *madame.*"

"I will have coffee only."

"Send up coffee with the light meal. You may change your mind about being hungry, *madame.* Now, I will examine your eyes. Miss Barton, please close the curtains on the window and the other side of the bed, and light a candle for me. I will be gentle, Madame Marie."

Before the room darkened, he spread the lids of each eye apart and leaned in. The scent of lilacs and oranges made his heart race.

The bed curtain opposite closed and then the one at the foot of the bed, and then Barton handed him a lit candle stub.

Marie flinched.

"I assure you; I will not set the bed afire." He scooted himself closer to her, his hip touching hers. "Close this side curtain over me as well, Madame Barton."

Barton pursed her lips and then did as he requested.

"Forgive me this impertinence, Marie," he murmured. "Open your eyes and tell me what you see."

CHAPTER THREE

OVERWHELMED, Marie pressed back into the mattress and pillows. The man's presence swamped her, taking her back years... How many was it?

Twenty-nine. She counted them out every year from the Christmas that was not a Christmas because it couldn't be celebrated. Twenty-nine years ago, a man had climbed into her bed, a man with a scent, and a voice, and a touch very much like this man's.

It wasn't him. It couldn't be him. Many men smelled of horses and had deep voices, and was not one man's touch much like another's?

Her eyes flashed open, and she raised her head, and then gasped. A light moved slowly from one side and then to the other, carrying the scent of burning wick with it, and she felt her eyes following it.

"Very good, Marie." She heard his smile and wanted to smile with him—or was she only being fanciful?

"Will I see again?" she asked. "Do not give me false hope."

"My dear, I will give you every bit of hope I can muster." With a sharp breath, the light extinguished. "I have seen this sort of ocular injury before in men exposed to explosives. All recovered their sight."

His hand touched her own, squeezed, and raised it up to receive the press of his lips. A shiver went through her. He tucked the blanket higher over her. *Mon Dieu*, the man took advantage.

She found she no longer minded.

The curtain rings squeaked, and a draft of air blew away the candle smoke.

"Well?" Barton asked.

"Tomorrow is Christmas Eve, and I don't think it's necessary for all of you to spend Christmas at this inn," Huber said. "Today, though it is growing late, and the road may become icy. I suggest that Madame stay the night here and travel in easy, slow stages tomorrow morning, if the weather is fair."

"But what of her condition?" Bakeley asked.

"I shall give you instructions, Madame Barton if you are willing to serve as nurse. The burn will heal, and the singed hair will grow out. As for her vision, as I told her, I believe in a few days she will be able to see again."

"We would welcome you to er, continue treatment at our home, sir," Bakeley said. "You are surely not spending Christmas in this inn."

"I thank you. I will be with friends if the fair weather holds."

Hazelcombe Lodge, Kent

"Madame La Fanelle arrived days ago." Edward Everly, the Earl of Shaldon, sent Angus Kincaid a sly grin. "She insists on keeping to her bed."

He himself had landed on the doorstep of Hazelcombe Lodge less than an hour ago, entering once again by the servants' door into a kitchen humming with Christmas cheer. The scents of roasted fowl, puddings, and sweets filled the air. The same little kitchen maid who'd greeted him upon his arrival from Dover a few days earlier had hurriedly put together a repast for him which he in short order devoured.

Seated now by a roaring fire in Hazelcombe's library, Angus Kincaid studied his oldest friend and comrade. Shaldon's hair had grayed a bit more and there were a few more lines on his face, but he was as fit as ever, with only a slight limp as evidence of old wounds.

His second marriage to Lady Jane Montfort had not taken the man completely out of the game; he still served the Crown and was still an arch meddler in his family and friend's affairs.

He was happy with his lady though. 'Twas a miracle when men their ages could find love and settle into it.

He himself had found love years ago and lost it. Unfairly. Unreasonably. Unpardonably. It would take more than a miracle for a hardheaded Frenchwoman to seek his forgiveness. And perhaps he, a hard-headed Scotsman, wouldn't grant it anyway.

Or perhaps they both needed to set aside their mutual feuding.

He took a sip of his whisky, beating back the annoying yearning that ate at him when she was near and studied the greenery festooning the mantel. Lady Bakeley had decorated every nook and cranny of the Lodge for this special Yuletide, celebrating a new member of the Shaldon clan and the health of both mother and child.

Mistletoe and kissing boughs were everywhere, the footman escorting him warned. Good thing that Marie was still abed.

"And, your lordship? Have you told her I'm here?"

"For some reason, it was agreed amongst the females that your arrival would be kept a secret from Madame. Even by them. That will be a challenge for my daughters and my lady, but Madame is being tended to by Barton and my wife's maid, Jenny. If you recall both women can be closed mouth when loyalty demands."

In fact, Shaldon had once tried to recruit the maid Jenny, who grew up in the Seven Dials, into spying for England.

"Why not tell Marie I'm here? Let her fret over my presence."

"She won't fret," Shaldon said. "She'll fume and perhaps knock over another lamp and start a new fire. I'm told that you caused the first accident."

"*I* did?" He shook his head, recalling the maid, Libby's story.

"Yes. Jane knew she'd change horses at the Black Horse. When she heard you had landed at Dover, she sent a note to the inn warning that you would be present for the christening. Madame was fiddling with embellishments to a gown, hoping to impress you."

He gripped his glass tighter and made himself scoff. Marie's beauty marched hand in hand with her pride. There was no sense getting his hopes up about Madame seeking to put her best foot forward. It had naught to do with him.

"If I were in her shoes, I would want to know if she was nearby when I was feeling defenseless. Someone ought to tell her I'm here."

"And interfere with her recovery? It's not like you to be so cruel, Kincaid."

It wasn't cruelty; it was leveling the field for a duel between old enemies.

"I know you are merely trying to provoke me, your lordship."

"What are friends for?" Shaldon said. "La Fanelle is no fool. She'll suspect you've arrived and wonder why no one is telling her."

Kincaid shrugged. Marie was no fool, yet she was the most stubborn woman he'd ever met. "How is her recovery proceeding?"

"Apace, Jane tells me. Though to satisfy Barton, who did not have full faith in *Dr. Huber's* judgment, we've sent for another doctor."

"And her vision?"

"She is seeing shadows. The burn, Barton fears, will leave a rather more formidable scar than Dr. Huber predicted."

Kincaid rose and refilled his glass. "Do you recall the soldiers we saw in Spain?" he asked. "The cannon that exploded?"

"I recall the scattered body parts."

Kincaid waved a hand. "The men further away survived. There were burns, yes, and two of them were blinded but their vision returned. I spoke with Dr. Saunders at Moorfields Hospital. He concurred that an optical burn like this will often heal. When she returns to London, he will examine her, if she wishes."

"Let us hope her injury follows the same course. The ladies will continue to flock to her shop even if she is scarred, but she will need her eyesight to draw her designs."

The dinner gong sounded and Shaldon stood. "Come and bring

your drink along. Bakeley is hosting a Boxing Day reception for the locals. Lady Bakeley has ordered me to be present."

Kincaid laughed. Lady Bakeley, Shaldon's spitfire of a daughter-in-law, daughter of an Irish earl, was dear to his lordship, yet he obeyed or disobeyed her orders as he wished.

"'Twas a long, cold ride from London today," he said. "I'll stay here by the fire drinking your son's whisky, if you don't mind."

"As you wish. Madame is ensconced in a chamber at the end of the hall of the south wing. I am telling you so that you may not stumble into the wrong bedchamber."

Shaldon crossed the room, barely limping at all, and stopped at the door, sending him another grin before exiting.

Squashing his own smile and a rising hope, he studied the amber liquid again, remembering another Christmas

Paris 1793

It was just as well that the Republic had banned Christmas, since so very little food could be found for celebrating, except in the salons of the members of the Committee of Public Safety. The day of Christ's birth had become the mere fifth of Nivôse on the revolutionary calendar.

Nor had Christmas been celebrated during his childhood in Scotland, yet the erstwhile James Murray had hoisted many a wassail cup among the English. Only fool governments banned holidays that soothed people's nerves and met their needs to have something to rejoice about.

"A chicken, James. A whole chicken." Marie whispered the words, perhaps afraid that a sansculotte would be shuffling about on the staircase. But he knew their neighbors to be gone—her roommate, Jeanne, off with her lover, and the family below gone to watch the macabre celebration substituted for Christmas by the state—more executions by Madame Guillotine.

He shook off the dark thoughts and dropped a kiss on her forehead. "A scrawny one, I fear. But I also have a morsel of beef."

The scent of roasting meat he could do nothing about except to add more onions and garlic to convince those nearby that he hadn't exceeded the meager daily ration of bread, meat and vegetables delivered to his lodging because of his official employment as one of several men engraving and printing the missives put out by the Committee of Public Safety. This feast had come courtesy of his other endeavors.

He pulled out a chair for her and she sat, raising her dark eyes to him, a look of wonder on her face. She reached for him, pulling him down for a lingering kiss that sent him to his knees.

"Ah, Marie, Marie," he said, moving his lips to her neck. "*Ma chère.* See here." He straightened and reached for a paper-wrapped package he'd set on the table. "This is for you."

She blinked. "A gift?"

"A Christmas gift. It is illicit, I fear. I made it myself. You may throw it into the fire if the good *citoyens* come poking around."

She untied the string and peeled back the paper and gasped. Her reaction brightened the dismal gloom of this day.

A smile lit her face. "A crèche."

Five carved wooden figures nestled within, two men, one of them holding a staff, a four-legged animal of sorts, a woman, and a babe in a box. He had learned to carve wood from his grandfather, who'd also taught him his other skills with the blade.

"How lovely. We had one like this made by my grand-père. Joseph, Mary, and this one is a shepherd, no? With his sheep?"

"You may call it his sheepdog if you think that is more apropos."

She laughed. "No angels or kings with camels?"

"Am I not a good Republican, disavowing kings and spiritual fantasies?"

"Except for the Christ child," she whispered.

Marie wore as large a revolutionary rosette as any other lady wishing to preserve her life. She was cynical, as well. In their many weeks of courtship—he'd grown to think of this friendship as that—she'd come to trust him with stories of the hypocrisies of the ladies who graced the modiste's shop, trading husbands and lovers as survival demanded. Seemingly useless information that often revealed more than Marie might think.

The neighbors whispered that Marie was his mistress. Try as he might—and he couldn't help himself, he had tried—she'd never allowed more than kisses. Perhaps it was her Catholic upbringing—three of her uncles had been priests. Or perhaps it was that, at her core, Marie knew her own value.

"I have no gift for you," she said. "Except…" Color rose in her cheeks. "The gift of myself. Today, if you will have me."

If he would have her? Pulse pounding, he smoothed back her hair. "*Mo chridhe.*"

"What?"

"*Mon Coeur*, it means, in the Scots."

A tap at the door brought her to her feet, her look of alarm quickly masked.

He rose with her and caressed her cheek. "Don't be afraid. We have one more dinner guest. You will know him."

The old man he ushered in handed over a bottle of wine and flashed her a bright grin. Marie blinked and rushed to greet him, dropping to her knees to kiss his hand.

"*Mon oncle,*" she said. "You're alive? But they took you. How—"

"God spared me for his service in this moment." The old man raised her to her feet. "And one last good meal, I hope? After the sacrament."

"The sacrament?"

"I have not asked her yet," he said. "Marie, will you marry me?"

"Marriage? But my work—your work…"

Though the modiste who employed her turned a blind eye to girls kept by lovers, as they remained childless, married women were let go, Marie had told him.

"Marry me here and now. The Committee need not know, your employer need not know, but we'll know, and God will know. Your uncle will perform the marriage."

"And I shall remind the Lord most high of your vows after I am guillotined," the old man said, affably.

132

"But…" Marie chewed her lip. "My work…"

"You offered me a most treasured gift," he whispered, leaning even closer and lowering his voice more. "I won't take it without vows. You won't lose your position. I will take precautions to delay getting you with child."

Her eyes searched his, her lips quivering, and he feared she would turn him down.

"It's madness, perhaps, given the times we live in," he said. "I know you wish to pursue your work, and I won't stop you. In fact…" He reached for another package and handed it to her. "I meant this to be a wedding gift, but you may keep it whether you say yes or no."

Hands shaking, she untied the string and unrolled the paper.

"Shears," she whispered, hooking her thumb and fingers and spreading the blades, her lips turning up.

"For your dress making."

"They are very fine. It is too much."

"They're from Thiers. The finest blades come from there."

"Thiers? When did you visit Thiers?"

"A friend brought them for me."

Her gaze flitted over his face. The suspicion he saw in her, the hesitation, tore at his heart. He wouldn't force her. "Come, let us eat."

"Wait." She reached for his hand. "Yes, James," she said. "Yes, I will marry you."

The priest cleared his throat. "Ah. At last. Then let us begin," he said. "James Murray and Marie La Fanelle, join hands."

He shook off the faintest of misgivings about his deception. His cover had been carefully crafted, was rigidly preserved and ran very deep. He dare not tell his beloved that James Murray was not his true name, but the same God who witnessed this union would know it, and someday Marie would as well.

CHAPTER FOUR

Hazelcombe Lodge

MARIE RESTED against the pillows plumped into place by Lady Jane's maid, Jenny. The bandage had been removed and her skin stretched taut, tender, and itchy under the housekeeper's thick burn ointment. Her eyes, covered now by a dark sleep mask, ached from the earlier effort of trying to see, and from a niggling despair creeping over her.

"Are you sure you won't take a drop of laudanum?" Jenny asked. "Dr. Ossington said—"

"*Non.*" That fool. That quack.

Barton was now showing the good doctor to the door after his second visit and probably interrogating him further. Her dear friend and business partner had insisted Marie be seen by a second doctor, though Barton had denied doubting Dr. Huber's optimistic diagnosis.

Both times he visited, the quack had loomed, a shadow beside her bedside, squeaky-voiced and smelling as though he'd doused himself in a lady's perfume instead of washing.

On that first visit, he'd tut-tutted about the carelessness of knocking over an oil lamp, as if speaking to a small child or an imbecile. And then,

without so much as lifting her wrist to check her pulse, he pronounced his opinion that her skin was healing nicely though she must still be wary of infection, that she would carry a scar for life, and that it was unlikely her sight would fully return—though not impossible. Until then, she must wear a sleep mask at all times and continue to rest.

At Barton's insistence, she'd followed those orders. When she removed the mask for his examination, she found the shadows had grown more defined. The quack discouraged her from getting her hopes up and told her to continue to rest.

She had been an unruly patient—peevish as Dr. Huber said. As to that, the quack offered a bleeding to better restore her humors.

Merde. A cut with his bleeding knife, not a gentle clasp of strong fingers, not a tender stroke of her uninjured cheek, nor a reassuring whisper.

She wished Dr. Huber had accompanied them from the Black Horse.

The door opened and closed, bringing a whiff of Barton's lavender scent.

"I've shown him out," Barton said. "I've told him to not return."

"*Merci.*" She pushed back the covers and swung her legs over the edge of the bed. "Assist me to rise and dress, Barton. I can't abide in this bed any longer."

Barton helped her out of her nightgown and carefully settled a chemise over her head.

Had Dr. Ossington been honest? Was it true that she would spend the rest of her life blind, scarred, unable to do the work that she loved?

She'd fought to be able to practice her art. She'd given up everything for it.

She stood to accept the gown over her head and turned to allow Barton to fasten the tapes. "It's a pity Dr. Huber has vanished," she said.

A person needed to have hope.

A long, quiet pause ensued.

"What is it?" Marie asked. "Tell me true, Barton: did this Ossington tell you something that you're keeping from me?"

"No, my dear friend," Barton said quickly. "Shall I ask Lord Bakeley to send for Dr. Huber?"

A tingle went through her, and she craned her head back, wishing she could see her friend's face. "Does Lord Bakeley know where is this sanguine Bavarian who gave me hope? If you find him, I promise not to be a peevish patient again for him."

"It seems to me you have a right to be peevish," Jenny said as Barton fastened the last closure and helped Marie to be seated.

"There now," Jenny said. "You're sitting on the chaise. If you but lift your foot, I'll help you into your slippers and then if you grow tired of sitting you may either wander around the room or lay yourself down again." The chatty girl paused for a breath. "Did you like Dr. Huber, then, *madame?*"

Did she?

"He was kind. He reminded me of someone... someone I once knew who was once kind to me."

He'd been kind to her until he wasn't... Until he'd demanded from her the unacceptable, and the unacceptable had come for her anyway.

She heard the door open and turned her head that way. The scent of a familiar lady's cologne greeted her, along with other smells: soap, fresh linens, and—she sniffed—the faintest scent of urine?

"Lady Jane," she called, "is it you?"

"It is indeed, and you are up. How wonderful to find you feeling better. I've brought you a visitor to cheer you."

Her heart stirred within her. Lady Jane's gown brushed against her own as she sat down next to her.

"She's awake," Barton said from her other side. Marie heard the smile in her voice.

"Yes, and I've just fed her and changed her clout—though I'm wondering if she has already soiled this one."

"May I..." Marie caught her breath before she went on. "May I hold her?"

"Of course. That's why we're here."

She put out her arms and felt the slight, bundled weight settle into them.

"She's watching you, *madame*," Jenny said.

Marie still wore the eye mask, but her healing skin was bare.

"Am I frightening her with this hideous visage?"

"Not at all," Lady Jane said. "In fact…" A chuckle escaped her lips. "There it is. Another smile. Julia has been a happy baby so far."

"Because she knows she'll always be dressed in the height of fashion," Barton joked.

Please God, she would be able to see again and dress this little angel.

"Look how she quirks her lips. Watch out, *madame*," Jenny teased. "It might just be gas."

The swaddled little body stirred, and Marie adjusted the babe's head higher. "Take off this mask for me, Jenny."

"Madame, Barton will have my head if I do that."

"I am not totally blind. My vision was fuzzy when that quack visited."

"Keep it on a little bit longer, Marie," Barton said. "Give your eyes time to heal. Dr. Ossington said to wait until after New Year's."

"Oh, do not cry, my dear." Lady Jane moved nearer, and an arm came around her shoulder.

Tears. What was wrong with her? Madame La Fanelle did not cry.

She wanted to tell them that, but she couldn't find breath to speak without sobbing. While the mostly sweet smell of baby rose to her, and the soft bundle nestled against her, her own body was betraying her. Longing, deep and painful, swirled in her, regret for all that she'd given up. Had she been wrong in the choice she'd made all those years ago and the choices she'd made in all the years since? Tears rolled painfully over her damaged cheek.

"It is only the injury making my eyes water," she said, finally mustering words.

Silence reigned. They did not believe her.

Someone gingerly dried her cheek, and Lady Jane began to talk of the festivities planned for the coming week.

What good friends they were to not press her.

Paris
November 1794

SHE HAD NOT SEEN James for two weeks and besides not feeling the least bit charitable toward him, she was beginning to worry.

The Terror had ended in the summer, the people of Paris having had their fill of the rivers of blood and being satisfied with the mere trickle now produced since the Committee of Public Safety had disbanded and the Jacobins had been crushed.

She and James had weathered the storm, two bourgeois citizens keeping their heads down, grateful to have not been denounced. Their marriage was still secret; not even her friend Jeanne knew, and she would keep it that way or else lose her position in the shop.

That would be terrible. Fashion was changing, rapidly, in revolutionary ways, and Madame had smiled upon some of Marie's designs.

She'd had other work too. James had brought her small commissions, gowns to be fashioned here in her rooms. At first, she'd been suspicious; what sort of husband would have her sew for other ladies?

She'd fussed so much that on an evening stroll, he'd arranged for her to encounter the lady demanding garments of different sizes. The customer—it had only been one—was an elderly woman who wanted extra pockets to conceal the weapons she and her maids carried with them on the dangerous streets of Paris.

It had been weeks since the last such commission; perhaps the lady had been taken up, for Madame Guillotine was still plying her craft.

She shoved aside her thread, pins and shears, moved the candle closer and set her pencil to the precious piece of blank paper she'd found in James's room. Normally a tidy man, this time he'd left it in such disorder, she'd begun setting it to rights until she ran out of light.

She hoped that when they were able to live together properly, he didn't think she would be constantly tidying up after him.

Or... she studied the flame. A rough man had come to the shop, questioning her about him. While her employer looked on with curiosity and suspicion, Marie had mustered some calm and denied any intimate knowledge of James Murray, except to say that he was a neighbor who said he worked in the Tuileries, and who lived one floor down from her. When pressed, she admitted she'd done some mending for an elderly woman friend of his, nothing that interfered with her work for Citoyenne Raspal.

She had not betrayed him. In truth, she knew nothing about him to betray except for his marriage to her.

Still, the visit had shaken her nerves, in no small part because of the way Madame had eyed her afterwards. Until she had the means to set up her own shop, she must find her way back into the modiste's good graces. Despite the chaos, Paris was still the center of fashion, and fashion was changing.

She reached into her memory of Citoyenne Cabarrus, mistress to Monsieur Tallien, who'd visited the shop, wearing a frock in the simple lines of the new silhouette in lady's gowns. It was said the new style had been inspired by the deprivations suffered by the woman when she was held in the wretched Paris prison, La Force. One did not need stays, stomacher and panniers whilst awaiting trial and execution.

Sleek lines rolled from the pencil, fashioning a higher-waisted gown with a flowing skirt. James was an engraver; perhaps he could make a print of this.

"That's lovely."

Marie looked up. "James."

She rose to greet him, stopping suddenly to hold him at arms' length and then drawing him closer to the candlelight. Bruises mottled his face from forehead to chin.

"What happened to you?"

"A bit of trouble."

"Sit down and let me—"

"No, no. I'm ahead of them, but… I came back for you. We must leave."

"Leave?"

"Yes, *mo chridhe*. We must leave France."

"And go where?"

"England. And we must move quickly."

She shook her head and glanced down at the paper. "No. Not now. You cannot demand that of me."

"They'll come for me, and they'll come for you too."

She let out a breath, worry rising inside her. "Who will come?"

"Agents from the Convention. Marie, please listen: my real name is Kincaid. I really am Scottish, but I am employed by England."

"You're a spy." She plopped into a chair. She'd suspected as much, hadn't she, whilst denying to herself that this could end—blissful nights making love while madness circled all around this tiny lodging.

Sooner or later the madness was bound to catch up to them—hadn't she always feared it?

He dropped to one knee. "Marie, I love you. You're my wife and I can't leave you here to their mercy, nor can I stay." He stood and drew her up by her hands. "We have to go now."

"They have already come, James. I was visited by a man at my place of work. Don't you see? Nothing happened. They won't bother me, and I can't leave Paris now."

His face hardened and his grip on her hands firmed. "What did you tell them?"

His palpable distrust spurred her anger. "You did not think to tell me your true name and that you were a spy? How could you conceal that from me?"

"It doesn't matter. We must go now."

"I will not."

Loud voices reached them, and footsteps on the stairs. James—or whoever he was, this stranger who'd lied to her, who'd disappeared for long days at a time, grasped her shoulders.

"They'll arrest you, Marie. I couldn't bear that."

"Let go." Her hand scrabbled for a weapon, the madness descending.

The madness of months, nay years of fearful waiting for a knock at the door, for a full plate of food, for a friend to help her. They wouldn't arrest her now. They'd had a chance already.

She couldn't trust this man, this liar, who'd taken her to his bed with false promises.

Her fingers closed on the shears, and she swung her arm.

With a yelp, James fell back, a look of heart-sick dismay quickly turning to fury.

And then he was gone, and she huddled in a weeping heap on the floor, her hand covered in blood that was not her own.

Rough arms took her up, swamping her in oniony breath and the odor of dirty wool over old sweat.

Days later, the old woman she'd sewn for escorted her out of the jail, and out of Paris, to an inn near the coast, where she handed Marie the remaining coins in the purse she'd drawn bribes from at every step of their journey, as well as a sack with all the contents gathered from her small room, and turned her over to three wily smugglers for the channel crossing.

Rummaging through her sack, she found her few gowns and undergarments, her pins, threads, and needles, and at the bottom of the sack, the one figure saved from the Christmas creche, the tiny manger containing the baby Jesu.

The shears were missing. That something so valuable would be stolen was not surprising. Or perhaps, her rescuers feared she would turn the sharp points on them.

The man, Kincaid, was not waiting for her. It was just as well. The moment she landed on English soil, he was dead to her, as she was to him.

Bah. Whether he lived or not, it didn't matter. She'd never wished to flee France, to come to this cold, wet, country. He'd taken from her everything; she resolved to find her way into the business she loved, to survive, to thrive even, and never be foolish again.

CHAPTER FIVE

Hazelcrest Lodge
New Year's Eve

"Go and see her, man," Shaldon said. "What are you waiting for?"

They were back in the Hazelcombe library again after a morning and afternoon spent riding the Hazelcombe estate, Bakeley proudly showing his father, his younger brother, and Kincaid first the stables that housed the horse breeding operation he shared with his horse-mad wife, and then the more mundane drainage projects he'd undertaken on the estate. Kincaid had tagged along out of sheer restlessness and a wish to delay seeing Marie again.

The day's outing had reminded him that he had a cottage and land of his own, in Scotland, looked after for years by his cousin, the laird of the nearby castle. He'd once thought, for brief moments during his youth, to finish his studies in Edinburgh, bring a wife there and raise a family. But then the trouble had started, first in Ireland and then in France, and duty had called, the desire to serve fed by his restlessness and yearning for adventure. He hadn't visited his home in years.

"Madame asked us to send for Dr. Huber," Lord Bakeley said with a smile as sly as his father's. "Dr. Ossington did not go over well. She was quite cross with him, Barton said. They've had the children up to see her the last couple of days. Hasn't cheered her up much though. Sirena found her in tears this morning after the nursery maids took the little ones away."

That could only mean that her vision had not returned. He crossed to the sideboard, and then thought better of refilling his glass, needing to keep a clear head.

He'd abandoned her to fate once; he wouldn't do it again.

He would escort her to Moorsfields Hospital himself. Damn her pride, and his own, he would look after her.

Leaving his empty glass, he faced the two men. "Have you told her I'm here?"

"No, and she has not asked."

"I'll go see her now."

"Bearding the dragon," Bakeley teased.

For a penny he'd slap this young man who he'd known since birth.

His face must have revealed his emotion because Bakeley raised both hands to ward him off. "A thousand pardons. Madame is a lovely lady and despite your, er, avoidance, I believe you care for her."

Kincaid nodded. "She *is* a lovely lady. Stubborn, headstrong, determined to have her own way." An image of her that Christmas so long ago rose in his memory. "And she is my *wife*."

On that note, he cast a defiant glare at Bakeley's astonished face. Shaldon only smiled. Though he'd never told his old comrade of his nuptials, Shaldon must have suspected, or he might have heard it from someone who'd served in Paris then. Marie had been rescued from jail and ferreted to England on the orders of their head of station in Paris, the one person he'd told of the marriage, the one person he'd begged to look after Marie when he was sent off with intelligence too important to trust to anyone else.

Against orders, he'd gone back for Marie, proving the folly of men like himself falling in love.

Treading softly along the richly carpeted hallways, he made his way to the upper corridor. The family would gather for a festive New Year's Eve dinner in less than an hour. Bakeley's Irish wife promised some Hogmanay touches to this Sassenach celebration, just for him. Perhaps he could convince Marie to join them after dinner for the New Year's party.

Marie's bedchamber was so close to his, the temptation to pay a call sooner had been nigh unbearable. He'd looked in on her once, late at night when she ought to have been sleeping, and found her awake, observant, and fretful. Jenny had spotted him from her chair by the bedside; at the shake of his head, she'd reassured Marie that it was only a footman checking whether anything was needed.

Guilt niggled at him for the way they'd all conspired to deceive her about his identity. Given the depth of her despair after the accident, and her hatred of him, it had seemed wise at the time.

Marie deserved better. For all that she'd cast him off, his sin had been worse—leaving her to the madness of revolutionary justice. The debt incurred by her rescue—well, he'd served the Crown for decades, working that off.

For years he'd considered her dead to him, even when he heard her name mentioned as a modiste in London. But when she was drawn into the Shaldon orbit a scant two years ago, he'd come face to face with Marie because of Bakeley's lady. Then, when Marie became involved in the dangerous game Lady Jane had been playing, they'd had actual words.

He hadn't been able to bear the thought of her in danger again.

He paused by his own bedchamber door, hesitated a moment, and proceeded on. He wouldn't bother to change out of his riding clothes —if he arrived by her bedside smelling of horse and boggy water, so be it.

Steeling himself, shaking off the character of Dr. Huber, he knocked, hesitated, then opened the door.

Barton looked over from a chair by a table, a gown spread before her, a needle and thread in hand. Marie lay stretched on a chaise by the fire, dressed for company in a blue gown, but with her dark hair loose and cascading over her shoulders. A black mask concealed her eyes. On the injured half of her face, the skin stretched painfully red and taut across her jaw and cheek. The blisters had dried and were beginning to scab at the edges.

She raised her sharp little chin, her lips turning down into a frown. "Who has arrived? I fear you have me at your mercy." She sniffed the air. "Shall I guess? Lord Bakeley, perhaps. You've returned from the stables and are here to harangue me about joining the dinner party."

How to proceed? His mind went blank.

"Surely, it is not the great Lord Shaldon?"

"It's... Dr. Huber." Barton had set aside her sewing and approached, a frowning question in her eyes.

Marie sat up and then stood, extending her hand. "Ah, la. Lord Bakeley found you. Have you just alighted from your mount and come to see me? Thank goodness. I am much in need of an optimistic physician. Unless... perhaps you have come to withdraw all hope and feed me laudanum or bleed me. Then you may turn around and take yourself away."

Despite her flirtatious words, her voice had quivered.

The ugliness of the burn did not diminish her beauty one whit. Yet 'twas not her beauty, but the force of her character, her strength, reminding him how much he had once loved her.

How much he still loved her.

He fought a sudden urge to rush to her and take her into his arms. The cautious young girl she'd once been hadn't welcomed a move like that. So much less, this mature woman of the world who'd carved a place for herself in the London world of fashion.

"Laudanum has its uses," he said, finding his voice, "but I don't think much of leeches. Nasty little things. Will you leave us, Barton?"

Marie turned her head, searching for her friend's location.

"You *do* have something awful to tell me."

"*No.* That is..." He paused, considering.

Telling her his identity now after so much deception, yes, that *was* awful. He'd adopted the persona of Dr. Huber because he had to see her, and he knew she'd never have allowed Angus Kincaid to visit.

Coward that he had always been around her, he hesitated. The stakes were high for her. The loss of her vision would be terrible for her business. To have him swoop in, admit his deception, to ask to take care of her...

He couldn't deny it anymore. He wanted to be part of her life.

It would be foolish to rush her as he'd tried to do that fateful November in Paris. He would proceed carefully.

"After I left the Black Horse, my business took me to London. I visited Dr. Saunders at Moorfield's Hospital. Have you heard of it?"

"The eye hospital." She groped behind her for the chaise and perched on the edge, patting the space next to her. "You did that for me? Come. Sit and tell me what you learned."

He seated himself a hand's width apart from her. Barton took the wing chair across from them and raised her eyebrows.

Whatever Marie might decide, if she turned him away, at least she would not be alone. She had loyal friends.

"Dr. Saunders concurred with my evaluation. These sorts of injuries to the eye very often resolve themselves. I'm told you were able to see people?"

"Blurred figures. The other doctor insisted I wear this mask to rest my eyes."

"But you have taken it off sometimes?"

"Only to replace it with a fresh one. Barton has insisted it must be done in the dark." She took in a small breath. "The burn—it is awful?"

Her hands lay in her lap, twisted together, the evidence of her nerves sending his own pulse pounding with a need to touch her.

"It is *not* awful. It is in fact healing quite beautifully. You have done as I said, you have taken great care."

"Barton is a cruel nurse. She insists on covering it when I am in bed. It is a wonder she doesn't tie my hands to keep me from scratching."

"It has begun to itch? That is a good sign. Now, may I begin as before with measuring the beat of your heart, Madame?"

Ach, he had slipped into the Bavarian doctor again. Perhaps that was just as well for the moment.

She nodded and he untangled her hands, taking both in his with a squeeze that he meant to be gentle and reassuring.

He wrapped his fingers around the delicate skin of her wrist, feeling his way over tendons and bone to the shallow well of blood pounding, and felt the shiver that went through her.

The fire in the nearby hearth burned too brightly for anyone to be cold. He didn't—couldn't count the beats of her heart. It had been a ruse anyway, a way to touch her. His own heart raced too quickly for any counting, and a bead of sweat trickled under his shirt between his shoulders.

When he shifted in his seat and captured her hands again, she angled her body to meet his, their knees touching.

"*Vous avez un bon Coeur*," she whispered. "*Pardon*. You are as good hearted as a man I once…"

She sniffed and swallowed, and he held his breath.

When the silence extended, he freed a hand and reached for the string holding her mask. One of them must be courageous.

"Marie, *mo chridhe*," he said. "Let us remove the mask."

Mo chridhe.

A CHILL WENT through her again, as the mask fell away and her eyes flew open. *Mo chridhe.* The guttural endearment burst in her memory. Her vision… She blinked, blinked again, dispelling most of the fuzziness, seeing a man in dark coats and buckskins and a woman in a gray dress.

He'd gone to his knees before her; his hair, as thick and dark as her own, though laced with gray, the eyes still dark and intelligent, the face broad and strong-jawed and now careworn from so many years serving his King.

In the few times they'd been in the same company these past few years, she'd tried desperately to *not* see him.

She couldn't avoid it now. She didn't want to.

"You can see." Barton smiled from her spot where she stood looking over his shoulder.

"You must leave us, Barton," she said. "You must truly leave us now."

Her friend nodded. "Dinner will be within the hour."

"Barton, my friend."

The persistent woman flashed her an even brighter smile. "I'll have the kitchen send up trays."

Marie heard the door close on her friend, but she kept her gaze fixed on him. He stared back at her, and she wondered if he was filling himself with a study of her or simply challenging her to break contact first, to push him away again first.

As she'd done almost thirty years ago.

He'd knelt before her other times—once on that Christmas day when he asked her to marry him, and the second time, to beg her to escape France with him.

All of her senses stirred. There'd been other times too, magical times, when they'd made love.

"What if I had said yes, Kincaid? What if I had left with you?"

He squeezed his eyes shut, a look of pain drawing his brows together. She waited.

"God's truth, Marie, it was a harrowing journey. More than once, I wondered how I might have managed to keep you safe. I begged our people to help you if you needed it. It was a year before I heard of your arrest and escape and that you'd made it safely to London."

"And then you chose not to look for me."

"Pride ate at me. Anger."

"You thought I'd betrayed you."

He shook his head. "I realized that no—"

"I did betray you. Not intentionally. The woman you had me sew for; I told them about her. When she came with her bribes for the guards, and they released me, I realized. That was how they found you out."

"I shouldn't have asked it of you."

Her heart lurched. "The sewing? Or... do you regret our... liaison."

"Never," he said, and the fierceness had warmth rippling through her. "I loved you, Marie."

The large hands squeezed her again and she felt tears threatening, as they had too often these last few days.

It was no use. She was becoming as the English called them, a watering pot.

She studied his face again: the faint gray afternoon whiskers rising along the curve of his jaw, the scar curling through one bushy eyebrow, the crooked tilt of his nose midway. While she had sketched and snipped and sewed after they'd parted, he had battled much and in many places.

He had loved her, he said, past tense.

"Did you... did you take lovers?" she asked. "Or a wife?"

He shook his head. "I have a wife, Marie."

He'd taken a wife. Her heart chilled at that news.

"And children? Do you have children, Angus?"

He blinked. "You're my wife, Marie. When we parted, were you..."

She gasped. "With child? No." Through the months of their love-making he'd told her he was taking precautions. A wise thing, she'd thought then, given their circumstances.

She didn't understand how he was going about his precautions until later, after listening more closely to the gossip of her fellow seamstresses and her clients. When she'd finally worked out that he'd never... never planted a seed within her, as it were, she realized how green she was. Too green then and later, too careful to say yes to any of the men who offered their services through the years.

Plus, until she learned otherwise, she was still married. Her conscience would not allow for adultery.

But she would never design a beautiful gown for a daughter of her own.

"You ought to have married and had children," she said.

It was an argument she'd occasionally, in moments of despair, had with herself.

"We'd said vows, Marie."

"Vows that were never recorded. I lost track of my old uncle, but he is surely dead by now. You might have taken a wife. No one would have known."

"I would have known. You would have known. God would have known."

"You believe in God, Kincaid?"

"Countless times, I've had naught but a prayer to raise in my defense." He bit his lip. "Would that I had swallowed my pride and come and talked to you sooner. We might have had children."

Emotion clogged her throat. She was still having her courses. Older women had children—look at Lady Jane. Though a first at her age...

"It is a regret I am finding every year harder to bear. But I must bear it."

He cupped her good cheek and swept his thumb over her lips. "I would bear it with you if you will allow it."

Startled by his tenderness, she lifted his hand away in self-defense. "James Murray. Kincaid. Dr. Huber. How could you pretend to examine me and assess my injuries? You have gall, sir."

"I also have medical training. Studied for two years at Edinburgh College, and I've tended more than a few wounds and injuries. Black powder in a poorly maintained weapon can be dangerous. I didn't lie. I've seen men with such injuries recover."

"My sight has mostly returned. *Mon dieu*, I hope I do not require spectacles. Bring me a mirror so I may see my face."

He shook his head. "Not yet. Let me prepare you." While he described the appearance of the injury to her cheek in detail she closed her eyes, picturing the wounds. She'd seen a seamstress burned like this leaning too close to the flame while she worked on an urgent commission. The plain-faced, plucky girl bore the scar with aplomb, even going on to marry.

"Now let me describe the state of your other cheek." He traced a finger from her forehead to her jaw, his touch sending a tingle of awareness through her, such as she hadn't felt in years.

"Dr. Huber's touch," she whispered. "I might have known it was you."

She clamped her hand over his. "No, I believe I did know it was you. A part of me recognized your tenderness."

"I've been a terrible fool, Marie. Will you take me back?"

"You would have me?" she asked. "Tell me it is not out of pity because of..." she pointed to her cheek, "this and the ugly scar it will leave."

"I have a few scars of my own. Would you like to see them?"

Her heart quickened, memories stirring again, desire melting the armor she'd built around her heart. "*Oui.* I see the one cutting through your eyebrow. Where are the others?"

"Here." He placed her hand on his chest. "And on my back as well. And lower down."

Before he could move her hand to a more interesting spot, a knock came at the door, and without waiting for a response, two maids entered carrying trays, shepherded by Barton.

Kincaid did no more than glance back at them.

"Ah, you haven't harmed each other," Barton said. "Marie, Lady Jane begs you to come down after dinner to help usher in the New Year. And Kincaid you must come down. Lady Sirena says you *must* appear because she has gone to the trouble of arranging a Hogmanay celebration for you."

"What say you, Marie? May I escort you down to the party after dinner?" He leaned in and whispered, "and then we'll return, and I'll show you my scars?"

"You don't need to hide from him anymore, Marie," Barton said.

Irritation flared. Her friend's managing ways could be annoying, even when she was right.

She sighed. "It's true, Kincaid. I've been hiding from you. No one announced your arrival or even mentioned your name, so I knew you must be here. I couldn't bear you to see me like this, burned and blinded. I might have known you would... you would find a way. You would deceive me."

His smile disappeared and he got to his feet. "You're not blind anymore, Marie."

She stood as well, clutching his shoulders and looking up at him.

"No, I'm not blind anymore. Don't..." She took a deep breath and swallowed the bitter bile of her pride, her anger, her years of stubborn denial. "Thank you for bringing me hope. Don't leave me again."

He swept her into his arms, and leaned down, studying her lips. "Will a kiss cause you pain?"

Giggling erupted behind him, along with the sound of shushing, and Marie went up on her toes as she'd done so long ago on that Paris street. "Let us experiment, Dr. Huber."

THE DARK-HAIRED young footman they'd enlisted to serve as the First Foot ushering in the New Year had a dazed grin on his face as he snatched up the whisky offered him and tossed it back.

"Too much wine below stairs," Shaldon said. "Bakeley sent a few bottles down to the servants for their party."

"What comes next in our Hogmanay celebration, Kincaid?" Lady Jane asked.

The smile he beamed down at Marie sent warmth bubbling through her. He lifted the glass that a servant had just handed him and linked arms with her.

"Raise your glasses," he said, in a booming voice Marie had never heard from the careful engraver. Perhaps at some point through the years he'd commanded men in battle. He had layers of secrets she must explore along with those scars.

"Out with the old year, and in with the new. Now we sing," he said, and in a very fine baritone led them in a song about old acquaintances being forgot.

The words had her weeping yet again.

"It's a song from Robbie Burns," he said, setting aside his drink and pulling out a handkerchief. "A Scots author."

"Yes, yes, I have heard of him."

He slipped an arm around Marie. "Shall we retire and as the song says, drink a cup of kindness?"

His whisper tickled her ears, evoking a laugh. They slid out of the parlor as surreptitiously as possible and went to her bedchamber.

She heard the click of the key in the lock. "Your Barton is a caring friend, but you don't need her nursing skills anymore."

"Not with Dr. Huber to attend me."

The only light came from a low fire in the grate, yet she saw the flash of his teeth as he smiled.

"Am I forgiven, Marie?"

She moved into his arms and pressed against him, her body remembering the feel of his muscular form.

"Perhaps." She slid her hands under the lapels of his coat. "Let us get you out of these coats and then you may light candles and lamps."

"I am at your service, *madame*."

Heart quickening as her eyes adjusted to the dark, she watched him shed coats and in only his shirtsleeves and trousers, make quick work of lighting the room and building the fire higher.

"Better?" he asked, taking her into his arms.

Better? Yes of course. She could see him.

He could also see her. Defiance made her lift her chin against a spurt of insecurity.

"Marie," he said, "underneath all the anger and pride, my love for you was always there. I never stopped wanting you, either. And I want you now."

She stared at his neckcloth, a million thoughts going through her head—regrets, and worries, and doubts. Her body was not the same—she'd grown plumper, softer. And then there was this ugly burn.

"L-like this?" She pointed to her cheek.

"We will be careful. Or, if you are afraid, we can simply talk."

She let out a long breath and began loosening his neckcloth. "I want no halfway measures, Kincaid. That is perhaps what we did wrong before. Let us talk after."

IN THE MORNING light trickling in through the window curtains, Marie lay on her side—her good side, studying the man stretched beside her. At some point in the night, Kincaid had risen to blow out the candles, dim the lamps, and feed the fire. The room was chilling again, and her face itched like the devil under the bandage Kincaid insisted on wrapping over her wound to protect it.

It was the only stitch of cloth she wore.

She burrowed under the covers and dragged a cold foot up his leg.

He instantly turned on her, alert and aroused, making her giggle like the silly sixteen-year-old she'd once been. "You weren't sleeping."

"I have learned to come awake quickly."

"Ah, *bien*. Your wife is cold."

"Are you, lass? Then let me see if I can warm you."

EPILOGUE

February 1823

KINCAID ENTERED through the workshop and made his way up to the study on the second floor where he found the esteemed Madame La Fanelle in conference with a seamstress.

She was still La Fanelle to her customers; in private, she told him she would be Mrs. Kincaid, or perhaps when required, Mrs. Murray or even Mrs. Huber.

The seamstress curtsied her way out of the room, a packet of designs clutched to her bosom, and he dropped a kiss on his wife's lips.

"How go the preparations for the Season?" he asked.

"We have studied the plates from Paris and the fashions have not changed so much from last year, though they are not what they once were. I predict that the sleeves, they will fatten more, the waistlines will descend another half inch, and the skirts will widen. How I should like to see with my own eyes what women are wearing in Paris."

"Indeed," he said.

"Ah la, the simpler gowns of my youth brought more comfort but for a modiste, less profit." She winked. "We can certainly charge more for these new designs and give employment to more girls. You will escort me to the warehouse *n'est ce pas*? I'm told the new shipment of fine silk has arrived."

"Of course. It will be my pleasure. Marie, my love, once the Season is finished and you've made all the new gowns for all the June brides, I'm taking you away for a while. Barton can manage without you."

Her chin shot up, the instant defiance making him laugh.

"If you wish to go. Only if you wish it."

"And where do you think to take me?"

"I thought we might go to visit my home in Scotland. Or perhaps we should go spying on the fashion houses in Paris. You may choose— meeting my family, or espionage."

Marie rose and came around the worktable. "Your home… oh we must see it and I must meet your people."

Her hand went to her scarred cheek.

"They won't see the burn for your beauty, and for your fashionable gowns of course."

She swatted him. "Yes, I must meet them. But, oh, Paris. It has been so many years, and you are right—I can *spy* what is coming from more than a drawing. Why not visit both places?"

"Both places." He tugged her close. "What a brilliant idea."

As he bent to kiss her, she put a finger to his lips. "You see what a good wife I am? I am becoming acquainted with my new family and joining my husband in his profession."

"At least fashion is a less deadly business."

"You think so, Kincaid? You will see."

He couldn't help grinning. "Then I will see that your shears are sharpened, Madame La Fanelle."

"Will you always remind me?" She pursed her lips in a pout.

"Only so I can demand compensation. A kiss, *madame*?"

Without waiting for an answer, he claimed her lips and they both surrendered.

ANGUS KINCAID first appeared in *Marrying Mr. Gibson*, book one in my Sons of the Spy Lord series, as the friend and sidekick to the Earl of Shaldon. When Marie La Fanelle stepped onto the pages of book two, *The Viscount's Seduction*, and cast a withering look at Kincaid, I knew these two old enemies would some day have their own story. And here it is! To find out more about the Sons of the Spy Lord series and my other books, visit my website at https://alinakfield.com/regency-romance/.

ABOUT ALINA K. FIELD

USA Today bestselling author Alina K. Field earned a Bachelor of Arts Degree in English and German literature but prefers the happier world of romance fiction. Her roots are in the Midwestern U.S., but after six very, very, very cold years in Chicago, she moved to Southern California where she shares a midcentury home with a golden-eyed terrier and a feisty chihuahua and only occasionally misses snow.

ALINA'S SOCIAL MEDIA

Website: https://alinakfield.com/
   Facebook: https://www.facebook.com/alinakfield
   BookBub: https://www.bookbub.com/authors/alina-k-field
   Goodreads: https://www.goodreads.com/author/show/7173518.
Alina_K_Field
   Newsletter signup: https://landing.mailerlite.com/webforms/land
ing/z6q6e3

MARYANNE AND THE TWELFTH KNIGHT

JUDE KNIGHT

Maryanne is only at the house party as chaperone for her half-sister. She is far too old and insignificant to attract the attention of a duke. Or, at least, if he is pursuing her it cannot be for honorable purposes.

Dell knows it is time to take a wife, but the offerings of the marriage mart bore him to tears. The only lady of interest at his sister's house party is the spinster chaperone. But she isn't eligible, is she?

CHAPTER ONE

December 27th, 1770, Fairclough Castle

THE DINING HALL at Fairclough Castle had sixty corners. Maryanne Beckingham, who was being ignored by the rest of the company at dinner this evening, had amused herself by counting. Sixty short walls. Sixty angles—which must, if she had calculated it correctly, each be one hundred and seventy-four degrees.

In effect, of course, the room appeared round, and was a fitting setting for the largest round table Maryanne had ever seen. By her reckoning, it could seat as many people as there were walls, with enough elbow room for them to manage their cutlery.

The Dowager Lady Kirkland had not been quite that ambitious for this first house party now she was out of mourning. Only twenty-three people were present. The hostess herself. Five couples. Four widowers. Two bachelors. Two widows. Three unmarried ladies—four, if one counted Maryanne, though nobody ever did, except as a spare female to make up numbers.

As evidence that Maryanne was entirely forgettable, the gentlemen on her either side were fully occupied with the ladies on the other side of them.

Maryanne had no objection. She was very aware that she was only here because her younger half-sister had been invited. "Lucette cannot go without a chaperone," their stepmother had told their father. "But it is such a chance for her."

"Kirkland is only fifteen," Papa had protested. "He is probably at school, and is certainly not old enough to be setting up his nursery."

Maryanne, who had begun wondering at what age a gentleman ought to set up his nursery, had lost track of the conversation, but Stepmama must have convinced Papa, for she heard her name mentioned and looked up to find all eyes on her.

"Yes, of course," Stepmama said. "Maryanne, you will be pleased to attend Lady Kirkland's house party as Lucette's chaperone."

If it had been a question, the answer would have been no. Maryanne would not be pleased. House parties, in her experience, were a special type of torment. But it was not a question. Maryanne wondered what she had missed. Presumably one of Lady Kirkland's guests was being auditioned as a prospective husband. Lucette's first season had been a great success, but thus far Papa had not been receptive to any of the offers for her hand.

"The chit is pretty enough and well-enough dowered to do better," he had said, but he was delighted with the interest shown by prospective suitors and their Mamas.

Indeed, Stepmama was much in favor with Papa at the moment. Not only had Lucette, under her chaperonage, been acclaimed as a diamond of Society, but Stepmama was with child again. This time, everyone hoped it would be the long-awaited heir, and even the chance of a brilliant match for Lucette could not be permitted to put her ladyship's health at risk.

That was why Maryanne made the journey to Whitecliffe Manor with Lucette, primed with instructions from both Papa and Stepmama about guarding her sister's safety and promoting her sister's interests.

It would not be so bad, Maryanne assured herself. True, the people she had met so far did not impress. If the gentlemen on either side of her were typical of the company, she could see a boring few days ahead of her. One spoke of nothing but horses, and the other was relating uninteresting gossip about people Maryanne had never met and never wished to.

However, unlike during her own first season, she no longer cared about what such fashionable fribbles thought, and that made all the difference. They would overlook her and sneer when they could not help but notice her? So be it. They might despise her as much as they liked. It made no difference to Maryanne, for she did not value their opinions.

She did care about being bored. Generally, she would escape to the library, but at this party, she was responsible for safeguarding her sister's reputation, so could not spend the party hidden away reading everything she could find.

The architecture of the castle must be her consolation. Parts of it dated back to medieval times, but it had been adapted and pieces added over many generations until it sprawled down the sides of its hill and up the sides of another. There was food for dreams here—in the rooms with their unlikely angles and niches, the passages that twisted in unexpected directions, the unexpected staircases and sudden windows.

Dreams, perhaps, of knights and ladies. This round table required a complement of each—beautiful of form and pure of heart. Today's inadequate showing would hardly do. Fewer than half of them qualified as beautiful of form, though their clothing certainly made up for any personal flaws. As for pure of heart, Maryanne had seldom met a Society lady or gentleman who qualified.

Still, she could imagine them as better than they were, and herself, too. Twelve lovely ladies (including the hostess), and eleven knights, the flower of chivalry. Surely, there must be another man to come? What, she wondered, had become of the twelfth knight?

As if her mental question had conjured him up, the door opened and a slightly harassed sounding butler announced, "His Grace, the Duke of Dellborough."

A tall handsome gentleman in his middle years strode into the room and crossed to where Lady Kirkland had risen to her feet.

The Duke of Dellborough? He was the one for whom Lady Kirkland had gathered three prospective brides and a camouflage of other guests? No wonder Stepmama had been so pleased with the invitation, and so determined that Lucette would accept it.

Maryanne vaguely remembered being told that Lady Kirkland was the duke's sister, so that explained it. Maryanne narrowed her eyes in the man's direction. She supposed her imagination might be up to the task of seeing the gentleman as the knight required by the architecture. She had not, of course, met the Duke of Dellborough, since mortals such as her were not presented to luminaries such as he, but she had observed him from the corners she haunted at ton events.

The man thought a great deal of himself. In fairness, though, he had reason. All of Society fawned over him. His arrival at an event, even late, would make any event a success. When he paid attention to a young lady, her reputation was made. When he ignored someone, they—in effect—ceased to exist.

Maryanne was quite ready to despise him, but he had not yet given her reason.

Indeed, if her suspicion was true and Lucette was being auditioned as a potential bride, then Lucette's sister had better give the man no hint that she even had an opinion.

The duke was speaking, his rich voice filling the room. "My dear Viviane, I must beg your pardon for arriving late, and a second time for coming to you in my dirt. If you and the company will hold me excused, I shall go and make myself fit to appear in company, but I first wanted to let you know that I have not failed you."

In his dirt? The Duke of Dellborough was immaculately dressed, his richly embroidered silk jacket over an even more ornate waistcoat, lace foaming at his neck and cuffs, breeches crisply pressed and embroidered to match the jacket. From curled wig to buckled shoe, he was as exquisite as if he had dressed to dine with the king.

Maryanne curled her lip at such obvious fabrication.

The Duke of Dellborough looked straight at her and winked.

THE LITTLE GREY dove attempting to go unnoticed in a flock of peacocks found his posturing contemptuous. Dell winked at her, just to give her a shock, a thrill, or a fright, depending on her nature. Instead of flinching back, leaning forward, or shrinking down, the unaccountable female laughed!

Dell dragged fascinated eyes from the presumptuous lady and did his best to appear fully focused on his sister, who was assuring him a place had been laid and nobody in the company would be offended at him being seated with them immediately.

Of course they would not. Dell was a duke, and could appear among them buck naked, and they would forgive him. Copy him, too, probably. The fools among them copied the silliest thing.

Once, when he was much younger, he rode a horse backward in the Hyde Park fashionable hour, telling those who asked that it was a training tactic used by the famous Polish hussars to teach horses not to be surprised by anything their riders asked of them. Within a week, five fools had been bucked off, two horses had escaped into traffic, and every afternoon the Park carriage ways were blocked by snarled traffic from incompetents losing control of their mounts.

It had been as hilarious as some of the fashion excesses he had adopted and then dropped, just for the fun of watching others try to copy him, but he had outgrown such tricks.

In any case, he had been prevaricating when he said he was not fit for company. When he'd been forced to stop this evening just five miles from Fairclough Castle, to have a wheel spoke replaced, he had washed and changed for dinner.

He took the place to which Viviane directed him, and greeted the ladies on either side. What a pity he was not seated next to the grey dove.

He watched her through several table settings, becoming increasingly irritated that the gentlemen placed at either side of her did not obey the dictates of polite custom, but ignored her through each change to continue their conversations with more richly-dressed ladies.

Not, now he came to consider the matter, that she was poorly dressed. The material was fine enough and well cut and the garments well made. But both fabric and trimmings had been designed to deflect attention. Who was she? And what was she trying to hide?

Dell would find out. It would give him something to do besides avoiding the lures and escaping the snares of the girls Viviane had invited for him. If any capturing was to be done, it would be by him and of his free volition.

He had met all three of the candidates in London. It was time he chose a wife, but the harsh light of a London marriage market had done none of the marriageable ladies any favors. He chose the three he found least objectionable, and asked Viviane to invite them to a house party. Over the course of several days, he hoped they would relax and he might find something to like about at least one of them.

His grey dove must be someone chosen to make up the numbers. He hoped she was a widow, or the wife of a gentleman who had interests elsewhere. Dell did not ruin innocents, and he would not make an exception for the lady who laughed at him, and who currently surveyed the company with calm interest despite being ignored by her dinner partners. If she was not an innocent, however... If she was available and interested, then he would take time from his wooing of a wife to seduce a lover.

It would require great discretion, of course. He could not offend his sister, the little grey dove, or his prospective brides by showing any public interest. Which would make the game more interesting, at that.

After dinner, he tolerated the male company at the table for thirty minutes. "On this first evening of the house party," he said, after that, "I'd like us to join the ladies. I am certain we will all be delighted to have the opportunity to greet those we know and be introduced to those we do not." He did not wait for agreement, but led them to the drawing room where the ladies waited, heading once more for his sister. "Viviane, my dear, will you introduce me to those of your guests I have not met?"

Not the three candidates for his hand, though of course he greeted them as Viviane conducted him around the drawing room. Miss Tollworthy was attending with her parents, Miss Thompson with her married sister and her husband, the Viscount and Viscountess Markham. There were three other couples, two of them already known to Dell, plus five eligible gentlemen—three of them widowers and two cubs barely out of the nest.

He smiled and nodded, made pleasant conversation, complimented the ladies, joked with the gentleman... and all the time he waited to meet the gray dove, who was sitting with Miss Beckingham. Not a wife, for the gentlemen were all accounted for. Perhaps a widow?

But he was about to find out. Viviane stopped before Miss Beckingham and began an introduction. "Miss Beckingham, may I make known to you His Grace the Duke of Dellborough." She was looking at the grey dove, and now she turned her attention to the younger woman. "Miss Lucette, I believe you and the duke have already met. Dell, Miss Beckingham has been kind enough to accompany her sister to the house party."

Not just a spinster and presumably a maiden, but the chaperone of one of his marriage prospects! Dash it all!

That should have been the end of it. He obviously could not pursue the lady as an object of amorous interest, and Viviane assured Dell that she was not suitable as a prospective duchess.

"Her mother was a merchant's daughter," Viviane said, when he followed her to her boudoir after the other guests had gone up to bed. "She is ladylike enough, Dell, but past her first youth and there is still the smell of trade. One cannot get past it. Viscount Beckingham, her father, married the mother for her dowry, of course. He inherited the title, the entailed lands, and little else. She died in childbed."

"Obliging of her," Dell drawled, to be provocative.

Viv chose to ignore him. "The mother had only the one child, leaving Beckingham much better off but without an heir. Beckingham married again, a girl from a good family this time. Lucette is her daughter. Much more suitable for you, Dell, and far prettier, too. She has three younger sisters, and Beckingham is on his third wife, who is nearing her second confinement, and so Miss Beckingham came to chaperone Miss Lucette."

"Include her," Dell told her. "When you are pairing me with the eligibles, Viviane. Include Miss Beckingham."

Viviane gave him a searching look, and he met her eyes, his face carefully bland.

"Very well," she said. "It would look odd otherwise, in any case. But I do not know what you are about, Dell. She does not at all fit what you told me you were looking for. She is past her first youth, her bloodlines are stained, she could not be described as beautiful, and I very much doubt she is the sort of woman to be biddable."

All of which was true. When he had given Viviane the three names, he had told her he wanted a wife who was young, well-bred, beautiful, and obedient. There were better born ladies in this year's offerings— daughters of earls and even the sister of a marquis. But these were the only three who had not managed to give him a disgust of them during the Season.

"They are all so boring," he told his sister.

"You are looking for a wife and a mother for your children," Viviane pointed out. "That requires you to choose one of them, marry her, and get her with child. There is no reason why you should spend time with your duchess outside of the necessary activities."

Which was, Dell thought, the truth. And unutterably sad.

CHAPTER TWO

THE ELIGIBLE LADIES WERE A DISAPPOINTMENT. Dell had sat beside each of them at dinner, partnered each of them in cards, turned the music for each of them, walked with each of them in the long gallery.

Miss Tollworthy, once she relaxed a little, proved to be a charming child. With the emphasis on the word child. On their walk, he coaxed her into half an hour of earnest discussion. Once they had exhausted the topic of whether kittens or puppies were more delightful, they moved on to how pretty the village looked and how sad it was that the planned visit to the drapers had been postponed because of the rain. Apparently, Miss Tollworthy needed a particular shade of silk for her embroidery, and she was hopeful that the drapers would have a supply.

I am old enough to be the chit's father, Dell thought. He was, in fact, more than twice her age, but surely even when he had been eighteen, he had not been so narrow in his interests? He tried his best to find something to talk about that would be interesting to them both, and failed. Miss Tollworthy gaped at him when he introduced the topic of unrest in France, but spoke wistfully of the marriage of the French Dauphin to an Austrian princess. "Oh, I do wish I could have seen her gown."

Dell allowed her to twitter on about the cloth of silver, the diamonds that covered the skirt and bodice, the enormous paniers. He had found a topic that enthralled her and his brain was slowly disintegrating with boredom.

He tried again when he partnered her for dinner, asking her about what she had studied with her governess. The three Rs, apparently, plus deportment, music, and French. "But I am not very good at French," she confided.

As a last gasp attempt to find some depth to the girl, Dell asked, "What do you like to read, Miss Tollworthy?"

The question drew a frown from her. "Read, your grace? I don't have lessons now that I am am grown."

"For pleasure, I meant. Poetry, perhaps? The Castle of Ontranto?"

Miss Tollworthy was shocked. "Oh no, sir. Mama says books of fiction are unsuitable for a lady. Besides, I do not enjoy reading. I can never remember what has happened. I like short poems, your grace, if they are about flowers or dogs. Or cats, but I do not believe I have ever heard a poem about a cat. Have you, your grace?"

"Perhaps you should write one, Miss Tollworthy," Dell said.

The girl's peal of laughter was delightful. What a pity she was such a nodcock. "Oh, I never could, sir," she replied. *Undoubtedly true.* "I know a poem about a dog," she said.

"I am the prince's dog at Kew;

Pray tell me. Whose dog are you?" Her eyebrows drew together into a worried frown. "Something like that."

Dell knew the poem. He had even, as a young man, met Prince Frederick, the Prince of Wales, who owned the dog. And Alexander Pope, who had given the prince the dog, with the poem he had written engraved on its collar. Miss Tollworthy had got it almost right. "I am his Highness' dog at Kew; Pray tell me, sir, whose dog are you?"

"A clever epigram," he said.

"Oh." Miss Tollworthy looked even more worried. "I thought it was a poem."

Viviane would say that he was being picky. After all, one did not need to talk to one's wife. It gave Dell an unsettling insight into Viv's marriage. She had been eighteen when she married a man in his forties. The earl had clearly managed to bed his wife, for Viv had two sons, but Dell had never seen any sign that they shared any other part of their lives.

Was Dell a fool for wanting more from marriage than distant tolerance and the occasional bedding? Even those, he would struggle to achieve with Miss Tolworthy. No. She would not do as his wife.

Miss Thompson was also shy, but once he managed to soothe her nerves, he found her much easier to talk to than Miss Tollworthy, provided they were talking about gardening and fashion, her two passions. She would not admit to reading novels, but was very fond of poetry, though the poems she mentioned were all dripping with sentiment, and she proved as incapable as Miss Tolworthy of understanding irony.

Heartened by some evidence of intelligence when she talked about gardens, he toyed with the idea of choosing a wife he could educate. But would she want to be educated? He could detect no sign of it.

Indeed, when he introduced a couple of the important issues of the day—the restlessness of the American colonies and the possibility of another war with France, she told him that ladies were not expected to know about such things.

"Surely you would like to know?" Dell suggested.

"For what reason?" she asked. "Men understand such things far better than we ladies."

"Only because ladies have not been educated as men have."

Miss Thompson shook her head. "My brother-in-law would never allow me to learn something unbecoming for a lady."

"What if your husband wished you to understand the affairs of the day?" Dell insisted. "Ladies do, you know."

"Ugly spinsters who wear blue stockings and meet for salons." Miss Thomson grimaced, then remembered what was at stake. "I daresay the rules for duchesses are different, your grace. I would study whatever my husband told me, I suppose."

She sounded as enthusiastic as if he was proposing she prepare for her own execution.

Which left the Beckingham sisters. Miss Lucette proved to be the most confident, which was useful, for he didn't have to work to discover that she was ambitious, ruthless, and aggressively stupid.

Miss Tollworthy had either been too foolish to know she was being auditioned for a position as his wife, or smart enough not to hint at it. Miss Thompson had made the single reference. Miss Lucette, however, was not only aware that the three of them were in contention for his hand, but seemed to assume she was the inevitable winner of the contest. "If I were a duchess…" was a favorite phrase.

Apparently, in Lucette's mind, a duchess's world comprised what people were wearing, who took precedence over whom, and various pieces of gossip she'd heard about members of the house party.

Some of her stories were designed to show her rivals in a poor light, but they were not her only targets. She had mocking tales about most members of the house party, including her own sister. She also seemed to think he would be interested in who was supposed to be sleeping with whom, which was not what he expected of an innocent maiden. Miss Lucette had a coarse mind.

He was vaguely amused to find himself shocked at the tone of her conversation. In fairness, she did not say anything he had not heard when the men dallied over their port. He had always supposed that the married ladies shared the same gossip as the men. Not the unmarried ladies, however. At least the lady should have the discretion to keep such salacious stories to herself.

Dell was down to one candidate. Miss Beckingham was nothing like her sister. Nor was she as silly as the other two maidens. Indeed, Miss Beckingham continued to impress.

"It is refreshing to speak to a lady who knows what I am talking about," he told her, after a vigorous fifteen-minute discussion over dinner comparing favorite poets.

To which she replied with a quote. "'Tis hard we should be by the men despised,

Yet kept from knowing what would make us prized;
Debarred from knowledge, banished from the schools,
And with the utmost industry bred fools."

"Ouch," Dell responded. "That's very good, and a fair comment. Is it yours?"

She chuckled, a delightful gurgle that had him imagining other situations in which he might make her laugh. "Not I, your grace. Lady Chudleigh. It is but four brief lines from 'The Ladies' Defense'."

"I shall have to see if I can find it in the Castle's library," he told her. "I have heard of the lady, but am not familiar with her poetry."

The following day, he offered his arm for a walk in the garden during a brief break in the weather. "I found a volume of Lady Chudleigh's writings, including 'The Ladies' Defense'," he told her. "She makes some good points. What education have you had, Miss Beckingham, if I make so bold to ask?"

Miss Beckingham sighed. "The usual, I am afraid. The simple reading, writing, and arithmetic I need to run a household, plus music, needlework, and deportment. Anything else, I have had to learn for myself. Fortunately, my father has an extensive library, and our village rector is very kind about answering questions."

"Your father allows you free rein in his library?" Dell asked.

The remark bought him another chuckle. "Say, rather, that he has little interest in what any of us girls do, provided he is not bothered by it. And my stepmothers have not interfered provided my chores are finished before I read."

Dell had an urgent desire to carry her away from an uncaring family and give her the liberty of his library. He resisted the impulse. For the moment.

"Lady Chudleigh is rather hard on men, I thought," he said. "In her opinion, they are unworthy of their wives."

"Those who bully their wives while keeping company with other women," Miss Beckingham pointed out. "If they demand faithfulness and obedience from their wives, surely it is only fair for them to offer faithfulness and respect in return?"

Keeping company with. Her sister would have said, 'sleeping with'. Miss Lucette's mother might have been better born than Miss Beckingham's, but he had no doubt which of the daughters was a lady.

LUCETTE WAS CONVINCED that the purpose of the house party was for His Grace the Duke of Dellborough to get to know her and the other two eligible ladies, so he could decide which he would have as his duchess.

Maryanne seldom agreed with Lucette, but in this instance, she was certain her half-sister was correct. Even the choice of bachelor guests made it obvious that the goal was a wife for the duke. None of the single gentlemen could possibly compete with His Grace.

Whether His Grace had a true interest in any of the three debutantes was an open question. In Maryanne's opinion, he was disappointed in all of them. Lady Kirkland had placed him at dinner beside each one in turn, and had appointed him to partner each one in a game and escort each one on a walk.

Maryanne had been near enough to observe several of the interactions. If she was reading the conversation of the gentleman's eyebrows correctly, she quite agreed with his opinion. They were unutterably silly, and Lucette was the worst of the lot. If she had an idea in her head beyond clothing, rank, and gossip, Maryanne had yet to see evidence of it.

If the duke had been the supercilious fop she had accounted him on first appearance, Maryanne would think the pair deserved one another, but Lady Kirkland had, undoubtedly out of courtesy, included Maryanne in her rotation of unmarried ladies, and Maryanne had discovered that the duke, despite a highly fashionable appearance and a cool and sardonic exterior, was an intelligent and interesting person.

They had read many of the same books, liked some of the same poets, and enjoyed the same music. When Maryanne played the pianoforte in the evening so others could dance, the duke chose to come and turn pages for her. He also insisted that someone else take a turn at the instrument so Maryanne could dance with him. And on the fourth day of the party, the duke demanded Maryanne as his partner for chess, for he pointed out, quite rightly, that none of the others could match him. Maryanne won two out of three games, causing Lucette to berate her once they were in private.

"Maryanne, it is not done to win against a duke. Do you know nothing? Men do not want intelligent wives. They want wives who are obedient and know their place. I know you do not want a match yourself, but think of me. If he takes a miff at your unwomanly intelligence, he may reject me, too, and if that happens, I shall never forgive you."

To emphasize her point, she dabbed a dry eye with a fine lawn handkerchief. Lucette was convinced that she was the front runner of the three debutantes. In Lucette's mind, the wedding was all but certain, and all that remained was to decide what color to redecorate the duchess's boudoir. (Pale blue, like Lucette's eyes. Lucette's answer to any color question was always pale blue.)

Lucette was wrong. Wrong to be concerned that anything Maryanne—or for that matter Lucette—could say or do would deflect the duke from any course he decided. Wrong that the duke would marry Lucette under any circumstances. And wrong that Maryanne did not want a match.

She would love to be married and have children. Her own family. She did not yearn for it so much that she would marry someone she could not respect or who did not respect her. Sadly, the six men who had proposed failed that basic criterion, and so, at twenty-three years of age, Maryanne was still single.

And likely to remain so, even if she wished otherwise. For fool that she was, after five Seasons and six refused proposals, Maryanne was falling in love with a tall cool sardonic peer who had come here to look over her sister and other possible brides, like a customer at a horse fair, checking their paces and viewing their teeth.

With a beautiful man who made her long to know what it was like to be desired—for she was clever enough to know it was desire she felt when she admired his fine calves in their silk stockings, or stared at his mobile lips, or floated on the dance floor with him, feeling delicate and graceful.

And he was a duke, as far beyond her reach as a star.

CHAPTER THREE

"ARE all of your gowns the colour of mud?" Dell, fell into step beside Miss Beckingham and frowned at the offensive garment. It was a robe a l'anglaise, well made, well fitted, and not too distant from the current fashion. But it was all in shades of brown—although he supposed he had to conceded the cream of the underskirt and trim.

Dell would take it out and burn it if he could. If he had the dressing of her, he would pick jewel tones—a luminous setting for her porcelain skin and her dark curls.

"I thought you were playing bowls," Miss Beckingham said. Scolded, rather. Her tone was discouraging, but she had known where he was. That must be hopeful, must it not?

"Your grace! Yoo hoo, your grace!" Bother. It was the sister, arm in arm with one of the other debutantes, both hurrying to catch up with him and Miss Beckingham.

"Were you looking for me, your grace?" Miss Lucette cooed, her smug smile suggesting she was certain of his answer.

"I was not, Miss Lucette," he informed her, his irritation making his voice curt. "I was attempting to hold a private conversation with your sister, in fact."

The girl gaped at him and then laughed as if he had made a joke.

"Silly," she commented. "Never mind. Miss Tollworthy and I will amuse you."

Miss Beckingham took a step to the side to allow her sister to grasp his arm and Miss Tollworthy boxed him in on the other side. "I shall leave you, then," Miss Beckingham said, her face suitably grave but her eyes dancing as they met his.

"You shall not," Dell demanded. "Your sister requires your chaperonage."

"Not when I am with you," Miss Lucette cooed. "I am certain, your grace, that my Papa would have no objection to me strolling with you. And with Sarah, of course."

Sarah Tollworthy giggled, which was her usual response to everything. In London, he had taken it for a pleasant nature, had perhaps that was true. But he was depressingly certain that another week of her giggles would drive him to homicide.

"Miss Beckingham?" Dell said. "If you abandon me now, I shall be forced to ungentlemanly measures." He raised his eyebrows and gestured with his head in the direction of the lake. She fell into step beside her sister, and he gave an internal sigh of relief. He was not quite certain where he was with Miss Beckingham.

"I suppose you can come too, Maryanne," Miss Lucette said, unwillingly.

Maryanne, Miss Lucette called her. A pretty name, and it suited her. Miss Lucette prattled and Miss Tollworthy giggled. Dell paid only sufficient attention to keep from committing to something he did not want to do. No, he did not think Miss Beckingham should take Miss Tollworthy back to the house to fetch a better bonnet. There would be shade enough under the trees, or alternatively, they could all go back together.

Yes, Miss Lucette's gown was a pretty shade of blue, but no, he had not noticed that it matched her eyes.

No, he would not demand all of Miss Lucette's dances at this evening's New Year's Ball. He must leave some dances for the other gentlemen, and besides, Miss Lucette needed to make allowances for his extreme age.

Miss Lucette assured him that he was not to mind being old. She thought older gentlemen were more interesting, and besides he was very fit, even if he must be all of forty.

Miss Beckingham was struck by a fit of coughing and Dell stopped to wait for her to recover, but every time she caught his eye she collapsed again, stuffing both hands over her mouth and coughing until the tears rolled down her cheeks.

"Really, Maryanne," said Lucette. "I hope you are not unwell."

"I must have accidentally swallowed something," Miss Beckingham managed to say. "An elderly insect, perhaps."

Minx.

The walk was interminable, but he was oddly content to have Miss Beckingham in the party, and to be able to at least watch her. And Miss Lucette was far less cunning than she imagined—he had a parry for each of her suggestions. He managed to snatch one more private word with Miss Beckingham before they parted back at the house. "I trust," he said, "that your ball gown is not mud colored. Will you dance with me, Miss Beckingham?"

The color was something awful. He could tell from the way her eyes danced. "I should not wish my clothing to offend your eyes, your grace," she said.

Dell sighed. "I can see it will be a purgatory," he said. "But I am determined to dance with you, Miss Beckingham, so I shall just have to bear it."

"Maryanne," said Miss Lucette impatiently.

"Miss Beckingham?" Dell insisted.

Miss Lucette snarled. "Maryanne! I need you."

"Yes," Miss Beckingham murmured, and hurried to follow her sister up the stairs.

January 3rd, 1771

DELL HAD FALLEN into the habit of having a cup of hot chocolate with his sister in her private sitting room before braving the dangers of the house party. For the most part, Viviane was restful company. On this third day of the new year, she had clearly decided it was time for him to crown her house party with a successful betrothal.

"Well, Dellborough," she said, "you have spent time with all the girls and Miss Beckingham. Have you made your decision?"

"I am grateful to you, Viv," he replied. "What a dreadful mistake I would have been making had I married one of them without meeting them again in the more relaxed atmosphere of a house party."

Viv pouted. "I suppose that means you have decided against all three," she said.

"Miss Tollworthy would drive me to murder in a week," he said. "Miss Thompson is determined to be stupid, which is even worse than being born that way. Miss Lucette is stupid and vain, which is a toxic combination."

Viv shook her head, even as she laughed. "I take it I am not announcing your choice of bride, Dellborough. Never mind. We can try again this coming Season."

"You did not ask about Miss Beckingham," Dell pointed out.

His sister laughed again. "Nonsense, Dell. You have more sense than that. Even Miss Lucette would be a better choice than Miss Beckingham."

Dell disagreed that Lucette was more suitable than Maryanne. Lucette had the brains of a peahen, though her plumage and self-centered behavior was more suitable for the male of that same species. Maryanne could beat him at chess, hold her own in a discussion on politics, science, the classics, or any topic he introduced, and correctly interpret his jocular comments to treat them with the amusement he intended rather than the awed agreement he usually received.

Furthermore, her passion for music and literature always set him thinking of another passion he would like to explore with her. Would the glimpses of passion he had seen in her when they talked translate into passion for bed sports? He had seen evidence when they danced —showed her evidence, too, though she was too innocent to know it

—that the passion was there to be ignited. Her dowdy attire could not disguise how lovely she was. Not from him, in any case. He wanted Miss Beckingham with a fierce desire that surprised him. Delighted him, too. He had hoped to feel something for his future wife, but such an intense longing promised far more than tepid affection.

Of the four unmarried females his sister had gathered under her roof, only Maryanne had captured and held his interest. So much so, that he had ignored the subtle indications of attraction from some of the other ladies of the assembly, and had even refused a direct invitation to share the bed of a former lover, one of the widows.

His little grey dove did not dress to attract, did not flirt, did not lay down lures. But she had him caught, nonetheless.

He had made up his mind. Maryanne Beckingham would be the next Duchess of Dellborough. Viviane would be surprised, but not more surprised than Maryanne. Would she be glad? Dell, who was confident in everything he did, was unsure about this. Surely, any girl would want to be a duchess?

There was only one way to find out, and that was to ask her. But how to detach her from her charge? Maryanne was a faithful and devoted chaperone, and Dell was reluctant to take Viviane into his confidence to cut his quarry out of the flock.

Examining the reason, he was alarmed to discover that he truly feared the lady would reject him. If nobody knew he had asked, he would not have the embarrassment of a public failure. The situation required careful thought.

THE DUKE OF DELLBOROUGH had landed Maryanne in the basket.

He had rejected every available female at the house party, and—from what Maryanne could ascertain—several of those who should not be available. He had become colder and more remote than ever, no longer greeting girlish inanities with more than chilly civility.

Maryanne was present on several occasions when he went beyond civility to skirt the edges of outright insult. For example, at afternoon tea one day, Miss Thompson made an inane remark about the group known as The Bluestocking Society.

"As I explained to his grace, it may be all very well for women who are too old and ugly to attract a husband, but no proper lady talks about such matters."

"And is this the opinion of the other young ladies you know, Miss Thompson?" asked the duke.

Miss Thompson stuck her nose in the air and sucked an audible breath into her nose. "Of all proper young ladies," she declared. "Too much education rots the female brain and," she lowered her voice, "is dangerous for morals."

The duke sighed. "I fear for the intelligence of the next generation if this Season's debutantes are their mothers," he declared. "Personally, I would like the mother of my children to use the brains God has given her.

That evening, Lucette was the target of his acid tongue. She had noticed his rejection of her rivals with satisfaction. When she saw him waiting with Maryanne to go into dinner, she glided up to them and boldly said, "Here I am, your grace. Maryanne, you can go, now."

"On the contrary, Miss Lucette, Miss Beckingham must remain," the duke replied, resting his own hand on the hand Maryanne was about to withdraw from his sleeve. "I am escorting her in to dinner."

"But I am here," Lucette objected. "Would you not rather take me into dinner?"

Maryanne was well aware of how rude the duke would need to be to get through to her cousin, and concerned that he would not hesitate. "Lady Kirkland has assigned Lord Martin as your escort this evening, Lucette," she said.

Any hope that her gentle reminder might cause Lucette to follow the dictates of good manners was soon dashed. "But why should I go into dinner with a second son when I can go in with a duke?" Lucette asked her, gifting the duke in question with a brilliant smile.

"You cannot," he told her, bluntly. "I am escorting Miss Beckingham this evening."

Lucette stared at him, her pale blue eyes expressing her bewilderment.

Those around them had stopped to listen. *Go away, Lucette,* Maryanne thought, hoping that her sister would not further embarrass herself. No such luck.

"But your grace, everyone knows you are here to choose a bride because you need an heir or your cousin might inherit. Why would you want to spend time with my sister?"

"Miss Lucette," said the duke, the exasperation in his voice warning Maryanne that Lucette was about to be roasted. "I can assure you I would rather allow the estate go to my half-wit cousin than be married to a half-wit myself. At least I would be dead in the first instance. Go and find Lord Martin, Miss Lucette."

He prevented any further comment from Lucette by walking away from her and into the dining room, the doors of which the butler had just fortuitously opened.

Maryanne was also an unwilling witness to a masterly put down of one of the group of widows and merry wives who had been chasing him just as vigorously and with just as little success. She had been up to her bedchamber to fetch a shawl, and was returning to the alcove where he had promised to wait for her, but the most obvious of the predatory wives was before her.

She stopped, just out of sight, when she heard the woman purr, "None of those ninnies can possibly amuse you, Dellborough. Now that you have established that for yourself, why not console yourself with me? Here is the key to my bedchamber door."

His eyebrows were as hidden as the rest of him, but Maryanne could imagine them, signaling incredulity as his frosty voice replied, "I have not given up on finding a suitable bride, Lady Dench. I have concluded, furthermore, that the best way to ensure the faithfulness of my future wife is to practice that virtue myself. I shall be sure to recommend the practice to your husband."

Maryanne had nothing more than Lady Dench's huff of outrage to warn her to turn her back and pretend that she had not heard the exchange. She was certain Lady Dench did not believe the pretense.

The duke turned her pages while she played for the company, then challenged her to another game of chess, and she had almost forgotten the earlier conversations by the time she went up to bed. But Lucette was waiting for her in her bedchamber, incandescent with rage.

"You have spoiled my chances," she hissed, and nothing Maryanne said made any difference.

Lucette, who had not spoken to Maryanne since she had thought about the half-wit remark and realized that the duke had rejected her on the grounds she was stupid. It was, Lucette decided, because Maryanne had embarrassed Lucette by winning against the duke at chess. "Just wait until Papa hears that you ruined my chance to be a duchess!" she threatened. "Of course, he doesn't want to align himself to a family with such an unnatural woman in it. I shall never forgive you."

She flew at Maryanne ready to slap. Maryanne had never before been the target of one of Lucette's tantrums, but she knew what to expect, having dragged Lucette off an unfortunate maid more than a few times. She grabbed the girl's wrists and told her to pull herself together. "I am not going to let you hit or kick me, and you will only make yourself look foolish if you try."

In the end, Lucette went to Lady Kirkland and begged to be moved into another room. "She has asked me to chaperone her in your place, Miss Beckingham," Lady Kirkland explained. "I thought it best to agree—she is very overwrought. And besides, why should you not have time to enjoy yourself without being bothered with the silly girl."

Lady Kirkland really was very kind. Most of the other guests were not. Especially those to whom the duke had addressed one of his barbs. Lady Dench spoke for many of them when she told Maryanne that she was not welcome in the morning room where the ladies were taking tea.

"You may think you are very smart to have attracted Dellborough's attention, girl, but mark my words, he is only pretending to court you to make fools of the rest of us. It suits his grace's wit to show us how little he thinks of us by pretending to address his suit to the ugliest, least fashionable, most graceless of us all. As if Dellborough could be serious about you! He'll bed you, girl. But he'll never marry you."

Maryanne was too shocked by the attack to argue. Afterward, sitting alone in the library, she thought of all the things she could have said. "Of course, he is not courting me. The idea is ridiculous. But he is not attempting to seduce me, either. He enjoys the company of someone who is not always trying to flatter him or impress him. He is bored with the likes of you and my sister, and he does not find me boring."

As for Dellborough trying to seduce her, that was as ridiculous as all the rest. He didn't flatter her. He didn't try to get her alone. When they were alone, he made no attempt to kiss her. He was a gentleman toward her in every way.

It shamed her to admit that she rather regretted the fact.

CHAPTER FOUR

Twelfth Night Eve, January 5th, 1771

THE LIBRARY WAS peaceful and empty. Since the confrontations with Lucette and then Lady Dench, Maryanne had found it a refuge from the chilly hauteur that settled on any company she attempted to join. The book collection was not vast, but this afternoon, Maryanne had found a copy of *Le Morte D'Arthur* and settled down on a couch near the fire to lose herself in the stories of the age of chivalry, somewhat hindered by occasional pauses to work out the meaning of the archaic English.

She was deeply immersed when she became aware that someone had seated himself in the chair opposite her. Even before she looked up, she knew who it was. Only the Duke of Dellborough made her heart beat faster just by walking into the room.

"Your grace," she said.

"Dell," he replied, sitting uninvited next to her. "Call me Dell, and I shall call you Maryanne."

Dear heavens. Could the gossip really be true? Was he courting her? Or attempting to get her into his bed?

"Why?" she asked, bluntly. "Are you trying to seduce me, your grace?" The naughtiest part of her was leaping up and down, shouting *Yes! Pick Me!* She ignored it as best she could, schooling her face to show nothing but polite interest.

The duke's expressive eyebrows shot up? "Could I?" he wondered.

Probably. Almost certainly. Maryanne didn't dare reply for fear of what she might say.

DELL HAD HIS ANSWER. For a man of his experience, Maryanne's arousal was obvious. He clamped an iron control over his base urges. His aim was not seduction—or not today, he assured that baser self. His aim was to convince the lady to be his duchess. Once she was his wife, he would seduce her as often as possible.

His mouth was suddenly dry. He had not been this nervous since he was a boy at school, trying to convince the dean he had not climbed the flagpole on the main tower to nail the dean's wig to the top. He was as uncertain of the outcome today as he had been then.

He took a deep breath. There was nothing for it but to ask the question.

"Miss Beckingham. Maryanne. I have come to esteem you greatly. I admire your wit, your grace, and your kindness to others. It would please me beyond all things if you would consent to be my duchess."

The lady looked startled and then—*Dammit*—unhappy. "You honor me, Your Grace. Do you think I would be good at it? At being a duchess, I mean."

She hadn't said no! That was a start. "You will be superb," he said.

"What makes you think so?" Maryanne asked.

Dell was stuck for words for a moment. When he had rehearsed this scene in his mind, she had rejected him or accepted him—he had imagined everything from enthusiasm to shy agreement to polite disdain. It had never occurred to him that she might doubt her qualifications to be his bride.

"I am sure of it," he said. "You are already a lady, and you have told me you know how to run a household. I have several, but I also have excellent housekeepers."

"And that is enough to be a duchess?" Her tone expressed considerable doubt, and she held herself so rigid he thought she might break if he touched her.

"Being wed to a duke is enough to be a duchess," he told her. "Maryanne, I do not know how to answer you. Except to say that all the duchesses I know are very different people. Also, if it helps, as my duchess, you would be the social superior of all but a handful of people in these realms. Whatever a duke chooses to do is the right thing. I imagine the same applies to a duchess."

"You imagine," she repeated.

"What can I say or offer that would convince you to agree to be my wife?"

Her eyes lit up and she began to smile. "Wife? If that position is on offer, Your Grace, I might be interested. Why do you want me to be your wife?"

"The position is the same one," he pointed out. "My duchess will be my wife."

The look she gave him said, as clearly as words, that he was evading the question. Which he was. His heart pounding, he told her the truth. "I want you for my wife, my dove, because I have become convinced that I cannot live without you." He could barely bring himself to look at her. He had known she had the power to destroy him, and now she knew it too.

But she was gazing back at him with soft melting eyes, all the rigidity gone from her body. "Your grace," she said, on a sigh.

"Call me Dell," he instructed.

"There he goes again," Maryanne observed, her eyes dancing. "The arrogant duke. The thing is, I don't want to marry Dellborough, or Dell for that matter. I would very much like to marry the man who happens to be the duke, but I don't have a name for him. What name were you given at your baptism?"

His heart was singing. How peculiar. Dell had been convinced that was just poetic nonsense. "You will marry me?"

"You will tell me your name?"

If that was her condition, he would meet it gladly. "Bedivere. But I was the Marquess of Thornstead from my cradle, and always called Thorn until I became duke when I was eighteen."

"No wonder you are rude and arrogant," she observed. "But I suppose I must marry you, nonetheless. For I love you, Bedivere."

Love! That was unexpected, yet he could feel it growing inside him, warming him as he had not been warm for a long time. He took her hands and was about to lean in for a kiss, when she added, "That is, if you truly want me."

"Oh, I want you," he told her. Then, after a kiss that threatened to become much more than he thought appropriate for the maiden who would be his bride, particularly since he had not had the foresight to lock the door, he distracted himself by picking the discarded book from her lap.

"Tales of knights and maidens?" he asked. "I enjoyed those when I was a boy." He settled at her feet, resting one shoulder against the front of her chair arm. "I cannot stop being a duke, my dove, even for love of you, and that, I fear, means you must be a duchess. Yet when we are private together, consider me your knight, and you shall be my lady."

Dell thought it a fine and romantic notion, and was disconcerted when the lady giggled. "The twelfth night," he thought she said.

"Yes," he agreed. "It is Twelfth Night eve today and Twelfth Night tomorrow, the last of the twelve days of Christmastide."

She shook her head, and put a finger on the crease between his brows as if to smooth it out. "Not the day, my love. It was a silly joke I amused myself with when I first sat at your sister's round table. Eleven gentlemen at the round table, and I thought, eleven knights, and where is the twelfth? Then in you came, as if you were the answer to my question."

He chuckled. "I shall, from now on, and officially as soon as I can get the consent of your father and a special license from London, be the answer to all of your questions, and your twelfth knight."

She leaned closer to kiss him again. "No, Bedivere. You shall always and forever be my First Knight."

DELL AND MARYANNE had four sons and four daughters, all of whom appear or are mentioned in one or more of Jude's Regency novels. Dell himself appears in "The Sincerest Flattery", the story of Percy, their eldest son. The other three sons all have their own stories, Lance in "The Talons of a Lyon", Artie as secondary lead in "One Perfect Dance", and Tris in "The Kindest Gentleman", a short story in "Chasing the Tale Volume 2". The four sisters also appear in these stories, and may one day have stories of their own.

ABOUT JUDE KNIGHT

Jude always wanted to be a novelist. She started in her teens, but life kept getting in the way. Years passed, and with them dozens of unfinished manuscripts. The fear grew. What if she tried, failed, and lost the dream forever? The years since 2014 have brought more than 20 novels, 20 novellas, 6 volumes of short stories, several awards, and hundreds of positive reviews. The dream is alive.

 X

JUDE'S SOCIAL MEDIA

Website and blog: http://judeknightauthor.com/
Subscribe to newsletter: http://judeknightauthor.com/newsletter/
Bookshop: https://judeknight.selz.com/
Facebook: https://www.facebook.com/JudeKnightAuthor/
Twitter: https://twitter.com/JudeKnightBooks
Pinterest: https://nz.pinterest.com/jknight1033/
Bookbub: https://www.bookbub.com/profile/jude-knight
Books + Main Bites: https://bookandmainbites.com/JudeKnight Author
Goodreads: https://www.goodreads.com/author/show/8603586. Jude_Knight
LinkedIn: https://linkedin.com/in/jude-knight-465557166/

HER HOGMANAY SPY

RUE ALLYN

A Du Grace Family Tale

Two Spies, One Secret—In the winter of 1296, can a Scottish Lady and an English knight survive shipwreck, winter in the wilderness, and a betrayal that could break hearts to bring in the new year with a love for all time?

CHAPTER ONE

A tavern in a village outside of Rotterdam, the Netherlands
December 28, 1296

AT A ROUGH-HEWN TABLE near the hearth, in the farthest corner of the tavern, Sir Amis Du Grace nursed his ale as late afternoon darkened to dusk. He stared out the mullioned window at the intermittent rain obscuring the sea beyond. Even had the weather permitted, he could not have left. He was here under orders to receive a packet, which he would then take to Edward of England's spy master, currently in York. Delivering the packet was the latest in a chain of actions on his part designed to discover who in the French court was sending false information to England about France's plans and its alliance with Scotland.

The tavern door opened letting in wind, rain, cold, and a woman. She surveyed the public room, shook water from her sodden skirts then put back the hood of her cloak and headed for the opposite side of the hearth to warm and dry herself.

He only caught a glimpse of night dark hair and chill-reddened cheeks in a perfectly oval face. He did not need to see more to know what she looked like. He was familiar with her very expressive face, every curve of her body, all the textures of her skin, the siren song of her voice, and especially the purr of sound that announced she would soon scream out her pleasure.

Raven black hair. Bright blue eyes that sparkled as if she knew some secret joke. Alabaster skin. High cheekbones. Lips of lust inspiring red. A delicate frame of perfect proportions for making love. The talk of the French court had been whether the widowed Lady Caitrin Drew-De Garrone's intelligence exceeded the lady's beauty or her skills in bed.

Amis knew the answer, but he planned to keep that information to himself. Let the world wonder how skilled a lover was Lady Caitrin.

He also knew she was a spy—for Scotland, despite her French marriage.

Would she recognize him?

Of course, she would.

One did not forget the kind of intense affair they had shared. He had known even as he said his farewells, that she would remain in his memory for his entire life.

He watched Caitrin remove her cloak and gloves. She made a slow, complete turn, taking in every detail before she faced his table. Her expression grew from a cat like smile to a small O of surprise. At least that is what he believed she wanted him to think.

"Sir, Amis Du Grace," she said as she approached.

Every graceful step called to mind the night they had first yielded to desire, and all the subsequent nights, afternoons, and early morning rendezvous.

"How lovely to encounter a friend in such a backward place. May I join you?" Siren-like, her voice could lure a thousand men to their deaths. She placed a hand on the chair opposite his.

He stood quickly and moved the chair for her to sit.

"Please. I have missed you. Though, in all honesty I did not expect to see you again." It was perhaps one of the few honest things he had told her.

She settled herself comfortable, and he returned to his seat.

"Nor I you." Her blue eyes, captured him now, as they had the first time they met.

"When we parted, you said you had been called home to Scotland to tend to your mother who was ill," he said, relaxing against the wooden back of his chair.

The corners of Caitrin's lovely mouth lifted. "I did say that, and I will be sailing west from here." She did not, however, confirm or deny her destination.

You travel to Scotland, but not to your family home in the lowlands.

"Have you had word? Is your mother recovered, I pray?" Amis asked.

He maintained the back and forth of light conversation, but could not empty from his mind all he knew *of La Belle Dame, le Cygne Ecossai, the Swan of Scotland*, or the memories of their first night together.

Le Bel Philip had given a midsummer masquerade. Both Amis and Caitrin attended. For the same reasons, he suspected. To gather what information they could from lips loosened by being masked and by too much drink. They had both worn masks, of course, but once seen, no one could believe those depthless blue eyes belonged to anyone else. Dressed as a Roman empress, her costume had been both daring and natural.

Months earlier, when he first arrived in Paris, he had asked who the current favorite was. His contact at the court had pointed her out and warned Amis of her loyalty to Scotland.

Amis had waited weeks to gain control of his deep physical attraction before approaching the damsel to request a dance that midsummer night. He could not allow her to know he was smitten. She could use that to very destructive advantage. Thus, he guarded his heart as carefully as his true allegiance.

They had flirted before and during that dance. She demonstrated a surprisingly sharp wit when he commented on some of the events occurring since his arrival in France.

"Lady Isabel du Crecy appears to be a favorite of King Philip." He had said, wanting to gauge how perceptive she was of the currents underlying the surface actions of the court.

Lady Drew-De Garrone had laughed as the steps of the Farandole slowed. "Madame du Crecy knows better than to attempt to steal Le Bel Roi's affections. He is devoted to his wife. The du Crecy simply wishes to inspire some jealousy in her lump of a spouse, Comte Alaine du Crecy."

Again, the pace of the chain of dancers picked up. Amis waited until the steps slowed once more and he regained his breath. "I remember jousting with the man. He's rather large, in a Norman warrior sort of way and, if I recall correctly, defeated most who challenged him."

"Indeed." Keeping her arms linked with his and the fellow on her other side, Lady Drew-De Garrone twisted and turned with the music. When a brief pause allowed, she eye his garments. "All challengers save you, Seigneur Du Grace. I was there the day you won the king's prize. I could tell then you had little need of that purse of French Silver Marks."

She could not have been so naïve as to believe him rich, although letting him think she did made sense. He surmised the comment had been intended as a probe. Whether to further her interest in achieving another wealthy marriage or simply to gain information about a new man in the court, he could not be certain. But the probe itself had reinforced his knowledge that there was more to Lady Drew-De Garrone than appeared on her bon vivant surface.

"You are quite perceptive," he had said allowing her to think he had been fooled. "I was fortunate to find a very expert *tailour* whose wife is even more expert with *embrouden*." It was a lie, of course, he'd gone deeply into debt in order to present the appearance of a wealthy visitor to the French court. His prize money had paid most of his debts. He did not plan to be in France long enough to pay the rest, though once he received his reward for services to England, he would send payment back to those few merchants.

She'd spent the next several steps examining his rich carmine-dyed velvet cotehardie embroidered with gold thread and tiny pearls at the sleeves and cuffs. Then her gaze moved lower, and her smile broadened. Evidently, she, like many women of the French court, appreciated a well-turned male calf and thigh.

His were adorned in fine hose decorated with thin stripes of gold thread. On his feet were dancing slippers of gold embroidered carmine leather. The shorter style cotehardie allowed him to draw the attention of most of the ladies. While discreetly admiring his form, he often had opportunity to ask questions which a preoccupied woman would answer less discreetly.

"Quite impressive," she cooed. "You must give me the cutter's name and location so I may order a few of my plainer items to be embroidered."

"Certainly," he lied again. The tailour's wife had been quite talkative. Whether she'd discerned the English origins of his traveling clothes or not, he refused to risk any possible exposure of his true purpose in France. No, Lady Drew-De Garrone's plainer items would remain the victims of Seigneur du Grace's deplorable forgetfulness. A trait he cultivated amongst the denizens of the court to defray suspicion that he might remember any political details let slip in his hearing. His entire purpose for being in France had him alert for mention of misinformation received by England's spy-master.

CAITRIN BABBLED SOCIAL NOTHINGS, as she considered the man seated across the table. She should not have been surprised to see her erstwhile lover. This tavern was located in an obscure little Dutch port where one might hire the fastest ships to make the crossing to Berwick on Tweed. She'd known before their first dance together that Du Grace was Le Bel Philip's agent. Her contact at the French Court, that king's own spy master, Seigneur Aboyeur, had told her of Du Grace's loyalties. However, Aboyeur had acknowledged doubts about the depth of an Englishman's dedication to France and warned her to take care in her seduction of the man. Aboyeur wished her to discover if Du Grace were the person delivering false information about England to France.

During the months of their affair, she'd learned nothing to discredit Du Grace's allegiance to Philip. She had reported the same to Aboyeur. It was her own secret, which delighted her no end. She had deceived Aboyeur into believing she spied for Scotland, when in reality she would do all she could to destroy those nobles who had made a misery of her life. Once satisfied with her revenge, she planned to hand them over to Edward of England.

"Enough about me and my family," she brought the conversation around to a topic of interest to her.

What is Du Grace doing here?

"When we parted," she continued. "I was told that you had been recalled to Bourgogne by your father. I was certain you were a scion of the French Comte Du Grace. However, your presence here, suggests that I misunderstood." She had never believed that nonsense but had behaved as if she did.

In her guise as a loyal Scot, she had asked about it. Aboyeur had revealed to her that Sir Amis's family once enjoyed the favor of England's king. However, that favor and their position in the English court was in jeopardy due to the recent marriage of Lady Jessamyn Du Grace to a highlander. The marriage had been intended to smooth the way for the troops Edward sent to invade Scotland through the highlander's lands. The English army had met with betrayal and suffered ignominious defeat at the hands of the highlander's family. Hence, Sir Amis had come to France and offered his services against Edward who now regarded the Du Grace family with suspicion and disdain.

"I cannot imagine how you could think I was French, or who might try to suggest I belonged to the French Du Grace branch of the family," Amis said. "I've certainly never made any secret of my origins."

You never bother to explain them either. Instead, you let others assume, often incorrectly. 'Tis just what I would do were I a spy for England. In fact, I have done the same by allowing all to believe I am loyal to Scotland.

But Aboyeur had been firm that, while he had some small doubt, Du Grace's loyalty lay with France.

Could he be wrong? And if so, is he misled or attempting to mislead?

Regardless, Caitrin understood the warnings implicit in Aboyeur's information no matter how flawed.

Still, she had thrilled at the challenge of seducing Du Grace. She'd won his attentions despite the many French ladies pursuing him. Because she'd been told Du Grace spied for France, she could not afford the luxury of trusting him with the knowledge of her true loyalties. Best for him to think she spied for France's ally, Scotland. Thus, she safeguarded her work and her heart from potential betrayal.

"So, your family is from Lancaster, and your father is a good friend of Edward of England?" Caitrin asked.

She acted as if she needed confirmation when what she really did was buy time to find out his true purpose for being in the Netherlands. If he thought her a bit slow to understand, all to the good. She was at her best when her opponent underestimated her.

As they continued talk of nothing particularly important, she cast her mind back over the months since she first met Sir Amis Du Grace. Knowing he spied for France, she'd been at pains to cause him to underestimate her. The task had been difficult, since she quickly learned he was attracted to intelligence as much a beauty. She did not admire stupidity, but it made an excellent disguise.

Weeks before he asked her to dance at the midsummer masquerade, she gained his interest. They had played a flirtatious sort of cat and mouse game up until the moment she decided to start an affair with him. What better way to learn a man's secrets than in bed?

Sir Amis had proved quite adept at blending into the social strata of the French court. He'd won a number of jousts, paid appropriate addresses to Philip, dressed like a peacock, and often sang to the queen's ladies while playing the lute.

When they'd become lovers, Caitrin discovered he actually enjoyed the lute. Their affair had been quite the coup for him. As the queen's current favorite, Caitrin had found herself courted by dozens of men. The attention suited her purposes. When she finally made her report in London, she'd be able to reveal a wide variety of secrets that her English masters could use to great advantage over their enemies.

Ending her affair with Du Grace had saddened her in a small way, even though she was safer without him. Du Grace was more dangerous, and thus a greater challenge, than any of her other suitors. Besides, she genuinely liked the man—a serious complication that she recognized. She could not pinpoint what it was about him that drew her. That is other than his speaking green eyes, the dark blond curls dusting the top edge of his tunic, the fine way his shoulders filled out that tunic, and the muscular legs she had noted when watching him dance or compete in the joust. Of course, she now knew just how muscular those legs were, and precisely how talented a lover was Amis Du Grace.

"Lady Caitrin?"

She straightened. She'd let her mind wander, never a smart thing to do when dealing with a man like Du Grace.

"I beg your pardon. I was recalling our very enjoyable liaison. Please forgive me." It never hurt to remind a man he was attractive or that they had been lovers. As if absent-minded, she placed her hand atop the table.

"'Tis naught to forgive." He took her hand, lifting it to his lips.

Just as she had hoped. Reminding him of other touches could prove useful. She would force him to recall the evening their affair had begun in earnest. The combination of excellent French wine, the soft warm breeze, and a flower-scented night had lured them into the gardens where they found a dark corner and embarked on some deliciously wicked behavior. Fortunately, or not, the interruption of the Queen and her ladies calling for Caitrin occurred after a serious, if most pleasurable, indiscretion. A fully intentional indiscretion on her part.

Now, his gaze locked with hers, he blew a gentle stream of breath across her knuckles.

She wished she had her cloak about her to disguise the shiver his gesture sent racing up her arm and through her entire body. The light was poor, so all she could do was hope he did not notice.

"Are you cold, Lady Caitrin?" He sat up abruptly and signaled to a serving wench.

The wench came at a run. "Yes, your lordship, how may I be of help."

"Bring hot cider and stew for the lady and myself," he ordered.

The wench hurried off.

"Are you always so autocratic?" asked Caitrin.

She knew he could be autocratic, when it came to pleasuring a woman, but he rarely gave orders to lovers outside of the bedchamber. Once he'd told her he always made certain the woman understood his expectations and could decline his attentions if she wished. But at present they sat at a public table pretending to be casual acquaintances. Her question was not unreasonable.

A dark blonde brow queried. "Autocratic?"

"An autocrat is a person who gives orders and makes decisions without consulting anyone as to their needs and desires."

The brow lowered. "Hmmm. I do tend to take charge when I see something that must be addressed. However, that is simple forethought in action."

"Call it what you will, you could have asked if I wished for cider or stew?"

"Do you dislike cider or stew?"

"On the contrary, I enjoy them very much."

He lay his forearms on the table, placing his palms together as if he were praying. "Then I do not see the problem."

"Of course not." Caitrin grinned. Very few men of her acquaintance would perceive any problem with ordering others to do their bidding. "What brings you to this benighted spot in such weather?" She gestured to the window.

He followed her movements, staring out at the rain pelting the ground.

He's deciding what lie to concoct to allay any suspicions I might have.

He returned his gaze to her face. "I am on my way to visit my sister in Scotland. She wed a highland laird this past June, and I was unable to attend. However, I must make a brief stop in Yorkshire before going on to Scotland."

Being a Scot by birth if not inclination, Caitrin smiled. "I know all of that."

"Really?"

"It cannot have escaped you that I am a Scot. Every Scot knows of the marriage between Lady Jessamyn du Grace and Baron Raeb MacKai and how the baron's family humiliated Edward of England by defeating his army without raising a single sword. However, I did not know that you were related to Lady Jessamyn."

"I am her brother, one of two." His smile broadened and laughter sparkled in his spring green eyes.

The wench returned with their meal.

"Will you be visiting your sister for a long while?"

"I hope to be able to stay for some time. However, kings like Le Bel Philip and Longshanks can be demanding, and my commitment to my king must take precedence over my own preferences."

"That's very loyal of you," she murmured and made note of the equivocation he'd used. He'd not named the king to whom he was committed.

"And you? Why depart from the Dutch coast? Would you not get to Scotland faster by taking ship from the north of France?"

"Perhaps, but the voyage from here to Berwick takes less time than leaving from France. Then the ride from Berwick to my family home is also shorter. The sea can be especially risky in winter, so the less time spent on ship the better."

"Why did I not know you rode?"

She shrugged. "Our acquaintance began less than a year ago. A few months is hardly sufficient time to learn every detail about a person."

"I would like to learn more about you Lady Caitrin." He leaned across the table when he whispered her name.

I'll just bet you want to know everything about me. But that is not going to happen.

"Please Seigneur," she chastised. "Remember we are not private."

"Ah yes, I forgot. Your beauty and grace do that to me. Did you know? I can scarce form a single sentence when you are near."

"What nonsense. You are well aware that I know better, and I don't respond favorably to flattery, sir."

"You respond very well to kisses, as I recall."

His kisses certainly. She had no need to manufacture her response when he kissed her on a bench in Le Bel Philip's Garden. The warm, feather light touch of his lips to hers had sizzled outward to her entire body. He followed that with a lick of his tongue. Intrigued by his taste, his cinnamon and oranges scent, his skill, she'd opened, and they'd engaged in a delightful duel that ended with them reclining on the bench. More kisses accompanied the play of his talented fingers with her decolletage and then her skirts. They had pleasured each other and come to an understanding that they would continue to please each other whenever time and circumstance would permit. She inhaled deeply, her body preparing itself for his attention. She could permit that tonight, given a modicum of circumspection.

The opening of the tavern's outer door, let in a man along with a copious amount of rain and disturbed her reverie. Across the table, Du Grace, who had released her hand, sipped his ale and seemed content to watch her as she remembered his touch, his scent, his taste.

She lifted her gaze to study the newcomer and failed to restrain a gasp.

"What is it?" Du Grace put his tankard down and turned to look. "I do believe it is our mutual friend Aboyeur."

He raised a hand and signaled to the Frenchman. *"Bonjour, mon ami. Par ici. Rejoignez-nous."*

"Why did you ask him to join us?" Caitrin hissed. The last thing she needed right now was another inquisitive male, and Aboyeur was more inquisitive than most.

Du Grace shot a quick glance at her. "It would be rude not to do so."

He was right. She should have thought of that herself. Speaking with Aboyeur guided her as she gained much of the information she sent to England. It would be wise to know what he was doing here now and where he was bound afterward. Perhaps he had some last-minute details to share with her.

Aboyeur returned the greeting, and after shucking his cloak and putting it along with his cap and gloves on a hook to dry he ambled in their direction. On his way, he stopped a serving wench.

"Well met, Lady Drew-de Garonne. Sir Du Grace. Are you waiting out the storm here before taking ship?"

Caitrin gave an elegant shrug and sipped at her cider.

"I am bound for York and eventually Dungarob in the highlands." Du Grace confirmed. "Lady Drew-de Garonne confided that she awaits transport to Berwick on Tweed where she will take horse to Scotland."

Caitrin restrained a glare. She'd not asked Du Grace to keep confident anything she'd told him. Still, she'd expected him to be more discreet.

"Ah yes," the Frenchman said. "I seem to recall that your mother is ill."

Caitrin nodded then drank and set her tankard down. Had she heard a very slight accent in his French? Something she thought she'd heard before. A slight shift of vowels that made her wonder if he was truly French or from some other country. She could not identify the country, however.

He gazed at her expectantly.

I'd best answer his question.

"According to the letter I received, the doctors do not know what ails her. I have some small skill with herbs and healing, but I would not wish to decide on a treatment for her without seeing her."

"Quite wise," Du Grace allowed. He dug into his stew.

"You must be quite concerned about her to be willing to go to Scotland," Aboyeur prompted.

"Think you, I care not about my family? They reside in Scotland, and thus, to Scotland I must go."

"Ah," replied Aboyeur, "I must have mistaken your preference for France as a dislike of Scotland."

It was an illusion she had fostered to disguise her true motives.

Verily, she had little difficulty with Scotland as a place. Most of her problem stemmed from the French marriage she'd been forced into because her father refused to oppose the desires of the Scottish crown. Once her decrepit husband died, she'd sworn to do all she could to bring down the governments of both Scotland and France.

Amis rested his spoon and lifted an eyebrow at her as he smiled and raised his tankard.

"I do not dislike my homeland, Seigneur Aboyeur," she said.

"In truth? I'd heard otherwise."

"Whoever would say such a thing is a liar."

"Ah, so you would challenge Madame du Crecy?"

"Pah!" Caitrin waved a dismissive hand. "I would not waste my time on such a one."

"But she, like you, is a lady of the Queen's court?"

"Queen Joan has many reasons for choosing the ladies who attend her. The Comtesse du Crecy is very much in love with her husband. The Queen in her wisdom hoped that some distance between husband and wife, might encourage the Comte to a greater appreciation of his wife's devotion."

Aboyeur laughed. "Oh, that is too funny."

"Why would you say that?" Du Grace asked.

So, Du Grace has finally decided to join the conversation.

Caitrin had almost thought Du Grace's silence too obvious a sign that he was listening for information.

Perhaps he sees Aboyeur more like a source of information than an ally, as I have, though I'm beginning to have doubts.

Aboyeur glanced at Amis then returned his attention to Caitrin.

"The queen's actions are amusing because, at the time she nominated Comtesse du Crecy to her ladies in waiting, she most likely did not know that the king expected to send Comte du Crecy to Gascony with new plans of attack for the fight with the English."

"*C'est dommage,*" Amis stated.

"It is indeed too bad," Caitrin echoed. "Do you know when the Comte departs? Perhaps there is still time for the queen's plan to work."

Looking very sober, Aboyeur leaned forward conspiratorially, patting a thick, wide wallet that hung from his shoulder. "I doubt there will be time. I have come from a recent visit to the Dutch court and am now tasked with delivering the King's orders directly to Du Crecy's hands before I return to Paris. I tell you this because I know you both to be Le Bel Philip's trusted agents."

Of course, Aboyeur would say that. Nonetheless, she'd begun to suspect that he spied in the service of Le Bon Philip, and made use of his connection with Du Grace, an Englishman despite his avowed loyalty to France, to dispense false information to Longshanks and his military leaders. She had no proof, but perhaps it was in the documents Aboyeur carried.

What a sweet achievement that would be, if I could with certainty identify the source of all the erroneous information coming to England about France's intentions.

The wench arrived with Aboyeur's order, and he sat back.

Amis glanced at Caitrin, tilting his head in the direction of the *serveuse*.

"*S'il vous plaît*," Caitrin nodded.

"Two more tankards of cider, please, mademoiselle."

"Is the food as good as it smells?" the Frenchman asked as he picked up his spoon to dip into his pottage.

"Most definitely, though not, of course, up to the standards at Le Bel Philip's court," Amis contributed.

"Nonetheless, I found it most filling," Caitrin said.

The cider arrived, and the three conversed casually for a while.

Amis set his tankard down with a thump and stood. "If you will excuse me, I must make arrangements for lodging with the keeper of this place. I asked when I arrived if beds were available, and the man allowed as how he had a few. Most in a shared space but one or two in rooms with doors that lock from the inside."

He bowed to Lady Caitrin.

"Did you also enquire about passage on a vessel going to Berwick?" She asked.

"I did that at the docks before seeking shelter at this tavern. I chose this place because the captain I contracted with will send someone here to rouse me. That way, when he is ready to set sail, I too will be ready."

"That was quite clever of you, Siegneur Du Grace. Do you think your captain would have room for one more passenger?" Caitrin asked.

"I believe so. However, to be certain, I will send a boy from here to the captain and secure passage for you."

She lowered her lashes and pale pink rose to her cheeks. "Please tell me in the morning, what I owe you."

"As you wish Madame." He inclined his head then turned to Aboyeur. "You are fortunate sir, that you need not take ship to Comte du Crecy's home."

"Fortunate indeed, especially if this rain ceases by tomorrow morning. I should be back in Paris within two weeks."

"Lucky you," Amis murmured. "I bid you both goodnight."

"*Bon soir*, Seigneur Du Grace." Caitrin and Aboyeur chorused.

She watched him move away to where the tavern keeper stood at the bar. The negotiations were very quiet, and quickly a few coins changed hands. Du Grace, she suspected from the number of coins exchanged, would be sleeping in the shared space. She herself would take one of the private rooms, if any were still available. Then she would spend her evening watching carefully to see where Aboyeur elected to sleep. That wallet of his contained papers of great interest to Edward of England and his spy master. She was determined to steal those papers from the Seigneur.

CHAPTER TWO

A tavern in a village near Rotterdam the Netherlands
Late evening, December 28, 1296

CAITRIN WAITED through another tankard of cider and idle conversation with Aboyeur before retiring to the last available private room. The tweeny who helped move her one traveling bag to the room was paid a silver mark with promise of another if she came to tell Caitrin when the French Seigneur retired to the shared space and all were asleep.

The time until the tweeny arrived proved useful. Caitrin occupied herself, preparing a sheaf of false documents to substitute for the papers she planned to steal. She also made an oiled leather pouch in which to place the originals once she had them. The writing on the false papers was all nonsense and would fool no one who actually read the documents. However, she trusted that Aboyeur, if he was the loyal Frenchman she believed him to be, would never actually read the items he carried. He would simply check to be certain they were secure then be on his way to Comte du Crecy.

Next, she changed into the dark clothing and soft slippers most useful for moving about undetected then settled to wait. With a braiser warming her feet, she sat near the room's small window and watched the rain slacken.

The girl's knock came just as Caitrin was nodding off. She'd begun to lose hope that she would be able to relieve Aboyeur of the papers he carried.

"Le Seigneur, he is asleep in the public room. He said he did not want to pay for lodging with so few hours left before he departed in the morning. He gave orders to be awakened at the hour of Prime with breakfast to follow as soon as possible."

False papers in hand, Caitrin gave the promised coin and followed the young girl down the stairs.

"Sit in that chair near the public room doors and pretend to be asleep," Caitrin directed her helper. "If someone approaches, make a loud noise."

"Yes Madame."

Caitrin cast a quick glance about then slipped soundlessly into the public room. She left the door very slightly ajar to be able to hear any sound from without.

She moved carefully to where Aboyeur snored. He lay, facing the hearth, stretched out on three chairs placed together. His belongings lay on the floor near to hand and partially covered with his cloak.

How careless you are Seigneur Aboyeur, to leave your messages where anyone could take them.

She continued to move with slow, deliberate, and soundless care. She set the cloak aside and found the wallet. Inside was a pouch of coins and an oiled packet. The documents she sought were in the packet. She exchanged her false papers for those signed by King Philip. Tucking the originals into a pocket beneath her skirts she left as quickly and silently as she came.

As she closed the door to the public room behind her, she smiled at the tweeny and sent the girl off to bed. Moments later Caitrin was back in her room.

Deep darkness outside her window suggested she had time to read the documents. She would be wise to do so as a check against the loss or theft of the papers. Should that happen, she would still be able to recite the information she'd read, and her mission would be a success.

By the light of a shielded lantern, she opened the royal documents and began to read. The king of France addressed his remarks to the Guardians of Scotland and the Comte du Crecy. In it he gave the outline of a plan to force England into war on two fronts.

To the Respected and Noble Guardians of Scotland,

> *I, Philip of France regret that I will be unable to send men, arms or money from France in support of your cause. Nonetheless, I believe we can be of great help to each other in our opposition to Edward of England...*

Much later, Caitrin folded the documents and placed them within the oiled pouch she had prepared earlier. The king of France had one of the most devious minds she'd ever encountered. Yet he seemed such a friendly and amiable sovereign. Deceptive appearances should not surprise her, even in a king.

The missive had gone into great detail, but she went over in her mind the essential points.

Philip had confirmed that he shared the Guardians displeasure over the English King's on-going efforts to conquer Scotland as well as defend Aquitaine and Gascony, territories in France Philip strongly believed belonged to France. The French king had been appalled to learn that Edward and his army were decimating Scotland with the aim of achieving John de Balloil's surrender before the end of July and the eventual success of that attempt.

Still Philip declined to send any sort of direct aid to Scotland. Instead, he planned to pursue war with Edward in Gascony, hoping to drain Edward's financial and human resources by forcing the king of England to battle on two fronts.

Then the French king recommended detailed plans of escape for most of the Scottish nobles and knights imprisoned by Edward after the Scottish defeat at Dunbar and the subsequent surrender Scotland's King John Balliol.

If the proposed escape of the Scottish nobles and knights succeeded, rebellion in Scotland was a near certainty. Edward would be forced to give that rebellion most of his attention and whatever funds remained in his exchequer. The conflicts with France and elsewhere would continue to be neglected to the detriment of the realm. If not neglected, certainly the English barons would revolt against the heavy taxation needed to finance war with both France and Scotland. Edward could be brought low by an English rebellion. It had nearly happened before, during the reign of Edward's father. Philip was certain that with proper management, Scotland and France could both find peace and Edward's destruction.

The situation was dire. Caitrin knew she must warn Edward or his spy master against the planned escapes and the increasing potential for revolt in Scotland. She could let no one interfere, especially not Sir Amis Du Grace.

She lifted the long strap of the pouch over her head so it lay across her body. Next, she put her remaining things into her single bag before reaching for her cloak.

She would go down to the stables and hire a horse then ride south until she found a village with a large enough harbor to have a ship, which she could hire to carry her across to England. She'd no intention of going to Berwick on Tweed. Thank heaven the rain was slowing.

She lifted the hood of her cloak. Any observer would see a cloaked figure leaving the tavern. Only later would it be clear that she was that figure.

A draft from somewhere blew under her skirts, and she shivered.

She reached for her bag only to find her arms anchored to her sides within her cloak. Strong male arms encircled her and lifted her feet from the floor. The familiar scent of orange and cinnamon struck her.

"Seigneur Du Grace, release me this instant." To her surprise, she was returned to the floor, and the arms loosened. They remained long enough to be certain she regained her balance. Then she was free.

She whirled and stabbed a glare at the man. Within her cloak one

219

hand moved to the hilt of her dagger. "To what do I owe the displeasure of your appearance in my private quarters."

His generous lips quirked. "You must know that I want Aboyeur's papers you so conveniently stole for me." He extended his hand, clearly expecting her to turn over the documents without any resistance.

"So, you are not Aboyeur's agent for France?"

Du Grace shrugged.

She laughed. "Regardless of where your loyalties lie, you are destined to disappointment. I stole the documents for my own purposes. Now get out of my way."

She shrugged her cloak aside and threatened with her dagger, while her free hand reached for the traveling bag.

His smile broadened. "I regret that it is you who shall be disappointed."

She'd never seen a man move so quickly. In a trice he stripped her weapon away, turned her so her back was to him, one arm twisted behind her and held her own dagger to her throat.

I've seen him on the jousting field and knew he was quick, but not this quick.

She'd failed to account for it. She had no one but herself--and the miscreant Du Grace--to blame for her present predicament.

"Now, have I your parole that you will cooperate and come quietly to the ship waiting for us? I would hate to have to gag and drag you, or worse."

Worse?

Caitrin could imagine a number of events that would be worse. Somehow, she did not think he meant rapine or murder. Regardless, cooperation might actually serve her best. If he had a ship waiting, she might as well make use of it to take her to England. She could use the entire journey to plot Du Grace's defeat.

"Why not simply leave me behind?"

"You would expose me to Aboyeur as less than loyal to France and claim that I stole the documents, overpowering you when you attempted to stop me."

"Very well, you have my word that I will accompany you to your ship quietly and without any trouble."

"Excellent." He released her but retained her dagger, looking at it then hefting it. "A well-made weapon. Damascus steel?"

She nodded and extended her hand. "I would like it back, please. It was a gift." The blade had indeed been a gift from the elder guard at her childhood home who had taught her its use. She missed very few things from those years, but Sir Gringold was one. He'd understood her frustration at being used as a political pawn.

"Eventually perhaps." He secured the dagger in his belt. Taking the traveling bag in one hand he grasped her elbow in the other. Then he cast a glance out the small window. "We must hurry. We need to be on the ship before the tide turns."

She followed his gaze to where a very thin line of scarlet dawn pierced the clouds that dominated what she could see of the sky. It was not yet Prime, so supposedly Aboyeur still slept.

She held her breath as they moved from room to stairs to entry and out the door into the tavern yard. No mounts or conveyance waited for them.

"You intend to walk?" she asked.

"The harbor is close enough. Besides taking mounts or a carriage, even a cart, would leave more evidence of our passing than is wise. If we walk, our footsteps will be nothing more than so many tracks through the mud, indistinguishable from other tracks, if they are not erased by the rain before any are aware we are gone."

"I wish I had been able to change into my boots." She bundled her skirts high to keep them out of the muck, showing her pretty ankles and calves.

"You must resign yourself to the loss of those slippers. I will furnish you with a new pair once we reach England."

Meanwhile he will keep me barefoot to aid in preventing my escape. Du Grace is no fool, he knows better than to trust my word completely.

Nonetheless, she followed, pleased in at least one respect. He'd forgotten to take the papers from her.

They reached the ship and were escorted on board.

221

"You did not say your guest was a woman." The captain leered at Caitrin when Du Grace requested a second cabin. "I'm afraid I only have the one cabin. You'll have to share."

With the weather uncertain there was no telling how long she would be cooped up with Du Grace. Perhaps he would be chivalrous enough to leave her alone and spend most of the crossing on deck.

Clouds moved in to block the weak sunlight, taking on an ominous purple-green shade. Or perhaps he would remain in the cabin. She doubted the captain or crew would ever be able to gossip about the unwed couple who shared a cabin. She shrugged mentally. She could plan nothing until she knew more. Still, she was determined to escape Du Grace with the papers then proudly deliver them to Edward's spy master. Fortunately, Amis had not removed the oiled pouch from her person. She had to wonder why?

THEY FELT the ship cast off as they made their way to their quarters.

"Stay here," said Amis. "I did not care for the way the captain looked at you when we came aboard. However, I must leave you to get sustenance with which to break our fast. Given this storm, I doubt very much the cook will produce much to eat during the crossing."

"Aye," she agreed. "By the look of the sky, we're in for a rough time of it."

"Agreed. I'll return soon." He left, taking her dagger with him. Now they were at sea, Lady Caitrin had nowhere to go. Nonetheless, he hurried to get their breakfast. It would be a serious mistake to leave her too long to her own devices. The woman was nothing if not clever. He'd never seen the dagger she carried. Subduing her by force had not been his original plan.

He returned with some hard biscuits, a round of cheese, and a flask of warmed cider spiked with a bit of whisky all held in a large cloth he thought might normally be used to cover the captain's table when he dined.

Since there was no table in sight, he spread the cloth on the floor, placing the food and flask on the cloth. He took a cushion from the room's only seat, a cross-framed backless chair, and placed it on the floor between the bed and the cloth then taking her hand, he guided Lady Caitrin to the cushion.

Her grip tightened a bit as she lifted her skirts displaying those lovely ankles once more, then lowered herself to the cushion before releasing her grip.

Unable to look away, he stared as her bottom met the pillow then her hips wriggled a bit making the seat more comfortable.

Amis swallowed.

I loved having those hips...

"Sir Du Grace? Are you planning to join me?"

He blinked.

Eyes wide, she looked up at him over her shoulder.

Surely that innocence is feigned.

She grinned, almost as if she knew what he'd been thinking.

"Yes." He lurched into motion, crossing to the other side of the cloth and seating himself on the bare, somewhat damp floorboards where the food was more easily accessible. He inhaled deeply as he sat, attempting to rein in the rampant lust that made sitting difficult and very uncomfortable. Nonetheless he endured. He could hardly adjust his hose without revealing his physical response to Caitrin. Though she was quite familiar with his body and its responses, she was his captive. Insisting on her attentions now would be cruel. For once he felt rather uncomfortable in his skin. Fortunately, even though he wore a short cotehardie, his more rampant parts were hidden from sight.

She reached for a biscuit and the flask, pouring a trickle of the cider atop the flat disc before handing him the flask.

Her white teeth bit into the biscuit, tearing off a chunk. She chewed a bit then her tongue flicked out of her mouth and circled her lips removing any crumbs that clung. She held out her hand.

His gaze remained fixed on her mouth, unable to stare anywhere else. He recalled those lips, that tongue doing to him what she'd done after biting into the biscuit. His male parts swelled, forcing him to shift. Even when he settled, his discomfort continued.

"Could you pass me the flask, please?"

Her words registered. He raised the flask with an unsteady hand.

She leaned forward quickly and snatched it from him. Her brow wrinkled, and her gaze narrowed. "Are you well, sir? Your hand shook, and nearly spilt our precious supply of warm drink on the cloth. You seem distracted. Perhaps you are ill?"

She placed everything she held on the cloth, lifted to her knees and leaned across. Her hand reached out...

He held his breath.

She stroked the back of her hand across his forehead then resumed sitting.

He shivered at the caress.

"You do not seem to have a fever." Her pretty mouth frowned. "Does your stomach pain you. You've eaten nothing, and you shiver as if you suffer chills."

"No!"

Why did I shout? She only expresses concern for me.

"That is, no," he moderated his tone, speaking just loud enough to be heard over the storm that had broken as the ship gained open water. "I am not ill. My stomach is fine."

That is if a raging erection could be described as fine.

"As for chills, there is a draft coming from beneath the cabin door. It cools my back. I should light the braiser."

The iron pot stood near to hand in a corner beside the door. He reached for it. Took flint and steel from a pouch at his belt. From his peripheral vision he could see her continue her meal. However, he felt her eyes studying his every move--studying him.

"There, much better." He pushed the lit braiser to a spot between them. It meant only part of him was warmed, while the other suffered the breeze from the ill-fitted doorway.

They ate in silence, and Amis kept his gaze lowered to the food on the cloth. He dared not look at Lady Caitrin. A woman like her could enchant a man so that he would do anything she bid. Since she was his captive, he could not allow that.

"You'd best get some sleep," he suggested, when the last crumb of biscuit was a distant memory.

She covered a yawn. "I did have an early morning. I will do as you suggest."

She stretched her arms, drawing the cloth of her bliaut tight across her breasts.

Amis was forced to look away else he should leap on her like the beast his manhood was proving him to be.

Then she arched her back.

Just to be able to take some action other than follow the urge to take her to the bed and swive her senseless, he jumped to his feet with a groan.

Continuing her torture of him she reached behind her with her arms, tightening the cloth over her breasts even further. Her hands found the edge of the bed's baseboard, and pushing, she hoisted herself onto the mattress. She gathered her skirts up around her hips, showing her long shapely legs, removed the ruined slippers then straightened the dress.

Too late for comfort, Amis, turned his back to her. He fisted his hands, digging his fingernails into the flesh of his palm until his eyes watered with the pain.

Only then, when his body was under control, did he wipe his eyes and turn back to look at her. It was a mistake.

She lay in splendid disarray, her dark curls spread across the pillow, her legs covered but relaxed. Her face turned toward him. Her eyes sparkled. Her mouth tilted up in a smile that begged for kisses.

Whether an intentional invitation or not, he must refuse the enticement. He searched in a chest at the foot of the bed, found a blanket, and tossed it over her, covering her from toe to chin. Then he pushed the braiser closer to the bed.

"Thank you." Her voice was low and husky.

Fear for his soul and her safety drove Amis to drag the cross-framed chair as far as he could from the bed. He pushed the backless seat up against the door and restored the cushion to its former place before sitting.

Being farther away was a good thing. However, with his back to the door for support, he was forced to look directly at Lady Caitrin.

"Sleep well, my lady." He spoke as sternly as he knew how then dropped his chin to his chest and closed his eyes. He was glad, truly, that all the warmth was across the room and out of reach, while he sat chilled and lonely on guard. The cold would smother the heat of his lust for Caitrin. At least, that is what he hoped.

"Good night, Sir Amis may your rest be peaceful." Her gentle words floated across the room. Against the noise of the storm, he could not even be certain he'd heard them. However, his heart accepted that he not only heard but welcomed them. He was in serious trouble.

Trouble or not, once he was certain she slept, he crept toward her. Thank heaven for the thunder and crash of waves. They covered any small sound he might make. At her side finally, he lifted the blanket he'd given her earlier. There, strapped across her torso lay his goal. He pulled the dagger he'd taken from her earlier. Fingered the blade and found it well honed. Then he slipped the knife beneath the pouch strap and her body to gently saw the strap in two. He repeated the action at the opposite end of the strap. With the pouch freed, he returned the dagger to his belt then lifted his prize from her torso before replacing the blanket to its original position.

He returned to the chair and spent enough time in the dim light perusing the documents with the French king's seal to understand the essential points of the proposed plan.

Finished, he placed the papers in the oiled pouch and put it inside his shirt, securing the leather beneath his belt. It was the best he could do to take care of them. Caitrin would not be able to retrieve them without touching him, and he knew how her touch stimulated him. He'd not sleep through that. Satisfied with the measures he taken, he allowed himself to nod off to sleep.

CHAPTER THREE

Late afternoon, at sea
December 29, 1296

A HORRENDOUS LOUD rending sound woke Caitrin. She threw off the blanket, sat up, placed her bare feet on the floor and found herself ankle deep in water.

"Amis!"

He startled awake at the same moment the ship lurched and tilted on its side, dumping him from his seat and hurtling the chair across the room to splinter into pieces against the head of the bed.

Caitrin lifted her arms against flying shards of wood but felt the sting of one slice against her cheek.

Soaking wet, Amis had righted himself and stumbled across the room grabbing her from the bed.

"We need to get out of here. The ship is sinking."

Together they managed to force the door open against the rising flood. Then they fought their way to the gangway, where Amis lifted her onto the stairs, placed a hand on her rump and fairly pushed her up the ladder.

They emerged to a deck tilted at a near forty-five-degree angle.

Amis grabbed her waist and pulled her against him. She looked to see him gripping the hatchway frame with his other hand. It was a tenuous hold at best. Boxes, crates, rope, slid to the rail then toppled over the side. Men, struggled to stay upright as they fought with the sail.

What they were trying to do she had too little experience at sea to say. Nonetheless, what she saw alarmed her.

The open sea lay to one side. The opposite side of the ship was wedged at an angle against tall rocks. Waves taller than the rocks and the ship broke against the stone again and again. Each time water sheeted across the slanting deck pushing everything it could into the sea and against the rocks.

A brief look about located the captain behind them on the raised deck at the wheel. The few men remaining at the ropes tried to set the sail so the wind would push the ship away from the rocks and directly into the waves. However, nature was stronger than they could manage.

A gust came of such force that she was lifted from her feet. Had it not been for Amis' grip on her, she would have flown over the side into the sea.

As it was, the wind whipped the men on the ropes like a flail in battle. With no tension on the ropes, the sails filled and crushed further onto the rocks. The deck was torn in two.

"Jump," Amis yelled in her ear, pointing past her to a rocky ledge as he pushed her forward. He must have leapt as well for his hand never left her waist.

"Abandon ship," yelled the captain behind them, scarcely audible above the roar of wind and wave.

She tucked her body into a ball and rolled rather than break her legs landing on the ledge.

She came to a halt at the far side. Lifted herself upward and looked. Amis had disappeared, and a huge wave crashed around the ship. She heard the mast snap. As the wave retreated, the craft rolled loose of the rocks to be tossed about in the waves like a child's toy.

She plastered herself against the niche between the wall of rock and the ledge as more waves pushed and pulled at her. One push thrust her against an outcrop. Pain lanced through her shoulder, but she hugged the outcrop with all her might. Her life depended on it.

How much time passed before the force of the waves lessened, she could not say, but the wind remained fierce, tearing at her clothing and freezing her to the marrow.

I have to get off of this ledge and find shelter.

She searched in the direction of the shore for any sort of break that might indicate a beach or safe harbor. As she looked, she saw something bobbing in the maelstrom that swirled between the rocks and the shore. Probably some flotsam from the ship.

To assure herself she hunted for safety in the right direction she looked back to where the ship had been. Nothing visible remained of the vessel or the men who'd sailed her. The still roiling waves of the open sea looked gentle by comparison to the maelstrom between the rocks. Nonetheless, she knew better than to imagine anything like safety lay in the direction of open water.

She would have to brave the rocky vortices and pray the current would carry her to safety. She began to look for a way to climb down.

"Help!"

The bobbing flotsam was closer now. It was a man. He struggled to swim against the current of the maelstrom but his strength was failing.

Did she have any more strength than he? She doubted so. Even if she did, how could she help from here?

Before she could think more carefully, she closed her mouth and leapt from the ledge at the same moment that the tide lifted the swirling water closer to the ledge. Some instinct had her kicking and stroking through the water in the direction of the man.

The current was indeed too strong to fight, she tried to cut across it but failed and lost sight of him.

The current between the rocks whipped her from side to side of the swirling stream. Still, she was able to keep her head above water.

Some obstacle stretched between the rocks, forcing the water to pile up. The current lifted her, and for a long instant Caitrin could see a flat area of land emerging from the sea below.

Then she plunged with the current over the blockage and down, down to an oddly sheltered pool.

The fall submerged her, and she struggled to make her way to the surface. She ripped away as much as she could of her storm-torn skirts. Sheer grit gave her the strength to breach the surface. She was still a long way from the shore but in much calmer water.

Splinters of wood that had once been part of some ship--possibly hers--lay scattered across the surface of the tide pool. One piece floated near enough for her to grab. What part of a ship it had been, she could not tell, but it was twice as long as she was tall, nearly as thick and very slippery. She would have been unable to hold on had she not discovered the remnants of a rope tied around the wood's girth.

She folded one hand around the line and hauled herself atop the wood. Once there, she anchored her fingers beneath the sodden hemp with the pressure of her own body. The position was awkward in the extreme, and her shoulder screamed with pain. Nonetheless, she managed to free her legs enough from the grip of her skirts to wrap them around the entire thickness of her makeshift raft then link her ankles together.

The timber bobbed and dipped. Save for having her face washed frequently in stinging salt water, it was rather like riding an unschooled horse. Of course, she lacked reins, stirrups or spurs to aid her in guiding her wooden steed.

Battered and bruised, she began to lose hope that she could hold on when something bumped into the beam. Weary as she was, she looked in the direction of impact.

Amis.

He floated unconscious but face up, thank Saint Clement.

She released her hold on the rope and leaned forward with both hands. Her fingertips touched his shirt, but not enough to grip. She stretched and managed to dig her fingers into the cloth. She tugged and pulled. Exerting more force, she dragged him from the sea onto the wood. Something popped in the pain ridden shoulder as she gave the last heave to bring him to what little safety she'd found.

She shrieked with the pain. Any sound was drowned by the wind. A wave rolled her craft to one side and filled her mouth with seawater. Still, she rammed her fingers into Amis' shirt and flesh. She tightened the grip of her legs around the wood.

For an eternity, she fought the eddies in the pool and the wind to keep herself and Amis from a watery grave. She was nearly at the end of her strength when the restless water smoothed to large gentle swells.

She looked about her but could see nothing. The line between sky and sea appeared to have been erased. The air around her thickened. She could scarce see where her hands held Amis onto the wood.

Fog.

That was when she shivered, becoming aware of how very cold she was. She could barely feel her legs where they circled the wood. Her fingers were numb from cold and lack of motion required to keep Amis in place. Her shoulder shouted at her to lay down and rest. Her eyelids drooped.

She shook her head violently.

I must not fall asleep. We'll both drown if I do.

Whether Amis still lived she could not tell. She peered through the fog, trying to see if his chest rose and fell. Between the obscuring mist plus the heave and roll of the water any determination was impossible.

She was so very weary. If she released him into the ocean she might rest, just a little. Doing so would be tantamount to murder, as she could not be certain he was already dead. She resigned herself to floating in an endless sea locked by her fingers to a man she knew she could not trust. She might be better off if he drowned. Perhaps, but as long as the chance of life existed, her conscience would not permit her to let go.

The air around her darkened but did not clear. Night must have fallen. How long had she slept when they first boarded the ship? The storm had obscured all sight of the sun and sky. It had to have been afternoon, since they'd boarded close to dawn. How far had they traveled? Had they been blown off course? Her mind circled through useless questions she could not possibly answer.

Her eyes closed. She jerked awake when her cheek hit wet wood. Time after time, she woke herself until she didn't.

AMIS LAY on a hard rough surface, his back to the sky, and opened his eyes to stare at a field of pebbles. He shrugged his shoulders trying to shake off the talons digging into him and burning pain all the way to his bones. When that failed, he forced his arms beneath himself and levered upward. Pain hissed from shoulder to bone and back, but he managed to dislodge the daggers piercing his flesh.

His arms trembled. However, he was able to look about him before his strength failed.

In the watery sunlight that filtered through the cloud cover, he saw a pebbled beach and hills or perhaps dunes rising from the area where he lay.

How long since he'd leapt into the water, certain of his death? The clouds made determining the time of day nearly impossible.

Prone once more, he turned his head, letting the small stones jab his cheek rather than his mouth and nose.

Tired. So tired. What happened?

His eyes closed.

No, don't sleep. Defenseless.

His lids fluttered. Beside him a face came into focus.

Caitrin. Caitrin is here.

Too weak to do more, he slid his hand along the pebbles and laid it on her shoulder before his world went black.

He was shaking. Was he still at sea?

"Amis Du Grace, you must wake up and stand. I cannot carry you." She sounded worried.

"I'm well."

Something struck his shoulder.

"I know you are well, you lummox. However, you must be well enough to stand and walk. The tide is rising. We need to get off this beach and find shelter."

He looked at her and saw her stuffing something inside her bodice. *The French documents!*

He felt carefully at his waist, but the pouch was gone. Farther down, stuck between his hose and his thigh the blade he'd taken from her pricked his leg. Some miracle had left him with a weapon. The pouch was lost at sea most likely. Or stolen back by Caitrin? He'd find a way to discover what she'd hidden.

"Damnation!" Abruptly he sat up. The motion brought a thousand aches and pains to life, so turning to face Caitrin was a slower effort. "Where are we? What happened? Are you well?"

"We can play question and answer after we find shelter." She stood, one arm akimbo, looking down at him. Her opposite shoulder drooped oddly.

He looked at her. How he could think her beautiful with seaweed and sand scattered through her hair and across her body he would never know. She was right; they must find shelter, warmth, water, food... His mind raced. He used that mental energy to heave himself to his feet.

"Finally. Let's go." She turned and staggered off toward the slope that bordered the beach.

"Wait, you're hurt!"

"I'll wait at the top of this hill. If I stop now, I'll never move again."

He understood and protested no more.

When he stood beside her, at the top of the rise, they groaned in unison.

Before them lay a plain of sandy dirt topped with tufted hillocks of dead grass and wildflowers.

"Where do you think we are?" she asked.

"Even with the storm, I doubt we reached Scotland. So, we're probably in England. Perhaps somewhere north of Berwick on Tweed."

"Hmmm. That makes some sense. We should probably move on. Staying here will serve no good purpose."

There was little space to walk between the mounds of vegetation and no direct path. Far in the distance--too far to guess--stood a heap of stones that might be a structure or simply a marker of some kind.

"What's that?" He pointed.

"In Scotland we call it a cairn. People, both ancient and modern, make stacks or piles of stones for a variety of reasons, sometimes as memorials for battles, or as grave markers. Frequently they are used to navigate where there is no obvious path."

Amis' gaze swiveled from one end of the horizon to the other. "That would certainly work for this area."

Using her good arm, Caitrin shielded her eyes from the glaring sun. "Usually, where there is one cairn, there is another. The suggested path then runs between the two. However, I don't see a second cairn. Sometimes there is no second cairn."

"Then how are we to decide which direction to follow."

"We walk to the cairn we can see and hope that from that vantage we see another." She lifted her ragged skirts and started down the landward side of the slope and into the endless plain of hillocks. But first I must arrange a way to secure my injured arm until we can find a time to fix it. Turn around." She lifted the edge of the rags she wore.

"Nonsense," he protested. "I've seen every inch of you. Now is no time to become modest. Nor will you tear more of your clothing. We will use a strip from my cotehardie. And sit down, while we bind your shoulder, I'll make some small protection for your feet."

"I don't want to sit. I might not get up."

He nodded. Tore three strips of material from his cotehardie and started with her arm. By dint of him kneeling and her holding onto him for balance, they managed to cover her feet without having her sit.

Soon she stood with her arm bound to her chest and her feet protected from stones and brambles.

"It pains you," he said.

"Aye, but we've no time to deal with it more. We need shelter and food first." She set off toward the cairn.

She looked nearly as exhausted as he felt. Amis considered simply lying down where he stood. He was too weary, and his body hurt too much to traverse difficult terrain. He'd starve to death for certain. He wanted rest, but he wanted survival more. He lurched forward and came up behind Caitrin. There wasn't space between the hillocks to walk two abreast.

"What if we get to this cairn and we don't see another?"

"Hopefully the construction of the cairn itself will provide a clue."

"Such as?"

"Such as, every stone has a point or a particularly jagged edge. Those similarities are lined up as the thing is built and aim in the correct direction for travel."

"That's a rather haphazard way to find direction."

"Earlier travelers used what materials were at hand. There are no trees to mark or fell to guide the way here. Signs left in the dirt would disappear with the wind or rain."

"What prevents some prankster from deliberately building a cairn to mis-guide other travelers."

She shrugged. "Nothing I suppose. In fact, with so much disagreement between clans, I can imagine a man might do so to misdirect his enemies."

"So, you and I could wander this near barren land until we die."

"We could. But I doubt that will happen."

"Why?"

"Scotland doesn't have coastal plains wide enough for that."

"You think we are in Scotland?"

"There or the very north of England."

"We were headed for Berwick on tweed. I suppose Scotland or such is possible. That storm blew for hours before the ship sank."

Caitrin made no reply. She was looking at the ground and stepping very carefully.

Amis did his best to follow where she stepped, but the ground was damp, almost squishy, and her footprints filled with muddy liquid, disappearing almost instantly.

They walked on like that for some distance. The ground would firm for several steps then become wet again. Every now and then, Amis would look up to judge the distance remaining to the cairn.

He made another check of the distance and was overjoyed to be able to see the outline of individual stones. Instinctively he hurried forward. Then his foot sank up to his ankle.

Quicksand.

He became aware of the difficulty just as his other foot swung forward and sank up to the knee. He tried to free his first foot, but the struggle only sank him deeper, so he stopped moving, both knees now covered in muck. He continued to feel himself sink.

This was not good.

"Caitrin." She didn't hear and kept moving on at a steady if slow pace.

"Caitrin, help!"

At last, she halted and looked back. Her irritated scowl changed quickly to a look of horror. She reversed course."

"Be wary," he shouted. "We don't need you to be caught too."

Moving as quickly as she could, she stopped a yard or so from the spot where he now stood covered to mid-thigh.

"Don't move," she said.

He looked down where he was mired to the hips. "I promise not to."

Her lips twitched. "We have to get you out of there."

"I agree." The conversation was absurd but oddly comforting.

She moved forward, cautiously, testing the ground before her and tugging with one hand on the grassy hillocks. Some came loose immediately. Others yielded only after several forceful pulls. Finally, she found one sturdy enough to resist all her efforts to dislodge it.

His descent into the quicksand slowed, but it still crept upward nearing his waist.

"Hand me your belt."

As it was yet uncovered by muck, he raced to remove it, throwing it to her.

She caught it.

"Here, take my cotehardie as well, if you can manage it. The belt alone won't be long enough."

Without the cotehardie, he became aware of the stiff breeze. Pain and exhaustion, he guessed, had kept him from noticing earlier.

She caught the cloth too, then sat and busily removed what was left of her dress, leaving herself in only her shift. When she had all the materials before her, she raced to improvise a rope. With only one useable arm, the work went too slowly.

He was now covered to his waist.

Eventually the rope was ready.

She looped the improvised length around the base of the sturdy hillock, securing the loop with the end of his belt. Then she tossed the length in his direction.

The rope fell in a heap just short of the mire.

He extended his torso, doing his best to avoid too great contact with the quicksand. His elbow struck solid ground, but the cloth lay about a hand's length from his reach.

Caitrin lay full length on the ground, then using one arm and her feet crawled forward.

When she reached the pile of material, she shoved it one-handed toward Amis.

He caught it and wound as much as he could around one hand. That allowed him to pull a bit more of length toward him until the line of clothing and belt stretched taut from him to the hillock.

He glanced at Caitrin, who lay where she'd stopped. Her lower lip was caught between her teeth.

"You can't help, can you."

She shook her head. "Sorry."

"Pray for me then."

She nodded, her lips moving as he began to pull on the cloth line. Hand over hand, he managed to inch closer to the solid edge of land.

The loose end of the line sank into the quicksand and anchored there giving him a small amount of stability. Before he was free of the muck, his feet touched something solid. Rock? Hard dirt? The bones of prior victims?

He pushed with his feet on whatever it was. His arms strained, and he tried to tighten his grip on the rope. The effort was rewarded with a great sucking sound as he freed himself from the quicksand. At the same moment the earth lost its grasp on the hillock which came flying toward him and smacked him in the face.

Spitting sand and grasses, he collapsed on terra firma. He was free of the quicksand.

"Thank you, Holy Mother," came from the direction where Caitrin lay.

Amis lifted his head and smiled at her.

She laughed. "You have grass in your teeth."

"I thank the heavens it is not quicksand. Your fast action saved me. Thank you."

"You are welcome, but I tell you now, I've no intention of moving any time soon."

"Nor do I," he replied.

He let his head sink to the ground and his eyes to close, but before he slept his outstretched hand found hers and twined their fingers together.

CHAPTER FOUR

Somewhere on the coast
Dusk December 30, 1296

CAITRIN WOKE to see Amis standing at the cairn examining it closely. Earlier she'd not had time to indulge the fear that had struck her along with the knowledge that he might die. He was the enemy, wasn't he? His death would be a relief.

A relief? Why? Because I care for the man. I promised myself, when De Garrone died, I would never trust another man. But I don't trust Du Grace, do I?

She should have left him to die, yet she'd saved his life not once but twice.

Well, it would be a shame to deprive the world of such a magnificent lover.

Yes, that was it. Her own lusts had rescued the man. He was naught to her but a convenient bed partner.

She spent a moment enjoying the play of muscles on his back under the thin material of his shirt before noticing how very uncomfortable she was. She sat up, pushing hair from her face and rubbing at the salt and sand irritating her skin. "What are you doing?"

"Trying to figure out which way this pile of rocks intends for us to go."

Standing, she gave up trying to get even a trifle more clean and joined him at the cairn. She gave the stones a brief glance, gazed up at the plain of hillocks and down, cast a quick glance at where the hillocks gave way to longer grasses and brush on the rise of land they faced.

"That way." She pointed to what she believed from the location of the sun was south."

"That's south,' Amis said, confirming her belief.

"Yes."

"Don't you want to go west, or north? England lies to the south."

How could she make her wish to go south seem like something a spy for Scotland would do? Survival would be easier with a second person to help. Besides, she enjoyed his company and had no wish to make him hate her by revealing that she spied for England. "Normally I would do so, but everything about this cairn indicates that the nearest habitation lies to the south. We need food, water, clothing and transportation. Going south would get me to Scotland faster."

"You'll have to escape me first."

"Hmpfh." She refused to dignify with reply his assumption that he still held her captive.

He didn't argue but set off in the direction she had pointed, walking parallel to the rise of land bordering the plain. He cast a glance back over his shoulder.

"Yes, I'm following you."

He stopped, and she caught up with him.

"What are you waiting for." She stumbled forward.

"Making sure I see you if you fall and need help getting up."

She smiled, knowing he could not see her expression. She could not recall a time when someone had truly cared if she needed help or not. Oh, court manners and politesse required that a man help a woman to sit or to her feet, but that was pro forma and not a matter of caring.

Here in this wasteland of weedy sand and rock there was no such requirement. Every action came from a need to survive. Help demonstrated at least some degree of caring.

She shook her head at the echo of her earlier thoughts. She wasn't a cruel person, of course she cared for anyone in trouble. Just as he did. Their actions meant nothing other than that they were smart enough to realize they had a better chance of survival together than apart.

How long they walked, she could not say, but dusk approached as they left the plain and something like a path formed beneath their feet. The path widened enough so they could walk abreast, and the distance between the plain and the rise of land to the west narrowed.

Soon they were traveling up a low incline. They kept on, making slow progress and shivering with cold until long after dark. They paused where the path topped the rise. Moon and starlight cast an ethereal glow on the grassy valley beyond the rise. An occasional tree dotted the landscape along with a number of large bushes.

In the light of the moon, one of the bushes separated itself from the others and began moving slowly down the valley.

"What is that?" Caitrin pointed.

Amis peered in that direction. "A horse, maybe? Or a cow? Perhaps a large dog."

"Scottish wolf hounds are large but not that large. I'm going to pray it's a horse."

"Either way, we should follow it. We can discuss how best to catch it when we get closer."

"Hmm. Even a cow would be a blessing. We could fill our bellies with milk."

"If it isn't a bull."

"Ugh. I want nothing to do with anything bull-headed."

He grinned, his teeth gleaming. "You don't think I'm bull-headed?"

"I don't think it. I know it. You're male, you can't help it." She was well aware that she'd contradicted herself, but she'd not abandon him. Not yet.

He chuckled. "I think you have no idea how stubborn I can be when I want something."

She couldn't see his eyes well enough to tell if he was flirting and mean her or if he was confessing a truth about himself. Truth or flirtation, he would find she could match him in determination. As long as their aims remained the same, she'd put up with his male foolishness. The time would come when they would part ways, and she would be glad. Yes, she would.

"Come on," she said, wanting to focus on something other than the man beside her. "If we want to catch that creature we'd best move faster."

"You're right there. I'm exhausted, but that animal gives me hope that food and shelter are close enough to warrant hurrying."

It took most of the night, but as the eve of the new year dawned, they were close enough to see the animal was a horse of a very pale color.

"*Thig each, thig each,*" Caitrin called.

The steed stopped and looked back in their direction.

"What are you doing?"

"I'm calling the horse."

"It doesn't know you. It won't come."

"A lot you know."

She reached inside her bodice and withdrew a lump of seaweed she'd placed there when she imagined she'd have nothing better to eat. Next, she advanced slowly on the horse murmuring quiet words.

The horse continued to stare at her.

It did not run away. That was a good sign. She extended her hand, palm open, the lump of kelp easily accessible.

The horse lifted its nose, sniffed then with a nicker, it advanced and began to nibble the seaweed from her palm.

"That's a good horse." Her empty hand being useless, she rubbed her cheek against the horse.

"Aye, you're a good fellow aren't you." Amis had come up on the opposite side of the horse and now stroked its withers.

As the sun crested the horizon, Caitrin could see the horse was in fairly rough shape. It looked as if it had been wandering outside for many days. However, the worn bridle over its head indicated it had once belonged to someone. If the bridle had a lead or reins, they'd long ago been lost.

"Do you think he'll let us ride him?" she asked.

"Perhaps. Set the rest of that seaweed on the ground, and I'll lift you up."

"Thank you, but shouldn't you ride? You're the one who almost drowned, first in the ocean then in quicksand."

"We'll take turns, but you first, please. If the horse doesn't want to be ridden, I'm better able to catch you, as I've two good arms."

She had to yield to that logic.

In moments, she sat astride the steed. Caitrin leaned forward and patted its neck. "Thank you for taking me up, Buttercup."

His hand on the mount's bridle, Amis looked back at her. "Buttercup?"

"I can't keep calling him, horse."

"Don't see why not. But Buttercup is a stupid name for a male animal, especially one that is a survivor."

"Have you a better suggestion?"

Amis looked off into the east before looking back at her. "Sunrise."

Caitrin smiled at him. "I like that. Sunrise he shall be. Sunrise is a good omen, and he's been an unexpected blessing."

Amis shrugged and set off, giving a slight tug on the bridle. Sunrise walked on beside him.

They traveled that way until the sun made half of its journey across the sky.

"Whoa." Amis stopped moving, so did Sunrise.

With nothing to occupy her, Caitrin had been dozing, but came quickly awake when the horse stopped.

"What is it?"

"There's a building up ahead."

"A house?"

"More of a hovel. Stay here," Amis ordered. "I'll go investigate."

"I'll go with you," Caitrin insisted.

"No." He turned, put a hand on her to prevent her dismount. "If there's danger, you'll need to go for help."

"You've a point. Very well. However, if you take too long and I get worried, I'm coming after you."

SHE MIGHT WORRY ABOUT ME?

Something warm spread in Amis' chest, as he resolved to take every precaution.

He approached the small building. Daub and wattle constructed, with a thatched roof and roughly shuttered windows of oiled skins. No smoke rose from the chimney. No light shone from any chink in the window covering. The door was the only thing well made about the place. He circled the building. A lean-to shed extended from the far end of the rear wall. A large, heavy length of leather covered the open end. The leather was weighted with stones sewn into a hem at the bottom edge.

Beside the lean-to was a second, less well-made door. He completed a circuit of the structure before returning to inspect the shed. He pulled aside the leather cover enough to step inside then waited for his vision to adjust to the dark, windowless space. A tangle of tools littered one side of the space where he stood. A lantern hung from a nail. He took the lantern and shook it. He heard the slosh of oil.

Thanks be to God.

He searched the area near the nail and found flint and steel and managed to light the lantern despite the dark. Lifting the light, he saw that the opposite half of the area was cleared showing a floor of hard-packed dirt. A small manger hung from the back wall of the cleared area. Whoever owned the place, at one time had a horse or cow. Nothing indicated which.

From the shed he made his way to the rear door. It opened easily when he lifted the latch. He stepped into the darkened space and raised the lantern once more. He stepped quickly outside and emptied his stomach to the side of the door.

"What is it?"

Caitrin's voice came from behind him.

"I told you to wait for me." He turned to glare at her, but he suspected the shadows prevented her from seeing the full extent of his displeasure.

"And I told you I would only wait for a while. You took too much time, so I decided to come and help you." She dismounted and headed for the door he'd left ajar.

"Don't go in there." He stepped between her and the doorway."

"Why not?"

"The folk who lived here…"

"Yes?"

"They're dead."

Her face paled. "How many?"

"Three from what I could see. But they've been dead a while. Rats and other vermin have fed on the bodies. It isn't a pretty sight."

She turned her head aside. "You cast up your accounts. It must be quite terrible. What do you think killed them?"

"I won't know until I get a closer look."

"I'll do it."

"No. It might have been plague or some other disease. I'll not permit you to risk yourself."

"But you will take the risk yourself." She folded her one good arm across her chest and tried to stare him down.

He was better at the game than she, for she finally dropped her arm and turned away.

"Fine. I'll take care of Sunrise while you risk your life."

"I doubt you'll find much in the way of fodder."

She shrugged as she took the horse by the bridle and walked away. "I've a bit of seaweed left. It should keep Sunrise satisfied until you and I can forage for other food."

As he watched her, an ache sprang to life where that warmth had earlier filled his chest. Why it mattered that he'd somehow hurt her feelings he couldn't say. He was a knight, anointed by a bishop on the day he won his spurs. Protecting others was his promise to God. He'd not foreswear that oath just to please a woman. A woman he shouldn't trust.

Do I trust her? She saved my life twice. Yet she has lied to me from the moment we met.

Not knowing what to make of Lady Caitrin Drew-De Garonne, he pushed the problem aside for a later time and entered the house.

All in all, he buried five bodies in an area that might once have been a vegetable garden. The earth had been turned and digging was easier. While he'd removed the bodies, Caitrin had taken a bucket from among the tools in the shed and gone in search of water to wash with and to drink.

He'd begun digging the graves when she returned.

"I need to find a peat bog, so we can have a fire before dark. Afterward, I'll find soap and scrub everything."

"But your arm." He gestured at where her one shoulder sagged.

"I can't let such a small hurt stop me."

"Small?"

"It isn't broken. In fact, now that we have shelter, I'll tell you how to help me fix it."

He lifted a brow. "Not broken?"

She nodded. "However, we have much to do before we can tend this small injury. Do you think you might try to find us some food when you are done with the burying? I saw a bow and arrows among the tools."

"I'll do what I can. But digging these graves will take time. There may not be light enough left to hunt."

"We'll find out when you finish." She left again. The sun hovered over the western horizon when she returned with an armload of peat.

Amis emerged from the lean-to with the bow and quiver of five arrows.

"You finished?"

"Aye. I dug one large grave instead of five separate ones. That family died together. I see no reason why they should be separated in death."

"We'll say some words over the grave when you return with our supper."

"We'd best both pray that I find a hare or other animal to cook and serve."

"Aye, I'll do that."

"As will I. The lantern is on the table. You'll have light for a while until you can get the fire started."

As he started to walk off, she put her hand on his arm. "Come back soon. I'd rather not have to save you a third time because you got lost in the dark." She smiled.

He grinned back. "If I'm not back before sunset, open the shutters of one of the windows. It will be a beacon to guide me back to you."

"Watch out for quicksand." She called to his retreating back, though she doubted this far from the shore such would be problem.

He laughed loud enough for her to hear.

She turned into the house, closing the door, and bending to the hearth. A few sticks of kindling remained in a basket beside the hearth. As she built the fire, she thought about what Amis had said.

"...To guide me back to you," he'd said. Not 'to this house', 'this place' or simply 'to guide him back.'

It mattered not what words he used. He means nothing by it.

Yet she couldn't stop the warmth that circled the region of her heart as the peat fire began to heat the room.

She found a pot of lye soap, extinguished the lamp to conserve what oil might remain. By the firelight she searched the space and found a rough bed behind a curtain that formed in an alcove. Whatever had been used as a mattress had disappeared. She doubted they would remain here long enough to warrant making a new mattress.

Still, the floor would make a better bed than the dirt or rocks where she and Amis had slept the past two nights.

She opened the shutters of one of the windows and unbarred the front door. Then she set to scrubbing every surface she could reach, removing heaven knew how many months of dirt and cobwebs. Hampered as she was with one useless arm, cleaning wasn't easy. Fortunately, the croft was small. The last thing she did was walk to the small pool she'd found earlier to get clean water. On returning, she collapsed onto a three-legged stool just as Amis entered the front door.

"I got very lucky. He lifted two large hares in one hand.

"That's wonderful." She smiled. "I'm ravenous."

"It will be a while before we can eat."

"That's fine. There's a clean pot on the shelf."

He busied himself cleaning and butchering the rabbits.

She let herself doze before the fire, warm for the first time in days.

His hand on her should woke her. "Our supper is ready, my lady."

"I didn't intend to fall asleep."

He handed her an earthen ware bowl and her dagger.

"It's probably best you did. I don't know what you plan for me to do to your arm and shoulder, but I suspect it will be painful."

"It will hurt very much for a brief moment or two, but the relief afterward will be like heaven. How did you manage to keep my dirk?"

"I don't know, but it was wedged between my belt and my body. When I gave you the belt to make the rope, the knife must have slipped down into my hose and stuck there, since I was covered in quicksand."

"And you didn't know it was there?"

"I thought it lost until I woke after my encounter with the bog. When I went to stand, it poked me in the knee. You still slept, so I removed the blade then walked over to the cairn. By the time you joined me, I'd managed to secure the dagger around my waist with a strip of cloth torn from my cotehardie."

"Ah. I'm sorry you did not trust me enough to tell me you still had it."

"Trust had nothing to do with it. I'm a knight and feel rather naked without a weapon close at hand."

"That's plausible." He lied; she knew. They may need each other's help to survive, but once they found themselves in a large enough town, all cooperation would end. It would have to end. They were enemies. She was surprised he'd not tried to murder her nearly as much as her own restraint with him astonished.

"You think I'm lying." He filled his mouth with boiled hare.

"Why would you say that?" She asked.

"Your disappointment at my supposed lack of trust speaks volumes about the absence of your trust in me."

"Yet I saved your life," she reminded.

"Twice, and I thank you for it."

"Do you mistrust everyone who saves your life?"

"I don't mistrust anyone."

"No?" She lifted a brow.

"No, and I shall prove it as soon as we fix your shoulder."

"I would have to trust you to allow you to lay hands on my injury."

He nodded. "That or continue as you are until other help can be found."

"We both know we can wait no longer."

"Then tell me what to do." He took her bowl and dagger, setting them aside near the water bucket along with his own bowl and the empty pot."

She slipped from the stool to the floor, shoving the stool a good distance away then stretched out on the floor near the hearth, the upper arm of her injured shoulder held at an angle to her body.

"Kneel or sit on the floor beside me then take hold of my arm at the wrist.

He followed her directions. "Now what?"

"You must pull my arm toward you. You must stop as soon as you hear the bones click together."

"It will be that loud?"

"Aye. Pull, straight, slow and steady, no matter how much I may weep. If you act too quickly or are not straight, you may do more damage."

She hoped she imagined the color leave his face.

He swallowed. "You are certain?"

"Definitely. I needed to do this for knights in my family home often."

He stroked her hand before securing his grip on her wrist and lower arm. "Did they weep?"

"Like babies. Now do it before I lose what little courage I have."

CHAPTER FIVE

Somewhere North of Berwick on Tweed
Night, December 31, 1296

HE COULDN'T IMAGINE her without courage. Cowering did not seem to be in her nature. Nor had she complained at any time since the shipwreck.

"Very well, I'm ready to start."

"Good." She turned her head away.

How long he pulled he could not have said, but neither could he tell if she cried. At one point he heard a small whimper from her, just before the loud click that signaled he could stop pulling.

She heaved a great sigh and turned her head to look at him. "Thank you."

Damp gleamed in her eyes, but her cheeks were dry. If the pain was so bad that it caused trained knights to weep, she was a woman of extraordinary prowess and determination.

"You know, I was in France to spy for King Edward."

She blinked at him then began to laugh. Loud, long, and nearly hysterical, she giggled and guffawed as she lay before him.

His brow wrinkled, and he waited for her fit to subside. Why he'd confessed his secret to her, he couldn't have said. But as he'd pulled on her arm, he wanted to be worthy of the trust she'd shown in asking his help. She might claim mistrust on both their parts, but he knew better now. She'd shown him nothing but trust from the moment he'd taken her captive in France. He couldn't explain it, but with the click of bone on bone, his thinking about this woman had changed completely, clicking into place like a well-worn pair of greaves.

At long last she lay still looking at him with a huge grin on her face.

"You'll share with me, please what you find so amusing about my confession to being a spy."

She shook her head.

"First explain why you tell me this now, please?"

He shrugged. "I can't explain. Not really. I can tell you that I had little difficulty deceiving the entire French court. However, I've been uncomfortable doing so with you. Especially after the mid-summer masquerade.

She nodded. "I think I understand."

"Then why do you find my confession so amusing?"

"It isn't your confession, but that you are spying for Edward. I always believed you a spy. Aboyeur assured me that your French father--the one whom I now know is a complete fiction--had ambitions to supplant Philip, and you were spying for your father to learn who might support his rebellion."

"Now you know I'm not French in the least."

"And you must know that I too am a spy."

"Oh, I knew that. Our mutual friend Aboyeur informed me you were the primary go between for secret messages between Philip and the Guardians of Scotland."

"But I'm not."

"Not a spy? I'm sorry but you stole those papers from Aboyeur."

"So, I could deliver them to Edward's spymaster, not to Scotland's guardians."

His jaw dropped. "You were spying for Edward too?"

"Unknown to Aboyeur, I never trusted the man, and now it seems I had good reason." She grinned.

"You're right. He is the one who warned me about your Scottish activities and background."

"And I suspect he is the source of the bad information being passed to Edward's spy master."

"As do I. Are you not a Scot?"

"Oh, I was born a Drew, but I was sold to de Garrone in marriage and lied to into the bargain. I wanted to marry a Scot, but my father and mother said I would be happier with the handsome, rich, courtly Frenchman, and that I must do so for the good of our family and Scotland."

"I met de Garrone years ago. He is none of those things."

"I was so deceived in my husband that I vowed revenge on Scotland. My parents died shortly after I left to marry in France, and the Guardians awarded their lands to a stranger. They too were betrayed, or I would have included them in my vow."

"So, we are left with the necessity of making our way to Edward's court to give our report."

"And to tell Edward that Aboyeur is Philip's tool."

"I wonder if those papers contained misleading information."

"Possibly." She yawned. "But since they were lost at sea, we'll never know."

"Not so."

She blinked at him. "Why do you say that?"

"Because I read them before we boarded that ship. I have a very good memory."

Caitrin smiled before covering a yawn. "I did the same. Perhaps between us we can recall more than the most general points of the French plan."

She covered a second yawn.

"You are weary. Indeed, we are both tired, and should get some sleep."

"There is a bed behind that curtain, but it has no mattress."

"Too bad. Stay here."

"I'm unlikely to go anywhere. The night is very cold."

He rose and walked to a chest that sat beneath the shelf holding the crockery. Fortunately, it was not locked. He opened it and rummaged inside for a moment. When he returned to Caitrin he carried three blankets.

"Lift your head."

She obeyed.

He slipped one of the folded blankets beneath her dark tresses. "Put your head down now."

He shook out a second blanket and covered her. Then he lay down beside her using the last blanket to cover them both. Turning on his side, he placed an arm around Caitrin's waist tugging her closer to his heat. Her bottom snug against him made finding his rest difficult, but he'd not attempt to make love to her when she was so weary.

Make love?

He'd had a healthy case of lust for her from the moment they'd met. He'd never loved a woman other than his mother and sister. However, he understood lust very well. What he wanted with Caitrin was certainly lustful, but also something more. Was that love?

I admire her greatly. She's determined on achieving her aims, as am I. She's beautiful, certainly. Intelligent, without doubt. I owe her my life twice over. What I feel for Caitrin is as far from gratitude as lust probably is from love. But do I love her?

The question intrigued him enough to distract him from his body's demands, and as the old year gave way to the new, he realized he would not sleep this night. He rose from the floor, tucking the second blanket carefully around Caitrin then left. She would be hungry in the morning, and he would make certain she had better than stewed rabbit bones and seaweed.

Caitrin woke alone to the New Year.

I'm glad. Yes, I am.

She stepped outside the back door and to the far side of the shed to relieve herself. If Amis Du Grace has taken himself off to Edward's court, then she need not worry about it.

She hurried back to the door wondering if she had enough seaweed left to break her fast? Her hand closed on the latch.

"Stop!"

Still holding the latch, she turned her head in the direction of Amis' voice. He walked in her direction, a priest at his side.

He hasn't deserted me after all.

"Why?" She tried to sound irritated.

I am not happy to see him.

Liar!

"Because, 'tis Hogmanay, and if either one of us is first foot, we'll have bad luck all year long. Doesn't every Scot know this?"

"I didn't think the English held Hogmanay as a tradition. Besides, I am dark-haired, which is half of what is required for good luck."

"Aye, and I am male, the other half of the requirement. Together we might make a lucky pair."

She straightened placing a fist on each hip. "Are you suggesting we cross the threshold together? Tradition speaks of one person not two."

"No, I am, however, suggesting we might continue together, after Father Eustace here, crosses the threshold."

They'd finally approached close enough for her to see the priest clearly. She also noted the heavy sack Amis carried.

The priest was possessed of tonsured, but shiny black curls.

"Welcome, Father Eustace, and God's blessings on you. 'Tis good of you to be first foot here."

"Blessings on you as well, child. I am told the family who lived here did not fare well."

"No, Father."

"I will bless the graves, after I make all well with this house." He stepped up to the door and began to chant in Latin then proceeded to walk around the house as he chanted.

Caitrin stepped aside to stand by Amis. "How did you find him?"

"More like, he found me on his way here from his village a few miles north of Berwick."

She turned her face to his and lifted a brow

"I could not sleep. I considered that a family such as they who died here would not live more than a day's walk from some sort of village. I met Father Eustace coming to check on them. He knew they had illness in the house, and for fear of contagion no one else from the village would go to help."

"And that sack which you carry?"

"Supplies the father was bringing to the family. He knew how poor they were and how they'd not been able to work to care for themselves when the sickness took hold."

She wanted to weep for those five souls. Their misfortune had been her blessing. "I should ask God's forgiveness for being glad I live."

"If you wish. I, however, will give thanks for the life he has given me and the chance to spend that life in better work than spying for kings."

She nodded. "Aye, thanks and forgiveness and for his blessing on the five souls who passed from here. May they live with him in heaven."

"Amen."

"Amen."

"Amen." Father Eustace returned from his circuit of the house and concluded his prayers.

"Thank you, Father," she said.

He opened the door, stepped onto the lintel, then turned to look at them both.

"I claim the honors and rights of first foot here. May your troubles be less and your blessings be more, and nothing but happiness come through your door. *Lang may yer lum reek.*"

Caitrin bounced up and down and clapped her hands. "I've not heard that blessing for many a year. Ye are a Scot then are ye, Father Eustace?"

"No, child. However, one of the Franciscan brothers who saw to my education was. 'Twas he who taught me to respect the old beliefs even as Christian faith replaces them. So, when I am asked to bless a Samhain or a Hogmanay or such, I do so, knowing that God understands the difference."

"I thank you for that courtesy. I feel much the same way. God is my salvation, but the old ways are important to many people I love and respect, so I respect those ways in their honor."

"Now that the blessings are complete," Amis said. "Might we all step within? 'Tis rather chilly out here."

"Aye." Caitrin agreed.

Soon all were comfortable. Bread, cheese and wine from the sack were spread on the table. Peat had been added to the fire. Amis stepped out to see that Sunrise had water and fed him some oats the priest had brought.

When he returned, the priest excused himself. "I'll be back in a few moments."

"Of course." Caitrin stood and watched the man go. Then she turned to the fire twisting her hands.

Amis' hand settled on her shoulders. "Something worries you?"

"Aye, but it is nothing to do with you."

"No?"

"No. Only while you were outside, Father Eustace reminded me that though I may be widowed, living with a man as I have with you might be perceived by some as sin--especially by King Edward, who you and I both know is very devout."

"The priest said much the same to me as we returned here. He suggested I ask you to marry."

"That's unnecessary," she said.

"True..."

"Father Eustace, could absolve us both."

"He might, but he has nothing here with which to write an absolution. Without that, none would believe us no matter what we claim." Amis pointed out the difficulties.

"We could go with him to his church, or wherever he lives, and get the absolutions there."

"Is that what you want?"

"It would make things easier when we finally get to court and Edward asks about our journey." She twisted her hands before her.

"So would our marriage."

"I saw you in the French court. You played with women like you play a lute, with great care and finesse." He smiled, as if she'd given him a tremendous compliment.

"Were we to wed, that care and finesse would be yours alone."

Something vaguely like hope stirred in her belly. Beneath his hands, she faced him. "Truly?"

"Truly, Caitrin."

"Would you like to marry with me?"

"Very much."

"Why?"

"I can think of a number of reasons, but none as great as how I would grieve for you were you not part of my life."

"You would grieve?"

"I would indeed."

"Why?"

"I am all but certain that I love you, Lady Caitrin Drew-De Garrone."

"Even though I am a Scot?"

"My sister wed a Scot."

"And caused no end of problems for the Du Grace family."

"Nothing we've not been able to survive. In fact, given my service to Edward and my father's long friendship with the king, our family thrives. One of my last letters from my father mentioned that his holding at Bowlands Castle is in need of a new chatelain. I don't know the details, but he implied he might offer the position to me, if I found myself in need of a home where I might live with a wife and family."

"I'm not certain I wish to be obliged to your father."

"Wed or not, I'll not allow you to be obligated to him. However, I have enough gold from my years as an errant knight, that I could purchase my own small demesne. Would you mind starting our lives together in a small place?"

She smiled up at him. "No, I would not mind."

"Then will you marry me, Caitrin?"

"Yes, Amis, I will be your wife."

He swept her into his arms, lifting her to her toes and kissed her.

She opened to him and felt the world fall away in the wonder of his caresses.

A gust of cold air recalled them to their senses.

Father Eustace entered the croft. "May I wish you both happy?"

Arm in arm they faced him.

"Aye Father. Would you do us the honor of seeing us wed immediately," Amis requested.

"I will do that, as long as you promise to repeat your vows in front of witnesses when we return to the village."

"Caitrin?" Amis captured her gaze.

"Yes. Yes, Father Eustace, I promise."

"As do I."

"Excellent. If we begin right now, we might be able to get back to the village before dark."

"Would someone there be willing to let us have a room for the night?"

The father smiled. "I think that can be arranged. Now let us begin."

Thus, in naught but her torn shift, with a rough blanket as a cloak and a circlet of seaweed as a ring, Caitrin plighted her troth to Amis who pledged to God to give her happy days forever after.

WHILE SIR AMIS DU GRACE has not appeared in any of my other tales, he receives mention in quite a few, from *Knight Defender*, which details the romance of his sister Jessamyn and Baron Raeb MacKai, to several of the MacKai Brides novellas. You may discover more about the MacKai family at my website, https://www.rueallyn.com/book snew/.

What to read next: Get the whole story about how the DuGrace family ended up entwined with a Scottish clan. Read *Knight Defender* - Knight Chronicles Book Three. **She would never wed a Scot. He would prefer death to marriage with an English woman. So why do these two natural enemies each pretend to agree to marry?**

She wants a life dedicated to the support of a nunnery not a love-less political marriage to an overbearing enemy. A growing passion for the man spoils all her plans. A weak simpering English woman is not his idea of the ideal wife. However, when she turns out to be more than a match for him, he cannot help but fall in love. Even when they discover love, can these two enemies create peace or will the hatred between countries separate them forever?

ABOUT RUE ALLYN

Hi, I'm Rue Allyn. Mostly, I write stories about heart melting romance. You know, the kind of story in which characters have great adventures and love triumphs at the darkest moment. I have done a few other things besides penning romances. Over the years I have, in no particular order, worked as an emergency room admitting clerk, receptionist, personal admin, US Naval Petty Officer, graduate student, and post-secondary English language arts instructor. I'm a mom of two children (both now adults), a spouse of more than forty years, and a caretaker to cats.

While nothing I write is 'autobiographical,' like most authors, I draw on my own knowledge and experience as well as copious research notes to create my stories. I love reading nearly as much as writing, and one of my favorite activities is talking with other book lovers about reading and writing.

Here are few little-known factoids about myself. At age six, I wanted to be an opera diva when I grew up—specifically a coloratura soprano. Sadly, I did not have the voice to make that dream come true. I did have other gifts. My first poem (never published) was titled "The Cloud Horse." I love looking at clouds and making up stories about the people and things I imagine from watching the shapes change. I wish someone would pay me to travel. Last, I have entirely too much formal education. I won't tell you how many years of school I attended, but I'll tell you I started at age two.

I'd love to get to know you better. A couple of ways to do that include **subscribing to my newsletter,** joining my Facebook group, **Rue Allyn's Daring Damsels,** and/or **Bookbub**

f

RUE'S SOCIAL MEDIA

Website: https://www.RueAllyn.com
Facebook: https://www.facebook.com/RueAllynAuthor

MEET THE BLUESTOCKING BELLES

The Bluestocking Belles (the "BellesInBlue") are eight very different writers united by a love of history and a history of writing about love. From sweet to steamy, from light-hearted fun to dark tortured tales full of angst, from London ballrooms to country cottages to the sultan's seraglio, one or more of us will have a tale to suit your tastes and mood.

https://bluestockingbelles.net/

THE BELLES' SOCIAL MEDIA

Website: https://www.BluestockingBelles.net/

Newsletter: http://eepurl.com/dAJU_9

Teatime Tattler twice-weekly gossip magazine: https://bluestock ingbelles.net/category/teatime-tattler/

Free books: https://bluestockingbelles.net/teatime-tattler-free-books/

X (Twitter): https://www.x.com/@bellesinblue

Facebook: https://www.facebook.com/bellesinblue

Bookbub: https://www.bookbub.com/profile/2577297493

Bluesky: https://bsky.app/profile/bellesinblue.bsky.social

Threads: https://www.threads.net/@bluestockingbelles4

Instagram: https://www.instagram.com/bluestockingbelles4

THE BELLES WOULD LIKE YOUR HELP!

Book reviews help readers to find books, and authors to find readers. Please consider writing a review for Belles & Beaux, even a couple of sentences telling people what you liked (or didn't like) about the stories. Reviews can be posted on BookBub, Goodreads and on most eRetailers websites. For links to this book on those sites, see the Belles & Beaux page on the Belles' website: https://bluestockingbelles.net/belles-joint-projects/belles-beaux/

Malala Fund

The Bluestocking Belles have chosen the Malala Fund as the charity they support, and to which they donate some of their royalties. Periodically, they take on projects intended to directly support this cause, which exemplifies their personal values and intentions: the right of girls and women to do whatever they choose with their lives.

How can you help?

Make a donation to malala.org

The Bluestocking Belles donate a portion of the proceeds to benefit the Malala Fund.

OTHER BOOKS BY THE BLUESTOCKING BELLES

Find buy links and story blurbs for all the following books on our website at https://bluestockingbelles.net/belles-joint-projects/

• **Holly & Hopeful Hearts** (2016)

Eight assorted heroes and heroines find more than they've bargained for when they set out for Hollystone Hall for a charity ball.

• **Never Too Late** (2017)

Eight authors and eight different takes on four dramatic elements selected by our readers—an older heroine, a wise man, a Bible, and a compromising situation that isn't.

• **Follow Your Star Home** (2018)

In eight stories, covering more than half the world and a thousand years, our heroes and heroines put the legend of the Viking ring to the test. Watch the star work its magic, as prodigals return home in the season of good will, uncertain of their welcome.

• **Valentines From Bath** (2019)

Music, candlelight, romance: Bath is made for lovers.

Holiday Escapes (2020)

Holidays, relatives, pressure to marry—sometimes it is all too much. Is it any wonder a woman may need to escape? The heroines in this collection of stories aren't afraid to take matters into their own hands when they've had enough.

- **Fire & Frost** (2020)

In a winter so cold the Thames freezes over, five couples venture onto the ice in pursuit of love to warm their hearts.

- **Storm & Shelter** (2021)

Winner RONE Award for best anthology of 2021

When a storm blows off the North Sea the villagers prepare for the inevitable: shipwreck, flood, land slips, and stranded travelers. One storm, eight authors, eight heartwarming novellas.

- **Desperate Daughters** (2022)

The penniless daughters of the Earl of Seahaven will pool their resources so that the youngest marriageable daughters might make successful matches, thereby saving them all. So start their adventures in York, amid a whirl of balls, lectures, and al fresco picnics. Is it possible each of them might find love by the time the York horse races bring the season to a close?

- **Belles & Beaux** (2022)

Just in time for Christmas comes this boxed set of eight charming stories of love, family, and miracles. Each Belle has contributed a tale set in the festive season—one just long enough to fit in between tasks at this busy time of the year.

- **Under the Harvest Moon** (2023)

Nine award winning and bestselling authors have combined their talents to create this engaging and enchanting collection of interrelated tales. An unforgettable read for fans of Regency romance.

- **Christmastide Kisses** (2023)

Six charming holiday season romances from award-winning and best-selling authors.